Jessica Huntley

MY REAL SELF

About Jessica Huntley

Jessica wrote her first book at age six. Between the ages of ten and eighteen, she had written ten full-length fiction novels as a hobby in her spare time between school and work.

At age eighteen, she left her hobby behind and joined the British Army as an Intelligence Analyst where she spent the next four and a half years as a soldier. She attempted to write more novels but was never able to finish them.

Jessica later left the Army and became a mature student at Southampton Solent University and studied Fitness and Personal Training, which later became her career. She still enjoys keeping fit and exercising daily.

She is now a wife and a stay-at-home mum to a crazy toddler and lives in Newbury. During the first national lockdown of 2020, she signed up on a whim to a novel writing course, and the rest is history. Her love of writing came flooding back, and she managed to write and finish her debut novel, The Darkness Within Ourselves, inspired by her love of horror and thriller novels. She has also finished writing the My ... Self trilogy, completed a Level 3 Diploma in Editing and Proofreading and has worked with four other authors on a collaborative horror novel entitled The Summoning.

She is now working on a new novel in her spare time, reads every day (thrillers...obviously) and is also a Thriller Ambassador for Tandem Collective.

Other Books By Jessica

The Darkness Series

The Darkness Within Ourselves

My ... Self Series

My Dark Self
My True Self
My Real Self

Standalone Thrillers

Jinx

**Writing in collaboration with
Dr. Stuart Knott, Harriet Everend,
Alice Stone and Shantel Brunton.**

The Summoning

Acknowledgements

First of all I'd like to thank my readers because without you there would be no book, which is nothing without its readers. A special thank you to my ARC team who read it early and helped me spread the word on its release. They are as follows; Cinthia Carmin Rangel Lopez, Megan Jackson, Becca Harris, Rebekah Bramall, Evelina Petitto, Leanne Jephcott, Gemma Nixon, Paige McAteer, Dr. Stuart Knott, Shannon Wing, Leigh Forshaw, Debbie Rumney, Sammantha Mouat, Natalie Chapman, Harriet Everend, Molly Emelia Roberts, Georgia Richardson and Rebecca Hopkins.

I'd also like to thank my editor, Jennifer Kay Davies, who has been editing the My … Self series from the start. She has supported me from the beginning and ensured my writing is at its best.

I always like to thank my twin sister Alice (my inspiration for Alicia) and my best friend Katie (who convinced me to turn this into a series). You two have always supported me and my writing and I know you both will always continue to do so.

Special thanks and mention always goes to my dad. He knew I was destined to be a writer from when I was five years old. Unfortunately, he cannot read my books himself, so my goal in life is to get my books on audio so he can listen to them.

Last but not least my thanks go to my husband, Scott. Without your support I wouldn't have been able to complete this series.

And to my son, Logan ... Thank you for napping during the day so I have time to write. One day I'll be able to show you what Mummy has accomplished while you've been asleep.

Connect With Jessica

Find and connect with Jessica online via the following platforms.

Sign up to her email list via her website to be notified of future books and receive her monthly author newsletter: www.jessicahuntleyauthor.com

Follow her page on Facebook: Jessica Huntley - Author - @jessica.reading.writing
Follow her on Instagram: @jessica_reading_writing
Follow her on Twitter: @jess_read_write
Follow her on TikTok: @jessica_reading_writing
Follow her on Goodreads: jessica_reading_writing
Follow her on her Amazon Author Page - Jessica Huntley

Prologue

Then …

'Hello, Frank,' I reply bluntly.

'I have been looking forward to speaking with you. I have heard a great many things about you.' His voice is deep, rough and mature. He speaks formally, something I can relate to. 'You may have a lot of questions for me.'

'I only have one … who are you? Your real name.' I can hear shuffling and movement on the end of the phone. There is possibly someone there with him, but I cannot be certain.

'My name is not important.'

'I believe it is.'

'My name is Frank Blake, but you can call me … *Father.*'

The word echoes around my head. Josslyn hears it too. I am momentarily stunned and the shock must be abundant on my face because Benjamin has stepped towards me, a look of concern on his face. I hold up my hand again, a warning to not take another step closer.

Father.

Frank Blake – The Hooded Man – the serial rapist … is our father.

'Now that I have your attention, Alicia … listen closely.'

I remain composed on the outside, but a burning rage ignites inside of me, spreading around my entire body

1

at lightning speed. It consumes me, threatening to punch a hole through my usually unwavering shield.

I cannot react ... must not react. I refuse to give this monster the satisfaction of knowing that he has rattled me to my very core. It feels as if he has stolen my breath, my life-force from my body.

My unblinking eyes focus directly ahead, ignoring Benjamin who keeps attempting to catch my attention. It is not about him; he can wait. In fact, he is acting rather like an irritating fly buzzing around my head. He is frowning at me, clearly aware that whoever is on the phone is telling me some exceptionally bad or important news. He makes a suggestive gesture to put the call on speaker phone so he can listen, but I blatantly ignore him by turning my back.

'Stop killing my men,' says the hardened voice on the phone.

I somehow manage to find my voice, despite my mouth feeling as dry as stale bread. 'Stop killing and raping women,' I answer back without so much as a second's pause.

'My child, you are in dangerous territory and you are trespassing where you do not belong, sticking your nose into something that is none of your business. I can guarantee if you do not step back and walk away from this, life will get extremely ugly and complicated very quickly.'

I grit my teeth, my jaw immediately beginning to ache. 'I can assure you that my life is already extremely ugly and complicated.'

'Ah yes, I am aware that you and your *sister* have dug yourselves a rather large hole you are now attempting to scrabble out of.'

I do not reply.

How does he know about me?

'I take it by your silence you are surprised I know about Josslyn.' He phrases it as a statement rather than as a question.

'Nothing surprises me anymore,' I reply coolly.

'I highly doubt that. Just now you were surprised to find out you are my daughter.'

'Disappointed yes, but not surprised,' I lie.

I can almost hear him smiling down the phone. 'I like you, Alicia. You are very special. It is exactly why I chose you.'

What the hell does he mean by that?

I sigh angrily, not aiming it at Josslyn, but at the arrogance in his voice. He is speaking as if he knows me, yet I have no recollection of ever meeting him. He is nothing more than a stranger.

'I know you are confused,' he continues, 'and I know you do not remember our time together, but maybe one day the wall you have built up will fall down—'

Wall? What wall?

'—and *then* you will remember. I can help you remember everything. Join me, Alicia.'

'Join you? Why the fuck would I join you? I am trying to get rid of you and your disgusting followers. The only way I will join you will be in hell.'

Nice line.

Thanks.

Frank stifles a low laugh. 'You have guts and you are not stupid. In fact, I believe you are cleverer than you give yourself credit. Therefore, you must know the threat against your life is extremely serious. There are men after you now, out for revenge. You have killed one of our own. I cannot stop them. The only way they will stop is if you join me.'

'And if I refuse … then what happens?'

'You know what will happen.'

'Humour me.'

Frank sighs. 'They will hunt you down and do unimaginable things to you … and to everyone you care about.'

At that point I turn my head and glance over my shoulder at Benjamin who is standing with his arms folded, his deep frown clearly conveying his annoyance at being left out of the conversation.

'No,' I say.

'No? Are you quite sure about that? I know you are a smart woman, Alicia. I am sure Josslyn is too. Please think logically about this. The only way to save yourself and the people you care about is to join me, otherwise, one day soon, you shall find yourself having lost everything and everyone. You will be alone. What is it to be?'

'No,' I repeat, firmer this time. I keep my voice low so that Benjamin does not overhear.

'That is the wrong answer, my child.'

4

'I wholeheartedly disagree.'

'I will break you, Alicia.'

'See you soon ... *Father.*'

I hang up.

Oh shit ... now you've done it.

I stand up straight and take a deep breath, running my fingers through my hair. I drop the phone on the floor and stamp on it, splintering the screen and destroying the plastic cover. Then I remove the SIM card and snap it in two.

'What the hell?' asks Benjamin, shrugging his shoulders. 'Who was that?'

'That was Frank Master.'

'And?'

'And he told me to join him or he would let his followers do unimaginable things to me ... and you.' The colour in Benjamin's face drains, leaving him a ghastly shade of greenish-white. He swallows hard and begins to shuffle from one foot to the other. Clearly receiving death threats still has him feeling nervous, whereas I have become accustomed to them now.

I wouldn't say that is a good thing.

'Do not worry,' I say. 'I have no intention of allowing Frank or his followers to come anywhere near us. Not yet anyway.'

'Not yet? What do you mean by that? What's going on inside your head, Alicia? What do you have planned?'

I smile at Benjamin, but he does not return it. 'I am making this up as I go along,' I say.

Well that's pretty fucking obvious.

'What else did he say?'

'Nothing.'

Wait ... you aren't going to tell him Frank Master is our dad?

No.

Why not?

For a start, there is a distinct and strong possibility Frank is lying and, secondly, I believe it is not worth mentioning right now. Even if he is our father it does not change the fact I am going to hunt him down and kill him.

You really think he's lying?

I do not know. He could be, but I feel something ... deep down ... a connection with him. I am unable to explain it.

I'm scared.

It appears that so is he.

He didn't sound scared.

He would not have called us and asked us to join him if he was not afraid of us. We are threatening to unravel his sick game. He believes he is untouchable and he is hiding behind whatever persona he has created in the outside world. We must find the real him and we must reveal him for who he truly is ... and his followers. That is our job now and we must do whatever it takes. He is afraid ... mark my words.

So how do we find him?

'Earth to Alicia ... are you there?'

I glare at Benjamin. 'I suggest you put the kettle on … we have work to do.'

I watch while Benjamin stomps out of the room towards the kitchen.

Benjamin does not like me.

Can you really blame him? So … the plan?

First, we must find Laura and Rebecca. I believe one of them holds the answer to finding him.

Chapter One
Alicia

Now … One month later …

You know who I am. There is no need for me to introduce myself. I will briefly remind you, however, that for all intents and purposes and to help shield myself from the outside world, my name is currently Alexis Grey, a disguise I manifested for myself. It will not last forever. There will come a time, hopefully in the not too distant future, when Alexis will cease to exist. I am determined to keep my *real* name a secret from the press and the authorities. No one knows who Alicia is; they only know me as Josslyn Reynolds.

The cracks, unfortunately, are beginning to appear. I wholeheartedly admit I was not as careful as I should have been when taking and setting up the fake name. There are situations I may have overlooked in my haste to flee the country, which means that my mask will not stay in place for long, so I must attempt to complete my mission as quickly as possible.

I dream of a time when I can finally be myself, entirely and completely myself, but that dream may never manifest, especially since currently I am being forced to hide from the world, yet again. This time, however, it is not through my own choice (but it is because of my previous actions). If I am not careful I will be captured, sentenced and locked away.

You may recall that a month ago I was captured and tortured by the twisted, vile human being called Peter Phillips, who exposed his disturbing fantasies to me in excruciating detail. Then I killed him, or more appropriately, Josslyn killed him, and a fine job she did of it too. She sliced his throat down to his cervical spine and we watched him bleed out together. He deserved to die; there is no point in denying that glorious fact. He also revealed that he had maliciously and violently slaughtered Josslyn's dog, Oscar, which had torn her apart in more ways than one. Yes, Peter Phillips was a man who had deserved his painful and sticky end, but his legacy, unfortunately, did not end with him. I intend to rectify that, which is why I cannot be seen and recognised by the outside world ... not yet.

Josslyn is a wanted fugitive and is being hunted down by the police as a *person of interest*. I cannot depend on my shorter blonde hair and slender figure to conceal my identity indefinitely. I am Josslyn and Josslyn is me. If I were spotted by someone who once knew Josslyn or who was able to see past the thin disguise then it would not take long before the authorities caught up with me. I do not know what specific evidence the police have, but I do know that her (my) DNA was found on the body of Daniel Russell (fucking Daniel), her ex-boyfriend, who I brutally murdered nearly two years ago (and what a fine and exhilarating moment that was). Therefore, her face is currently plastered over every news channel across the country, making my movements very restricted. My situation is predominantly a dire one and to be perfectly honest I really am making it up as I go along. Every day seems to bring with it more complications, more obstacles, but I will not give up.

I am eternally grateful that I have an assistant – some might call him a friend – helping me and allowing me to stay in his house while he does the majority of the leg work. Without him I would have been discovered weeks ago.

Benjamin Willis.

Josslyn and Benjamin have become quite the item over the past month; however, they have always ensured our mission comes first. Basically, the plan is to locate Benjamin's sister, Laura, and the elusive Rebecca, the currently unknown woman who was one of Peter's obsessions. Both of them, however, appear to have disappeared off the face of the planet without a single trace. Without them, the second phase of the plan is essentially null and void: to track down Frank Master and his evil online cult (or whatever you wish to call them), a cohort of abusive, power-hungry men who find it pleasurable to stalk, rape, torture and even kill women for entertainment purposes. These men need to be eradicated, but first I must ensure Laura and Rebecca are safe and I believe they may have information which could help me find my targets. I do not know these women, but I owe it to them to find them. Josslyn and I were stalked by Peter Phillips and I also had one of his apprentices attempt to rape me. I know how they must feel; trapped and alone, with nowhere to run and no one to turn to. I intend to relieve them of their burden and help them, but that is proving seemingly impossible because I cannot find them.

I have been scouring the internet for the past month for any clue as to where they may be, but as far as their online presence goes … they are not there. A part of me is envious about their situation; I wish I was as invisible as they appear to be.

After the phone call with Frank, Benjamin and I sat down and discussed our potential options. It was established that he would search for his sister and I would search for Rebecca. We did not want to waste time looking for them individually when our efforts could easily be doubled.

Benjamin revealed he had received a postcard from Laura over a year ago from India, so he had assumed she was residing there at the time; however, he has had no correspondence from her since. His first instinct was to fly to India and search for her, but I pointed out that not only was it a ridiculous waste of time (searching for one person in a country of nearly 1.4 billion), but it was also almost impossible due to the influx and the spread of the pandemic over there. So he set his sights elsewhere, convinced anyway that she had returned to the United Kingdom. He contacted her previous friends and even tracked down the drug dealer she had been in cohorts with all those years ago.

This led him down a very long and somewhat dark path as it was revealed to him exactly how much trouble Laura had gotten herself into, and yet Benjamin had disregarded her at the time, angry at the fact she had used his generosity to fuel her drug habit. Her friends seemed convinced she was still in India travelling, but her drug dealer told Benjamin he had sold her some heroine six months ago. It did not add up. Her trail ran cold at that point and no one has seen or heard from her since, which unfortunately could either mean that she is dead or she is exemplary at hiding.

I reckon she's dead in a ditch somewhere.

And here I was thinking you were always the tactful one.

I'm sorry, but it's true. She's probably overdosed and dead.

Right.

And another thing … she clearly doesn't want to be found. She ran off to India with some guy after stealing Ben's watch all those years ago and now she's probably returned to the UK after running out of money and living on the streets, begging for her next fix. It's no wonder we can't find her. It's like she doesn't even exist anymore.

It does appear that way.

I just wish we could find something out about her or Rebecca. It's been a whole month and yet we have nothing … absolutely fuck all!

Josslyn is growing more and more restless by the day, a result of being cooped up in Benjamin's house for the best part of a month.

You think!

I understand your impatience, but we must remain calm.

Why? Why should we stay calm? We have a group of serial murderers and rapists after us as well as the police and I'm wanted for murder … and you expect me to stay calm? I feel so bloody helpless.

The most logical thing we can do right now is stay safe and hidden until we have some solid evidence and a lead. We are doing everything we can do for now and must wait for the right time to conduct the next phase of the plan.

Fuck you and your logic.

As I said … Josslyn is becoming very restless and impatient and the situation is not helped by Benjamin being away. He is searching all of Laura's old haunts and hangouts, talking to anyone who may have any information about her. He has been gone nearly two weeks.

Okay … look … I'm sorry, I didn't mean what I said about Laura. I take it back. I'm just angry and frustrated. You won't tell Ben I said those horrible things about her, will you?

I will not.

Thanks.

Josslyn misses him and is worried for his safety. Frank and his allies are not only after Josslyn and myself, but Benjamin also. He made that abundantly clear on the phone even though he had not specifically mentioned Benjamin by name. Any person connected to me is in danger. Benjamin, however, does not appear to care about his own wellbeing and almost immediately set off in search of his sister, leaving me to fend for myself in the house he grew up in.

I still think we should've told him a month ago that Frank is quite possibly our father. I hate lying to him.

You are not lying to him. You are merely omitting a piece of information that has no relevance to him. It does not affect him in any way.

Okay, so if it doesn't affect him then why keep it a secret?

I am silent for a beat.

Are you too ashamed to tell Ben that you're the daughter of a rapist?

No.

Then what's the real reason you won't tell him?

I sigh in annoyance at Josslyn's persistence in this matter. She is so goddamn stubborn sometimes.

Pot ... meet kettle.

Whatever. Fine ... if you must know the reason ... I am afraid Benjamin will think I am capable of the same crimes. He already knows I am a murderer. If he knew who my father was ... he may hate me or take pity on me and, frankly, I do not want him to feel either of those things towards me. I would rather him not know, not yet, not until it is absolutely necessary for him to know the truth.

There are several long seconds of silence.

Fine, but I can guarantee you that Ben wouldn't think any less of you, or us, for knowing the truth. He's not that type of guy. He's one of the good ones.

I roll my eyes in silent sarcasm and rise to my feet from the overstuffed armchair, twisting and contorting my back and shoulders until I feel the blessed cracks of release in my stiff joints. I have been cooped up for so long in this house, unable to run outside and stretch my legs properly and I feel as if my body is giving out on me. I have been keeping as active as physically possible though.

Benjamin had retrieved his old punching bag from the attic and a dusty set of weights before he left, so I have been actively releasing my built-up tension and energy on them several times a day. The injuries I sustained from the days of torture I endured at the hands of Peter have almost fully healed; however, my once-broken little finger still throbs on occasion and it is still not quite as straight as it once was.

My phone clatters to the floor, but I ignore it and make my way into the kitchen in search of some sustenance. The fridge is almost empty bar an egg and there is the crust of a loaf of bread in the cupboard. I have been keeping my online food shopping to an absolute minimum and when the delivery driver knocks on the door I shout through the letterbox for them to leave the items on the doorstep and go away. I have barely interacted with another human being face to face for over two weeks. The old me would have revelled in it, but I must admit that I find myself becoming slightly stir crazy.

Thank God for the voice in my head ...

I retrieve the remaining food from the fridge and begin to prepare a basic meal. It is nearly six in the evening and I have barely eaten all day, having been glued to the laptop screen as per usual, searching for Rebecca, but my efforts remain fruitless (as per usual).

Yesterday I believed I had found a possible breakthrough, but the lead eventually came to a dead end ... literally. The Rebecca I located turned out to be deceased and she had been the wrong age and ethnicity anyway. With no last name to go on it has been beyond impossible and after nearly eight hours of searching I came up with nothing. I am not sure how much longer I can continue the search, but I know I must because somewhere out there Rebecca needs my help.

While the egg sizzles in the frying pan and the crust burns in the toaster, I glance out the window of the kitchen and into the back garden. I think back to the garden at Peter's house. I sometimes feel as if I am transported back there, often seeing the faint bare patch of earth; the spot where his body had burned to cinders. I remember watching the flames increase in size and heat as they had engulfed his body, his skin melting off his bones, his once strong and sizeable muscles dissolving into nothing, his bones reduced to ash. It had been a glorious sight, one which I shall never forget. I recall the smell of burning flesh as it stung my nostrils. Benjamin had gagged at the stench, but not I, and eventually the odour had evaporated into the air, gone forever, but sometimes I can still smell it, just tickling the back of my nose.

A rapid movement at the far end of the garden catches my eye, my daydream into the past broken. I look up and scan the area, but there is stillness once again, bar the wind blowing through the smaller branches of the trees.

What did you see?

I do not know. It was quite possibly the wind.

Then why are all your hairs on the back of your neck standing up? I know that feeling, Alicia. I know it well.

I do not respond, but instead draw the kitchen blinds, blocking out the waning sunlight of the day and then attend to my fried egg and toast.

I eat in silence, cross-legged on the armchair, my phone still on the floor where it had fallen previously. I usually watch the evening news, but I find myself needing some quiet time. There is only so much I can watch before it begins to repeat itself.

My phone suddenly vibrates, sending a small jolt of surprise through my body. I glance down and see Benjamin's face and name on the screen. I scoop it up without a moment's hesitation. It has been several days since I have heard from him and a part of me has begun to get ... what is the word for it ...?

Concerned?

Impatient.

'Benjamin,' I say curtly by way of a greeting.

17

'Hi, Alicia. How are you?'

'I am well.'

'Good to hear. I'm sorry I haven't called sooner ... I've been ... well, I've done a lot of driving.' His voice sounds strained and tired. Like me, his search for his sister has been relentless and every day has clearly been a struggle. 'Is Josslyn okay?' he asks.

I'm fine Ben. I miss you.

'Josslyn is fine. She misses you.'

'I miss you too, Josslyn.'

'So ... what have you found? The last thing you told me was that you were heading to Liverpool.'

'Yes. I went there and then I drove to Hull. I have news ... I think I've found her. I think I've found my sister.'

Chapter Two
Alicia

I can hear my heartbeat pounding in my ears, so loud in fact that it is deafening, as if a base drum is thumping directly beside me, ricocheting my entire body.

Finally, a fucking breakthrough.

I do not reply to Benjamin as I wait for him to continue, but he obviously expects an answer because he says, somewhat bluntly, 'Alicia … did you hear me?'

'Yes.'

'Sorry … I forgot you don't talk much.'

I do not respond, proving that he is indeed correct.

'Right, well … as I said I think I've found Laura, but there's no guarantee. It's a bit of a long shot and, to be completely honest, I don't know what I'm going to find.'

'Rather than providing me with cryptic clues perhaps you could get to the point.' I do not care if Benjamin thinks I am rude (he knows that already). He also is perfectly aware I hate random chit-chat and long, drawn-out conversations that have no real meaning.

'Right …,' he says again, 'okay, so basically, you remember the postcard she sent me from India over a year ago … the one I told you about? I don't think she actually sent it.'

I absorb the information, but warning bells start sounding in my brain; something does not sit right.

'What do you mean?'

'Well, when I looked at it properly I saw it had a Leh Ladakh stamp on it, meaning it was sent from that region … I managed to find some phone numbers and email addresses for several hostels and businesses in the area, so I contacted them and asked if they'd seen someone with her description. It was a bit of a long shot because it was so long ago, but one owner of a hotel said he thought he recognised her and he said she'd told him she was headed for the Phugtal Monastery, which is in the most remote region. She'd planned on staying there for some time. It's apparently one of the only Buddhist monasteries in Ladakh that can be reached by foot. It's built into a cliff side in the form of a honeycomb at the mouth of a cave.'

'Why the hell would your sister visit a monastery? From what you have told me about her it does not sound like the type of place she would want to visit, let alone stay at.'

I agree. Why would she be going to a monastery? She wasn't religious, was she? Unless she went there to hide, but I'm pretty sure a load of monks aren't going to let a British woman stay with them …

'Why would Laura go in search of a Buddhist monastery?' I ask again when I am met with silence.

Benjamin sighs. 'That's exactly my point. She didn't … she wouldn't. It's completely out of character for her.'

'That makes no sense.'

'Will you just hear me out?'

'Only if you hurry up and get to the fucking point!' As you can clearly tell Benjamin and I have been somewhat stressed lately and we often take it out on each other. Our fuses are exceptionally short.

Benjamin continues, a strained tone to his voice. 'The point is Laura was never there. She was never in India in the first place. She has clearly been leaving fake trails everywhere because she doesn't want to be found, even from all that time ago. I believe that she somehow convinced a woman who looked a bit like her to pose as her and tell everyone her name, so whoever came looking for her would think she was still in India. But she'd actually swapped passports with this other woman and remained in the UK.'

I frown. 'So ... what you are saying is that she never went to India and she is actually living in the United Kingdom?'

'Yes.'

'Why the fuck could you not have just said that straight away?'

'I thought you would want all the facts.'

'Are you trying to piss me off on purpose?'

'Why would I want to do that?'

I close my eyes and count to ten, taking a few deep, cleansing breaths. This man infuriates me so much.

'So why are you in Hull?' I ask finally, once my blood pressure has returned to a somewhat normal state. 'You said previously that her ex-drug dealer said he saw her six months ago. Is she there?'

'No. I think he lied. I think that was another fake trail.'

'But you said at the beginning of this ridiculously frustrating conversation that you thought you had found her.'

'I did … at least I thought I did. I've found the woman who was posing as Laura. She eventually came back to the UK and is now living in Hull. I'm about to go and speak to her now. I've been running around the country for the past two weeks, chasing shadows, but I've finally got a real lead.'

'Fine. Great. Good for you.'

'Excuse me?'

I am silent, perfectly aware I sound like a sarcastic teenager.

I hear Benjamin sigh. 'Look, I know it sounds as if I'm still chasing shadows, but I'm really close this time. I can feel it. It's better than doing nothing and sitting on my ass like …'

I grind my teeth together. 'Go on … say it … like *I am*.'

'That's not what I was going to say. I'm sure you're doing everything you can.'

'I *am* doing everything I can,' I seethe.

'I know!' he shouts.

I raise my eyebrows at the phone, which I have to remove from my ear due to his exceptionally loud voice, which leaves a shrill ringing noise in my head. I hear him muttering some words, quite possibly to random strangers around him.

'I'm sorry,' he finally says, his voice much lower and calmer now. 'I didn't mean to snap at you. I'm just tired and fed up … and I know you are too. Sometimes I forget that while I've been driving all over the country you've been stuck in my house all by yourself … well, technically not all by yourself, but … you know what I mean. I assume you've been keeping an eye on the news?'

'I have.'

'I'm so sorry this is all happening to you, and to Josslyn. I wish I could be there with you, but this is really important to me. We agreed that you'd be in charge of finding Rebecca and I'd be in charge of finding my sister. I'm so close to finding her; I just know it.'

I let out a long breath and lean back in the soft armchair.

Don't worry, Alicia. I'm sure one of you will find something solid soon.

I am beginning to think otherwise.

I think Ben just needs your support on this, otherwise he wouldn't have called you.

He is infuriating.

I know, but he's trying his best.

I roll my eyes.

'Fine,' I say finally. 'Call me once you've spoken to this woman.'

'I will. Thanks. Have you found anything on Rebecca?'

'Nothing.'

Benjamin sighs loudly. 'I'm beginning to think they don't want to be found.'

'You think?' That is the understatement of the century.

'Sometimes I think it would be easier to tell the police about my sister and about Frank Master and the Hooded Man and all that crap and they could just take over this investigation. They're set up for it. We're not. I have no idea what I'm doing or what I'm about to walk into and neither do you.'

'Do you want me to go to jail?' I snap.

'No, of course not. I'd leave you and Josslyn out of it.'

'I thought we discussed this before you left. I *have* to be the one to do this, so does Josslyn. We do not inform the police until the right time.'

'I know, but I just—'

'Do you want to speak to Josslyn now or not?' I interrupt.

'Yes ... thank you.'

'Oh ... and Benjamin?'

'Yeah?'

'Try and not get yourself killed while you are out traipsing around the country. I will not be avenging your death if you do happen to die.'

'That's comforting ... thanks.'

I close my eyes and allow Josslyn to take over.

Chapter Three
Josslyn

I can feel Alicia slipping away, her frustration with Ben subsiding with her. To be honest, I feel a little annoyed at him too. We've always had a plan, right from the start and I thought he was on board, so when he says he thinks it would be easier to just let the police handle it ... well, it pisses me off. We're supposed to be a team, a trio, a ... whatever the hell we are ... a threesome? Eww, no, not a threesome. The point is that we're all in this together (he's an accessory to murder for crying out loud!) and now he's having doubts out of nowhere and—

'Josslyn ... are you there?'

Ben's voice jolts me from my thoughts and I'm momentarily stunned at finding myself in the real world. It's very disconcerting switching between our mind and our body, although I've been spending a lot less time in control of our body lately, ever since Ben left for his ... travels. I don't really know what to do without him around. I used to enjoy spending time by myself; hell, I preferred it, but now spending time by myself fills me with dread.

Right ... Ben ...

'I'm sorry ... yes, I'm here.' I run my fingers through my hair. It feels greasy and in desperate need of a wash and a trim.

I thought you were supposed to be the one who looks after themselves properly? What's with the greasy hair, Alicia?

I have more important things to worry about than washing my fucking hair.

Okay, okay, calm down. Yeesh!

Note to self: after this phone call go and wash my hair.

Shit, I'm vaguely aware that Ben's been talking to me this whole time and I haven't heard a single word he's said. I'm a bad girlfriend. *Girlfriend.* It still feels weird to say, but I love saying it. I'm his *girlfriend* and he's my *boyfriend.*

'... so what do you think?' I catch the end of his sentence and there's a long pause while I mentally kick myself.

'... Um ... sure,' I say, elongating the final syllable.

'You didn't hear a word I said, did you?'

'... Um ... no, but I'd be happy to listen if you can just repeat it all again.'

Ben sighs loudly. I bet he's contemplating why the hell he's even with me. I mean, I'm the worst girlfriend ever, but then he starts laughing so I laugh too and my fears dissipate.

'I'm so sorry, Ben, but you know how it is with Alicia in my head. Well, I guess you don't, but you know what she's like. She's so distracting sometimes.'

'Uh huh, yeah I get that. She's still as pleasant to talk to as ever.'

'You know she can hear you, right?'

'Yeah I know, but some things are just hard to say directly to her.'

I smile. 'Are you still scared of her?'

'Hey, I never said I was scared of her,' he corrects.

'Right.'

'She's just ... you know ... actually there aren't any words to describe her.'

'I'll agree to that. So what was it you were saying?'

'Before I repeat myself again can I just say one thing?'

'Um ... sure?' I'm not really sure if I want to hear what he has to say now.

'I love you.'

I immediately hear Alicia making fake dry heaving noises.

I roll my eyes.

Quit it!

'I ... I ...' Oh shit, I still can't bloody say it. Ben's said the L word to me so many times lately, but I can't bring myself to say it back. What's wrong with me? It must make him feel so unloved, but the word just won't form in my mouth. It gets stuck at the back of my throat like a bad cough and makes me feel a bit sick.

'Josslyn? You okay? You still there?'

'Yes ... sorry ... miles away again ... um, me too.'

You are pathetic.

Shut up.

The annoying thing is that I really *do* love Ben, but something is stopping me from telling him. I'm not sure if it's Alicia or my actual brain (for want of a better word) that causes me to become mute whenever he says those three little words to me. I've never loved anyone before. Yes, I loved my parents (although since Peter told me they probably lied to me *again* I'm having trouble feeling love for them at the moment) and I loved Oscar (I still miss him) and, God forbid, I love Alicia too (although fuck knows why), but I've never actually been *in love* with anyone. Although, for a while in my teenage years, I was in madly in love with Duncan from the boy band Blue and then when I found out he was gay or bisexual or whatever, it actually made me love him even more … anyway, I digress … (I still love you, Duncan.)

'I miss you so much,' continues Ben, clearly skirting around the fact I've declined to answer him properly. It's always so fucking awkward. 'I can't wait for all this to be over so we can disappear, just the two of us and live normal, boring lives in a normal, boring house.'

'Me too,' I reply slowly.

I know full well that this ludicrous pipe dream of his will never happen, but who am I to squash his dreams? It's probably the only thing that's getting him through these tough times at the moment, having been roaming around the country by himself for the past few weeks, hitting one dead end after another. It's enough to drive anyone crazy and make them feel lonely. At least I've had Alicia to talk to (not that she's great at talking, but it's better than talking to a brick wall … well, sometimes). Now he's found another potential lead, which means he will be away even longer … Speaking of which …

'So … about Laura,' I say apprehensively. 'That's great you've found another lead.'

'Yeah … but listen, I'm sorry I didn't tell you before. It all happened so fast, you know how it is, but like I told Alicia, I feel like I'm so close to finding her now.'

'What if it turns out to be another dead end? You could be wrong about her not being in India. She could still be over there.'

'I know and I can't fly to India and look for her because of the pandemic being so bad over there. This lead may be my last chance to find her.'

'How long do you think it'll take you? I mean when do you think you'll be coming back?' I ask.

'That's what I was saying beforehand. If this does turn out to be a dead end like the rest of them, then I'll come straight home. Clearly Laura's got herself mixed up into something bad. Whether that involves Frank Master and his cronies, I don't know, but I still have this strange feeling … like … maybe she might be …'

Dead.

'… hiding for a reason.'

Or she is dead.

I have to agree with Alicia on this one. I don't, however, say those words aloud, but I think Ben hears them anyway in his own head even if he doesn't want to admit it's the most logical explanation as to why we can't find her. Let's be honest … we're all thinking it.

'Okay,' I say.

'You don't sound so sure.'

'No, it's not that. It's just ... I'm tired Ben. I feel like we're going round in circles. This Frank guy is messing with our heads. I need to stop him, but ... I feel like I'm in way over my head and the worst part is that I've dragged you into it too.'

'You haven't dragged me into anything. Phil was the one who dragged me into it when he stalked my sister and tortured you. I'm as deep into this mess as you are.'

Except you're not wanted for multiple murders.

I don't reply directly to him, but I can guarantee both of us are feeling the pressure. It's been a month since the whole fiasco with Peter and we basically haven't gotten anywhere, although, luckily, we haven't had any issues with Frank and his cohort since. In fact, the whole Hooded Man thing has quietened down in the news too. There've been no new rapes or attacks relating to him and no further women have come forward. Everything has dried up and ground to a halt and it's fucking infuriating.

'Well ... let's just keep going,' says Ben matter-of-factly, finally breaking the silence. 'Something is bound to pop up soon.'

That's Ben ... always trying to stay positive.

'Other than the obvious, how are you?' he asks, his tone softening.

'I'm okay,' I reply with a smile. Although to be perfectly honest I feel a bit sick. Anxiety and stress is never a good combination even at the best of times (not that there's ever a good time to be anxious and stressed). 'Just promise me you'll be back soon or at least message me whenever you can so I know you're safe and the minute you find and talk to this woman.'

'Of course I will ... Oh, shit ... babe, I have to go—'

'Wait. Why? What's happened?'

'Nothing, I ... I have to go, I'll call or text as soon as I can. I love you. Bye, girlfriend.'

'... Bye, boyfriend.'

I hang up before the awkward silence starts again as he realises I *still* haven't said those words back to him. Maybe he shouldn't say them! I mean, he's starting to sound a bit desperate ... right? But the whole *girlfriend* and *boyfriend* thing is sort of like an in-house joke between us ever since we agreed that's what we were. It's cute ... or maybe it's only cute to us.

I stare at my phone and sigh as I feel fresh tears brimming in my eyes. Dear God, what's happened to me? I've become this annoying, emotional wreck since being with Ben – everything I've always hated about being in a relationship. I'm not the overly emotional type of woman, never have been. Maybe because this time it's different. This time it's real and I actually care about him.

I know what you're going to say, Alicia.

I was not going to say anything.

Okay, but I know what you're thinking.

Which is?

That being with Ben is making me weak and it would be better if he weren't involved.

31

That is exactly what I am thinking, but there is nothing that can be done about it now. Benjamin made his choice when he chose to stay with us ... you ... He knows the risks involved.

No, he doesn't, not really. Neither you nor I have told him what was really said on the phone between you and Frank that day.

And it is best it stays that way for now.

I really hate keeping things from Ben, but Alicia is right (and you know I hate it when she's right). Ben can't know the truth about what Alicia and I've recently found out. It would kill him. He'd want to try and wrap me up in a protective bubble, try and shield me from everything. He'd want to hide me away so Frank would never find me, but I can't let that happen. Alicia and I need to face Frank and deal with him once and for all. Ben will be told everything when the time is right.

I have an idea.

Oh God ...

Since Benjamin is going to be away for a little longer how about you and I go on a road trip of our own ...

Um ... where exactly do you want to go? It's not like I have a warrant out for my arrest or anything ... Oh, wait!

Just shut up and listen. Remember before the phone call with Frank you told Benjamin you wanted to break into your parents' old house to look for the box where you found the ultrasound photo ...

Yeah ... and Ben said he'd help me, but then backed out of the idea and said finding Laura and Rebecca was more important and we should focus on them first.

Right ... well, since we have found out fuck all about Rebecca lately maybe we should ... take a break ...

I like your thinking, but we'll need to be careful. Going back home means there will be people around who are likely to recognise me. I'm probably the talk of the whole bloody village.

Then we shall be stealthy.

Stealthy. Right. I can do that.

Maybe you should let me handle this one. You have never been known for your ... stealth.

I've no idea what you're talking about.

Chapter Four
Alicia

The prospect of leaving this godforsaken abode is enough to fill me with giddy excitement as I grab my phone, a change of clothes (I have no idea how long I will be away), my toothbrush and the remaining bag of crisps I find at the back of the store cupboard.

Um, not to put a dampener on the whole idea or anything, but how the hell are we going to even get there? It's too risky to take public transport in case we're recognised, and Ben has his mum's car.

Fear not … I have a plan.

Right, and that fills me with the utmost confidence. What are you gonna do … steal a car?

I do not reply.

Oh fuck! No way. You're going to steal a car, aren't you? On top of murder you want to add stealing a car to our list of convictions. Do you have like a bucket list you're trying to tick off or something?

Lucky for you I have been very observant lately. There happens to be an old car parked opposite this house, which has been there for over a week. The owners are currently on holiday because they left with their luggage in an airport taxi, so I assume they have travelled to a different country. I will have the car back before they even know it is gone.

Wow, you really have been bored. Okay, but what about the fact neither one of us knows how to hot-wire a car? This isn't a bloody Hollywood movie.

I am sure it will be straightforward with an old car. Besides, that is what Google is for ...

I am already scrolling and searching for online instructions. It says that the older the car is the easier it is to hot-wire. According to the car's number plate it was built in the early 1990s, which leads me to believe that it must be a valuable car for the owners to have kept it for so long, but this happens to work in my favour.

Oh my God ... this is crazy. You're actually going to steal a car.

Relax ... I have done much worse.

Pfftt! You don't have to tell me that.

I don a cap and a hoodie (and also grab a screwdriver, a wire stripper and some electrical tape from Benjamin's toolbox under the stairs) and lock up the house before glancing up and down the street to check for pedestrians. It is late in the evening now, so most should be winding down for bed.

I approach the car. It is a red Vauxhall Corsa and I must say that it is in pristine condition, but I am having a hard time understanding why the owners would want to keep it. However, I ignore my curiosity and set about removing one of my shoelaces from my trainer.

What the hell are you doing?

Just shut up and watch. Maybe you will learn something.

I retrieve the shoelace and proceed to tie a slipknot in the middle of it so I am able to tighten it by pulling on the ends. Next, I hold one end of the string in each hand, slide it through the corner of the car door, and use a back-and-forth motion to work it down far enough until the knot slides over the doorknob. Once it is in place, I pull on the string to tighten it and pull up the doorknob, unlocking the car.

I hear slow clapping in my head.

Okay ... I'm mildly impressed. I'll be even more impressed if you can actually start the damn thing.

I slide behind the wheel and quietly close the door while I adjust the seat so it is as far back as possible. I quickly read through the instructions I have found online which specifically instructs how to hot-wire an old car such as this and I get to work.

First, I take the screwdriver and place it into the keyhole of the ignition system and turn it, saying a little prayer in the hopes it will start this way. It does not. Apparently it is possible to start a car this way in a small number of cases, but after several attempts I resign myself to the fact I will need to follow further instructions.

I take out the screwdriver and remove the screws on the steering column, revealing the access panel, which I remove by simply pulling it out, allowing me access to the wires of the ignition system. I check the instructions again.

There are many wires and it takes me a few minutes to deduce which ones are for the car lights, wipers and warmers, battery and finally, the ignition. Once I figure out which wires are for the ignition and battery I use the wire stripper to remove some of the insulation from each of the two wires. Then I twist the two wires together with my fingers and, amazingly, the ignition, radio and lights all turn on.

Holy fuck! You did it!

Calm down. I have not finished yet.

Next, I find the wire that connects to the starter motor, which takes me several minutes because I am not accustomed to a car's wiring system. Once I do I also remove a piece of the insulation and finally, I touch this live wire to the combined ends of the other two …

The car splutters and then starts, a low rumble emanating from the engine.

I am in awe of you right now. You're a freaking genius.

I smile to myself as I use the tape to cover the end of the live starter wire to avoid a nasty shock while I am driving. I then settle myself into a comfortable position and pull out into the road.

Do you even know the way to Brockenhurst?

I ignore Josslyn while I type the address into my phone's navigation system and then place it on the dashboard in front of me.

Okay … fine, I'll just shut up and let the genius work.

The drive is completed in relative silence other than Josslyn randomly breaking out into song to keep herself entertained. Honestly, it is like living with a fucking child sometimes. I know it is a big risk to show my face around the area where Josslyn grew up, but like Benjamin feels about this new lead, I feel like I have to do this ... for me. Questions need to be answered. I hope that a nosey neighbour does not recognise me or attempt to engage in conversation. Luckily, the cover of darkness helps and by the time I arrive it is gone midnight. I perform a drive-by of the house to assess the situation.

There it is: The Old Mill.

I feel Josslyn's emotions stirring within. She is anxious about being back here, but there is also a small element of hope, as if she is expecting her parents to be standing at the open door for her, ready to welcome her inside and supply her with an endless amount of tea and biscuits. There is the plant pot that Oscar used to pee in every time he visited, except now it is flourishing and at least three times the size. I guess now the supply of dog urine has ceased the plant has been able to grow to its full potential.

All the lights are off in the house, as I assumed they would be at this time of night. The driveway light is on, illuminating the entire area and this part of the road. Everywhere I look feels familiar, yet completely alien to me. This is Josslyn's world I have stepped into (well, her old world). The last time I was here I had been saying my final farewell to her parents before driving away and leaving them to perish. I had only been thinking of myself at the time; they had been merely an inconvenience I had been glad to leave behind.

I now feel like an outsider coming back here; a fraud.

Josslyn and I have never really discussed her parents in great detail. It is a sore subject, but being here is no doubt filling Josslyn with all sorts of questions.

I still can't believe they're dead. I'll never see them again. My old life seems so far away, like it happened a million years ago, but being back here is making everything come flooding back. I hope we find some answers, whatever they may be. What are you expecting or hoping to find?

Nothing. Anything. Something. We shall have to wait until morning when the new occupants leave for work.

Josslyn agrees so I park the car in a secluded spot down the road so I am able to keep an eye on the house during the night. I settle down into a semi-comfortable position and close my eyes.

Chapter Five
Alicia

The next morning I am crudely awakened by a horrendous pain in my lower back. It appears my body is not accustomed to sleeping in a cramped, cold car. After performing a few stretches, which help alleviate the stiffness and pain, I check out the house. The lights are on and it does not take long before a slightly overweight, middle-aged man appears, gets into a large black Range Rover and backs out of the driveway, a portable coffee mug in his hand. Next, a woman of around the same age, but with considerably less body fat, walks out of the house, locks it and casually slides into a small, grey Porsche, which whizzes up the road seconds later.

The time has arrived.

I slowly get out of the car, grimacing as another shooting pain erupts at the base of my spine. However, after walking a few steps it soon begins to disperse.

I feel like we're getting old. When did that start to happen?

We are only thirty.

I feel fifty.

The road is quiet as I approach the building, but I immediately spy a potential problem. There are CCTV cameras set up at the front of the house pointing at the door and the driveway; they are new.

Mum and Dad never had security cameras, never needed them. This is a safe neighbourhood.

Let us hope the new owners do not have them set up at the back of the house as well. Where is the spare key hidden again?

Round the back in the garden under a loose patio slab. We can get into the garden using the far end wall. I used to hop over it many times.

I remember. You fell off it on more than one occasion.

I circle the property, my feet knowing instinctively where to go and stop by the old stone wall. It has degraded even more over the past couple of years; the stones within it have become loose and several have now made their home on the ground. Vivid green moss covers the stones, making them slippery due to the light dew this morning, but I am easily able to pull myself up and over it, jumping down on the other side without making hardly any noise. The garden is severely overgrown compared to when Ronald and Amanda had lived here. Ronald had always doted on his garden and had tended to it almost every day, always ensuring that the flower beds were perfect and the grass was neatly cut. This garden, however, has now been left to its own devices, the weeds and vegetation growing wild. Clearly the new owners are far too busy enjoying their wealth and jobs to put any thought into their garden. Such a pity.

I cautiously walk over the long grass towards the patio at the back of the house, checking for a security camera, but it appears they do not care about protecting the back of the house, which suits me perfectly. I find the loose patio slab, wiggle my fingers into the dirt to get a grip and then lift up a corner ...

Bingo.

An old, rusty key is embedded in the earth, which is tightly packed. I pry the object out of its hiding place, leaving a key-shaped indentation in the earth, and then replace the slab. I quickly clean the dirt out of the crevices of the key.

What if they've changed the locks?

Then we shall have to break a window.

Great ... another crime to tick off the bucket list.

I ignore her and approach the back door. I say another silent prayer to whatever God is listening that the locks have not been changed.

They have not. The key is a little stiff, but after a few attempts the lock clicks open.

Wait!

What is it now?

What if they've installed an alarm system too?

I pause with my hand on the door handle. I have to admit that particular thought had not crossed my mind. However, it is too late to turn back now, so I hold my breath as I push the door open a tiny fraction, waiting for the piercing shriek of an alarm ... but it does not arrive.

Thank fuck for that.

Indeed. It appears that luck is on our side.

Let's just hurry up and get to the attic. Being here is creeping me out and I'm not sure how much more stress I can take.

I silently agree and make haste to the stairs, noting that a lot of the furniture is the same as when Josslyn's parents had lived here. When I originally sold the property I had included everything in the house, so it would have been up to the new owners as to whether they disposed of the furniture or kept it. It appears, for the most part, the items have been kept, but, despite this, the house feels different and nothing like Josslyn's home at all. There are a couple of new items; an enormous flat-screen HD television for a start, along with an expensive looking rug in front of the fireplace, which now has two enormous statues of elephants on either side.

I agree. It feels ... weird. Wait ... what's that noise?

What noise?

It sounds like a ... oh, shit ...

I slowly turn around and see a ginger cat staring at me with its beady green eyes, furiously swishing its tail from side to side and emitting a hissing sound.

Shit.

It could be worse. It could be a great big vicious attack dog.

I stare back at the cat, locking eyes with it, daring it to make a move. It hisses some more as it slowly raises its hackles and begins to back away. I watch as it scurries under a table and that is where it stays as I turn to head up the stairs. I jog up them two at a time and stop on the landing. I grasp the swinging handle and pull down the trapdoor above me; the metal stairs unfold on their own.

The stagnant, damp air from above wafts down through the open trapdoor, tickling my nose as I climb the rickety steps into the dark space. I search around for the light switch, which I know is up and to the left, but upon flicking it on I realise it no longer works. The light from my phone will have to suffice.

Oh my God, why do I feel like we're in a horror movie? This feels like that scene in The Grudge.

I smile to myself, knowing how much Josslyn had been terrified after watching that movie. She has always enjoyed her dark horrors and her serial killer documentaries, but apparently a movie about a vengeful spirit occupying a dead Japanese woman is one step too far.

Shut up. It's the horrible clicking noise she makes that freaks me out.

As if on cue I step on a loose floorboard and a loud creak echoes around the enclosed space. Josslyn screams in my head. She is giving me goose bumps. I must admit even my mouth is feeling rather parched, but that could be due to the dry air up here.

Just hurry up and find the fucking box.

I scan the light around, searching for the elusive box, but it does not help that there are dozens of cardboard boxes stacked up here, as well as numerous other household items, even old pieces of furniture that had once occupied the spare room downstairs.

If I remember correctly the box was right at the back in the corner. It may not still be up here. It might have been thrown away.

I follow her instructions and head in that direction, slowly making my way around the various stacked objects. I carefully begin to rearrange the boxes so I can reach the back of the attic. Like Josslyn said there is no guarantee the box will still be here. Ronald and Amanda could have thrown it away after Josslyn originally found it, or maybe the new owners have disposed of it. I am about to give up and begin searching elsewhere when I suddenly spy it sitting alone, tight into the back corner. It has big red words scrawled across the top that says 'Baby Stuff'.

This is it.

Oh my God, it's still here ... it's ...

But Josslyn is unable to finish her sentence. The last time she saw this box she had found out she had a twin sister, then after that her whole life had unravelled and fallen apart as her parents revealed they had lied about her being their biological daughter. What other secrets did this box hold? Josslyn had not finished searching through it at the time, as she had been too preoccupied with all the shocking revelations that had come from finding the photo. What would she have found had she stayed and searched the whole box?

Now it is here ...

I recall the words Peter had said only moments before his gruesome death ... 'No ... they lied about something else too. Everyone's been lying to you.'

Open it.

I place my phone on the floor so that the beam of light illuminates the space around the box and then drag it away from the cobwebs and dust. It is still partly open, the sticky tape having been previously ripped off by Josslyn. Pulling open the flaps I immediately spy an old teddy bear.

I saw that before, but I didn't recognise it. I still don't.

This time, instead of casting it aside, I thoroughly inspect the toy. It is very weathered and tatty, clearly having been well used by a child in the past, but, like Josslyn, I am unable to recollect any memory of this bear. I turn it over and notice a small tear in the seam on its back. I stick a finger into the hole, expecting to feel soft stuffing, but the tip of my finger almost immediately hits something solid. It appears to be a fairly large object, but the rip in the seam is too tiny to pull it out, so I pull it apart even more, widening it so that eventually I am able to retrieve the item.

It is an old cassette tape. There is a single word written on the faded white label: *Alicia.*

What the hell? Is this Alicia Phillips's stuff?

Neither one of us utters another word as I place the tape next to my phone and begin searching the box again. There is more treasure to be found, I am sure of it. I pull out a blue and pink crochet blanket, which has several unravelled ends of wool dangling from it.

I remember that. Apparently my mum made it for me when she was pregnant.

Since she was never pregnant with you that is not true.

So who gave it to me? Where did it come from?

I do not reply.

The next item I find is the empty wooden box, the one that had once held the illusive ultrasound photo of Josslyn and Alicia.

The photo that had started it all.

Where is the photo now? Did you keep it?

I did not. I burnt it.

Josslyn does not reply, but I get the feeling she is disappointed.

I open the lid of the box and peer inside. The darkness makes it difficult to see properly, but it does not appear to hold anything else. The lock had been smashed open by Josslyn that day; the remnants of the padlock are now nowhere to be seen. I place the cassette, blanket and bear into the wooden box and dig around in the cardboard box once more.

I bring out a plain white envelope, which is substantially thick for its size. It has two words on the front: *Alicia Reynolds.*

I stare at it. I have never been known by a surname. I have always been Alicia. I do not know how to feel about seeing Josslyn's surname attached to my own name. It is like we are really—

Family.

Yes.

Aren't you going to open it?

Not here, not yet.

It's weird ... why on earth is everything in this box addressed to you or maybe to Alicia Phillips when it's supposed to be my baby stuff? None of this is mine, but this was my house ...

The final item I retrieve from the box is a notebook, which is loaded with newspaper clippings and hand-written notes. I flick through it quickly, but due to the darkness I am unable to make out a lot of the content; however, I am overwhelmed with the feeling that this notebook holds the answers we are looking for.

I check the box once more, but there is nothing else inside.

So what now?

Now we head back to Cambridge and find out what is on the cassette tape and look through this notebook.

And open the letter.

I do not respond. The truth is I have a very strange feeling, deep down inside, like I am not supposed to allow Josslyn to see the contents of this letter – that it is for my eyes only, but how am I supposed to read it alone when I always have Josslyn in my head?

I collect all the items, dump them back into the cardboard box and then lift the whole thing off the dusty floor. It is all coming with us.

Chapter Six
Alicia

I am tempted to sit in the car and leaf through the notebook now because my curiosity is threatening to engulf me, but I do not. Instead, I place the notebook under the passenger seat, park the car outside an electrical store in the nearest town and enter, ensuring I keep my head down and avoid eye contact with anyone. I approach a young man who is stacking shelves.

'I need to buy a tape player,' I say.

'A cassette tape player?'

'Yes.'

'Er ... you do know it's 2021, right?'

'I am aware of the year.'

'Then you should know that people stopped using cassettes like twenty years ago. We barely use CDs anymore let alone cassettes,' he says with a chuckle, apparently not even caring he sounds exceptionally rude.

I clench my jaw. 'Then what do you suggest I do?'

'Try Amazon.'

I roll my eyes and leave. I should have known that attempting to speak to a real human being would result in failure.

Before I point the car in the direction of Cambridge I take a quick detour to the local graveyard where I was informed by the family lawyer when Ronald died that Josslyn's parents were buried there. It is a quaint cemetery on the outskirts of Brockenhurst and they were buried together under a big oak tree. I allow Josslyn to briefly take over so she can say goodbye. It is likely she may never get another chance to do so. It is a sombre moment, but one I feel is necessary.

While Josslyn is talking to them out loud (which I find very odd considering they are dead and unable to hear her) I take a moment to study the joint headstone. Luckily, Ronald dealt with Amanda's death and when Ronald died his solicitor dealt with his funeral because the plan had already been paid for upfront, almost as if Ronald knew he was going to die soon and there would be no one left to plan his funeral and burial.

I cast my eyes over the gold engravings on the shiny black marble.

Ronald Reginald Reynolds
Born 15th January 1964
Died 17th September 2020
Beloved Husband and Father

Amanda Mary Reynolds
Born 16th October 1969
Died 13th April 2020
Beloved Wife and Mother

May their spirits live on for eternity

I finally arrive back at Benjamin's house and slot the car into its original parking space. I even face it in the correct direction. The only difference being that it now has an extra three-hundred-odd miles on the clock, something the owners may or may not notice. In any case it is back safe and sound, exactly as I promised it would be. No harm done.

I immediately switch the kettle on and make myself a cup of tea, my stomach aching with hunger. I also turn on Benjamin's laptop, quickly order a food delivery from Tesco and then bring up the Amazon page. Luckily, Benjamin is a trustworthy idiot and leaves his login and password automatically saved on his devices. I find the cheapest cassette player they sell, add it to the basket, along with a few other things I may need in the future, and check out (using Benjamin's credit card details – I am sure he will not mind). It says the items will arrive tomorrow (thank you Amazon Prime).

I quickly take a shower and change into some clean clothes (jeans and a black t-shirt, nothing fancy) and then wrap my hands around the hot cup of tea and stare at the notebook on my lap. The other items I found in the attic are on the floor beside me, except for the white envelope which I have stored away in my backpack for safekeeping. Out of sight, out of mind ... for now.

I open the first page of the notebook and begin to read.

It is a complete jumble of words, newspaper clippings and scribbles and the handwriting is barely legible, most of it smudged. There are even some dark stains that look suspiciously like blood on some of the pages, causing them to stick to each other.

What the hell is all this?

I read the first newspaper headline, which is highlighted in yellow:

Woman Slain While Husband Slept. Jessica Thomas was brutally murdered in her own house while her husband slept upstairs. She was found by him the next morning sat upright in a kitchen chair, her throat slashed.

Another headline is highlighted yellow:

Missing Woman Found Outside Bath. Mandy Williams was reported missing by her family three days ago. Her body was found late last night in a ditch on the outskirts of Bath, stripped naked.

Another in yellow:

Mutilated Mother Found. Katherine Cooke, wife and mother, was found mutilated on the side of the road half eaten by wild animals.

The fourth headline I read is highlighted in green:

Dark Hood Rapes Woman. Charlotte Murray was attacked and raped last night by a man wearing a dark hood. She was badly beaten and was later found by a group of school boys in an alley. Later, her brother came to take her away to Scotland so he could look after her.

The one and only clipping that holds my attention is the one about Charlotte Murray and the man in the dark hood. I cannot help but notice it is highlighted green whereas the first three were in yellow. The clipping is from May, 1988. There's a woman and a man in the newspaper photo who I assume are Charlotte and her brother, but I barely take any notice.

I quickly flick through the next several pages and see there are dozens of other articles stuck or clipped into the notebook. All of them are about the torture, rape or murder of a woman, all of them in their late teens or twenties. None of the women are over thirty. Most of the articles are highlighted yellow, apart from a select few which are in green. I spend longer reading these ones, but not all of them mention a man in a dark hood. In fact, the Charlotte Murray article is the only one that mentions it.

Other than the fact all these women were roughly the same age when they were attacked there doesn't appear to be any official connection. None of the names jump out at me until I come across the last newspaper clipping and it is at this point my heart skips a beat and I feel the unmistakable pang of ... dread. This is the last article highlighted in green:

Pregnant Woman Found Badly Beaten In Road. A heavily pregnant woman was found badly beaten along the side of the A30 near Salisbury. She was taken to Salisbury Hospital where she later gave birth to twins, both of whom survived. She declined to provide details of what had happened to her and one of the twins was put up for adoption at her request. She kept the other.

I read the short paragraph several times, ensuring I have absorbed the words as much as possible.

Is that ... us? Me ... I mean, you and Alicia Phillips?

It is possible.

Holy fuck! That's our mum — that's Jane Daniels, right?

I check the date of the article — 1st June 1991 — the day after we were born. It all fits.

Okay, so ... I have an observation. It says here that Jane Daniels kept one of us, but my parents told me they adopted me from a baby and Alicia was adopted as a baby too, so this makes no sense.

Evidentially your parents lied.

But why? And who put all this together? Who made this scrapbook?

I do not know. The handwriting is unfamiliar. Plus, all these clippings are from thirty odd years ago, which clearly have nothing to do with Rebecca or Laura.

But they must be related to Frank Master, The Hooded Man. I mean one of them even mentions a dark hood. It can't be a coincidence. It almost looks as if whoever made this scrapbook was keeping tabs on all the rapes and attacks on women that fit a particular profile.

Indeed, you are correct.

But what the hell was it doing in my parents' attic! They can't have known about this ... surely. I know them and they wouldn't have covered this up.

Are you sure about that? Is this handwriting familiar to you? Could it belong to either Amanda or Ronald?

No, definitely not. My mum has weirdly neat handwriting and my dad used to do strange loops with his j's and g's. It's not theirs. I don't know who it belongs to.

Okay, which leaves us with the question ... who would be keeping track of these attacks thirty years ago, and why?

We are both silent for several minutes before I head upstairs. I need to think for a moment. There is an annoying buzz in the back of my mind that is telling me to look through Peter's *masterpiece*, as he liked to call it. I need something to jolt my brain into coming up with a solution.

I push open the door to Benjamin's mother's room and behold the chaos within. I stare at the back wall which I have covered in newspapers, printed out articles and Post-it Notes, all of which were pulled from Peter's old house. Yes, I am aware of the irony of this situation and the fact that Peter used to keep tabs on his women by doing the exact same thing, but at least I am doing it for a good reason.

The second wall contains relatively new articles about women who have recently been raped by The Hooded Man. Now that he is in the news (although it has quietened down somewhat lately) I have been able to create a loose timeframe of the assaults. It has taken me the best part of the last month to accomplish this; however, it has, unfortunately, brought me no closer to finding Rebecca's location because, according to the internet, her attack was never mentioned or published. Josslyn and I have gone through the enormous effort of organising these attacks by year and trying to find a pattern, but there does not seem to be one to find. I am not a detective; neither is Josslyn. For all we know the answer is staring us right in the face and we are too blind with rage and confusion to see it.

What are you looking for, Alicia?

I stay quiet while I scan the walls, searching for something … anything … that appears out of the ordinary. Why is nothing making any sense? I have all of this fucking information, but none of it adds up, nor does it help me in locating Rebecca.

I scream in frustration.

'Where the fuck are you Rebecca! Just fucking tell me where you are!'

I lunge forwards and punch the wall with my right fist and then for good measure I kick it, forgetting that I am bare foot.

'Fuck! … Motherfucker!' I shout. I collapse on the floor, clutching my injured toe and then have one of those light-bulb moments …

Mother …

Mother …

Rebecca's mother …

Wait … didn't Peter want to find her? Wasn't that stuck on one of his Post-it Notes somewhere?

I immediately lunge for the pile of Peter's notes that Josslyn and I took down from his spare room. I have not bothered to stick them to the walls. They are still in the black plastic bag I originally stuffed them into. I begin to search through them until I find it and I read it aloud: 'I know who Rebecca is now. I am unsure whether to tell The Master. Does he know? Does she know? I must find her mother …'

Peter wanted to find Rebecca's mother, but why?

It appears there was something about Rebecca that Frank did not know, but Peter did and he needed to speak to her mother to maybe confirm it, but what … wait …

Alicia? Talk to me. What are you thinking?

I think maybe Rebecca is Frank's daughter.

Oh, shit! Which means …

It appears we may have a half-sister.

Fuck! But how did Peter even find that out?

Hear me out on this.

I pace up and down as I speak to the empty room, blurting out my random thoughts as they come to me.

'Peter always seemed to stalk women he had some sort of connection with. First, it was his sister, then me and you and Laura, who was his best friend's sister … so why Rebecca? Who is she? What is so special about her? Maybe Rebecca told him her mother was raped and Peter put two and two together, or maybe he found out before that somehow. Maybe he was trying to find out if she was indeed Frank's daughter, but then Rebecca disappeared, so he started to search for her mother instead. Maybe her mother is one of those women in the scrapbook we found from thirty years ago.'

But which one? There are dozens of women in that book.

'The first one highlighted in green,' I reply out loud. 'Charlotte Murray.'

Well, it's a bit of a stretch, but it's all we have and I don't have any better ideas right now. So now we're looking for Charlotte Murray?

Yes. I believe she may know where her daughter is.

Chapter Seven
Josslyn

I take over for a while when Alicia becomes too exhausted to keep her eyes open, but it soon becomes abundantly clear Charlotte Murray is as elusive as her daughter. For fuck's sake, why does everyone feel the need to hide? Yes, granted, I'm hiding, but I have my reasons as you well know, but why is Charlotte Murray hiding? Do you know how many Google results pop up when you type in *Charlotte Murray, Scotland?* – over seven and a half million. I can't even narrow it down further because I have nothing else to go on. I keep looking over the short article in the notebook, but there's no further information that's relevant. I don't know the name of her brother who took her away to Scotland and I don't know what she looks like (because the photo is blurry), other than the fact she'd be in her fifties by now.

Yes, I've flicked through hundreds of LinkedIn and Facebook profiles, but I'm looking for a woman I've never seen before so it's proving to be rather difficult. I know she has a daughter called Rebecca, but that doesn't really help at all.

I eventually fall asleep and when I wake up I'm awkwardly lying on the hard floor with drool trailing down my cheek. I wipe it away and groan, rising myself into a sitting position. I gaze at the walls … the pictures of Laura and Rebecca stare back at me, torturing me. I'd be the worst detective or private investigator in the world. There must be databases on the internet with everyone's personal address and details on, right? Or am I just making that up?

The morning sun creeps in through the thin curtains. I traipse downstairs, hanging my head in shame and make a cup of tea, which will at least make everything better for a little while. My mum always used to say that a cup of tea would fix anything. Well, she's fucking wrong, isn't she? Because a cup of fucking tea isn't going to fix the fact I'm now searching for two women, neither of whom want to be found. If only I had something a bit more … tangible … to go on. Anything. A date of birth. The name of her brother. Anything more than *Charlotte Murray, Scotland.*

As I'm slurping my tea the doorbell goes, so I shout through the letterbox.

'What do you want?'

'Is Ben Willis in?'

'No.'

'I have a package for him.'

'Leave it on the doorstep.'

'I need him to sign for it.'

I sigh. 'I'll sign for it. Hang on.' I unlock the door and open it a crack, avoiding showing my face to the scrawny delivery guy. I quickly scribble a random signature and grab the box off him, slamming the door in his face.

'Have a nice day!' he shouts sarcastically to me.

I ignore him and rip open the box. It's the tape player.

Maybe the tape will reveal some more information.

Alicia ... you up yet? Hello?

Weird. Where the hell is she?

I shrug my shoulders, settle down on the sofa with my tea beside me and slide the tape into the player after inserting the batteries.

I press play ...

There's a weird static sound and something that sounds like feet scuffling on the floor and then a woman's voice plays through the small speakers and my heart rate literally doubles in speed as she begins to speak:

'Hello. I don't even know who I'm speaking to, but I hope it's you. I can only hope this has somehow found its way to you, my darling Alicia. I pray every day that one day you'll find this, but if this is you then it means I'm dead. That's such a cliché thing to say, right? But unfortunately it's true. I'm dead, but it means I'm no longer suffering and it's better this way, I promise. If I'm dead then it means I'm at peace, but if you're listening to this then it means that you aren't at peace and you've probably been searching for answers your entire life. I don't know how things have turned out for you, but I can only pray that you've been able to put the past behind you and find some happiness because no little girl should have to go through what you've been through since you've been born. I know this is a horrible thing to say as a mother, but ... I wish you'd never been born. Not because I don't love you ... I do ... so, so much, but because I wish I'd done more to protect you. I wish I hadn't brought a child into this world; this is no place for a child.

'I don't know if you'll remember me, but I'm your mother. I'm Jane Daniels. I expect you've been told by people and your adopted parents, whoever they may be, that I died in childbirth. It's not true. I never wanted you to come looking for me. I wanted you to have a whole new life and I never wanted you to think that you had to find me. I gave birth to you and your twin sister at Salisbury Hospital on the 31st of May 1991. Throughout my pregnancy I was kept in a locked room by your father. He fed me, clothed me and took me out for medical appointments when necessary. He looked after me. When we were told I was carrying twins I saw disappointment in his eyes, but he told me he had a plan. He only needed one of you, but then we found out you were both girls and he almost killed me because of it. He wanted a boy, but he took a few days to calm down and accepted the fact that you were girls.

'Anyway … when I went into labour he drove me as far away as he could and then dropped me on the side of the road near a hospital. He told me what I had to say to the doctors and what I had to do. I had no choice. I was his prisoner and I knew if I didn't obey him then … well, I don't like to think about what he might have done to me. I gave birth to you both. There were a few complications and you were starved of oxygen for longer than was deemed normal, but you pulled through. I told the doctors I wanted one of you to be put up for adoption straight away. I decided to keep you, the one who had nearly died at birth, and I handed Josslyn straight over, telling them her name. The doctors tried to change my mind and even tried to get me to see a psychiatrist, but then your father turned up and he took us both away again. That was his plan.

'That was six years ago. Your father is a sick, sick man. He is a rapist and I don't even know his real name so I had to put *unknown* on your birth certificates. He's done awful things to you, Alicia. I'm so sorry. I can't even begin to tell you how sorry I am, but I'm sick too. I keep staying with him. He lets me out for a few hours at a time, but I always have one of his friends with me. I don't really have an identity anymore. I'm just his play thing, but since he's had you he hasn't paid me as much attention. He never touches you though. Never. But he lets others touch you … I'm not going to explain exactly what your father has let those perverts do to you because I can't bring myself to even say the words. I've tried to protect you and have begged him to beat me instead, but he doesn't listen. He does it all for the glory. He shows you off to his sick friends and lets them do things to you … things you're too young to even understand. He says he's trying to break you. He keeps repeating it over and over. I'm so sorry my darling. Please forgive me. I wish I'd had an abortion all those years ago. I know it's a horrible thing to say, but at least you would have been spared this … evil … this … awful, despicable …

'Today he took you and you're never the same when you come back. I see a little bit more of you die each time it happens, but today it finally happened … *he broke you.* He brought you back to the room and you were different. You wouldn't look at me. You just kept holding your teddy bear against your chest, squeezing it around the neck. You're laying on the bed behind me now … broken … I-I can't …

'I have a plan, my baby. I have my own plan. I'm not going to let him take you anymore. I'm getting you out. It may already be too late, but all I ask is that you try and forget what has happened to you. I don't care how you do it. I don't even care if you get a head injury and get amnesia. I just want you to forget about me and everything that's happened to you. I'm going to put a few things in a bag for you to take and I'm getting you out of this house as soon as I can. I've been searching for an escape route and I've finally found one. You're a smart girl so I know you'll do as I tell you. If you manage to escape then you'll be free and someone will adopt you, I'm sure of it. I just hope the damage hasn't already been done.

'Don't worry about your sister. Josslyn is safe. Maybe one day you'll find one another, but maybe not. Whatever you have to do my darling to forget this awful place just do it. People will think you're crazy maybe, but that's okay. They could never understand anyway. You'll never be a normal girl because of what's happened to you, but I can at least try and get you out. I'm sorry if it doesn't work, but at least I'll know that I tried. Please, Alicia … promise me you'll forget everything, you'll block it out, you'll suppress all these memories … then you'll be okay …

you'll be safe. Goodbye, my darling. I love you. Mummy loves you.'

The recording splutters to a close and I'm left feeling ... feeling ... *nothing.* My body is completely numb from my head down to my toes. I feel as if all the air has been sucked out of the room ... I can't ... breathe ...

Oh God ... I think I'm having a panic attack ...

A heavy weight is forcing its way down, down, down ...

I need air!

I stagger to my feet, clutching my chest, but my legs aren't working and I stumble forwards onto the floor. I need oxygen ... I need ...

Someone help me!

Then the darkness engulfs me ...

Chapter Eight
Josslyn

The next thing I'm aware of is a bright light burning through my eyelids, which feels like searing hot needles are being stuck into them. I squeeze them tighter, but that only hurts more.

What the fuck just happened?

I open one eye at a time and all I see is black ... just black ... nothing else.

Where am I?

I assume we are in our own head.

Alicia!

I sit bolt upright, but instantly regret the sudden movement as my head begins to spin and I immediately see double. I clutch my head and groan.

Take it easy. Just breathe.

I don't understand ... Why are we in our head? Why aren't we in the real world?

My guess is you passed out and we now have to process what we have just learnt.

Did you ... I mean ... did you hear everything that was on the tape?

I did.

What does it all mean?

You know what it means, Josslyn.

Please … please explain it to me. I need to hear it from you.

At this point I feel a presence next to me; the darkness shifts slightly and I lift my head to see Alicia crouching down next to me. It's good to see her again, but she looks tired, as I'm sure I do too. She places a gentle hand on my shoulder, but I can't really feel it because she's not really there.

I blink several times as tears form in my eyes, blurring my vision. Now that she's in front of me I speak out loud.

'I don't want to believe it.' I know exactly what it means, but I can't bring myself to say it. If I say it then it's real and I don't want it to be real. Everything I've ever known has been a lie. Everything I have ever believed about myself and about Alicia … is … I'm … I've never been …

'You … you are not real,' says Alicia as she lightly squeezes my shoulder. 'Benjamin was correct about us. You are not a real person living inside my body. You are indeed a separate personality I have created in order to … to shield myself from … the horrific things that happened to me as a young child.'

I shake my head. 'B-but … the foetus in fetu … it was real. I was real. I lived a whole life up until the age of nearly thirty. I grew up on a farm. I was home-schooled. I went to university and became a vet. That was all real!'

'Yes, the foetus in fetu was real, but the doctor was correct. The tumour I had removed was merely a bundle of cells and tissue, nothing more. I have spent a lifetime believing that you truly exist, that you are completely separate from me and that you are my twin sister speaking to me. It is what we have always believed since you found out about having a twin, but we are one and the same. Josslyn ... you are a personality I created in order to cover up my dark past, but the real me eventually began to surface again and take control.'

'It can't be true. I ... I remember my childhood. I grew up with a mum and dad. I had a happy childhood. I don't understand ... You were there. You remember, right? We used to play in the fields ... remember ... Tornado and Milo ...'

'Yes. I remember, but what do you remember from before the farm ... before the age of seven?'

There's a sudden silence.

I shake my head slowly. 'Nothing. There's nothing before the farm, but a lot of kids don't remember things before the age of seven.'

We sit quietly for a few moments as a wave of reality sets in and I feel my heart sink lower and lower. I'm so confused ...

'But who's Josslyn? She said Josslyn was put up for adoption.'

'She was talking about Alicia Phillips. Somehow our birth certificates must have been mixed up, whether on purpose or not I do not know. Josslyn was always Alicia Phillips ... and Alicia was always me. You do not exist. You have never truly existed.'

'Alicia, this can't be true. It can't! I don't believe it. I won't believe it and neither should you.' I'm angry now. In fact, I'm more than angry. I'm furious!

I stand up on wobbly legs and pace up and down, staring at the floor, my fists clenched.

'I'm real goddammit!' I scream in Alicia's face.

Alicia doesn't even flinch.

I glare at her as tears stream down my face. 'I'm real!' I shout again, but this time it's with less conviction.

Alicia slowly shakes her head. 'We should have known this was the truth from the start. To believe a cluster of cells could really be a living person was my own brain shielding me from the truth. I am damaged. I am broken, but you helped fix me ... for a while at least.'

I choke back a sob that's stuck in my throat. 'But my mum and dad ... they lied to me about adopting me as a baby.'

'Peter told us they had lied to you about something else.'

'Why does everyone keep lying to us?'

It appears Alicia doesn't know the answer, so she doesn't reply. Instead we sit down on the floor, back to back and sit in silence for a long time, neither one of us knowing what to say or do next. Our entire world has been torn apart and I've no idea how we're supposed to put it back together and carry on.

Even though I can't actually *feel* Alicia's back pressing up against mine I can still feel a certain warmth coming from her. It's nice; comforting even. There's so much to say, but we choose not to say anything. Now isn't the right time. This isn't about me and Alicia. This is about Frank Master and bringing him and his sick reign to an end no matter what the cost. There will be time afterwards to address this … issue.

'Can we pretend like everything is normal for a bit longer?' I ask finally. 'I don't want to face reality right now.'

'Yes, I believe that is the most logical way forwards.'

'Not a word to Ben about this though, okay?'

'Agreed.'

Chapter Nine
Alicia

The first sensation I am aware of is a sharp pain on the left side of my head. With a shaking hand I feel around the area, checking for the wet, sticky sensation of blood. I find none, but there is a rather large bump, signalling the fact I obviously hit my head on the way down to the floor. I bring myself into a seated position and hang my head between my knees, inhaling deeply, waiting for the dizziness and nausea to pass.

Josslyn is ... taking some time out for a while.

I will not lie ... the contents of the recording has left me feeling a little shaken. I had not been expecting that, but now I think about it ... it makes perfect sense. I was abused as a child and in order to protect myself I created a new identity, a different personality ... Josslyn. She was the one who was in control for a long time until the real me decided to take over again. I had the foetus removed, which enabled my real self to come forwards as the dominant identity and Josslyn's personality to take a step back ... until she emerged a year and a half later.

Here we are now ...

I feel ... angry. It seems that anger is the only emotion I can comprehend at the moment. I need to somehow vent my frustration and right now the punch bag hanging from the ceiling in the corner of the spare room is

71

the only thing that can take the brunt of my abuse and survive it.

I stand up and head upstairs, grab the boxing gloves and put them on, using my teeth to pull at the restraints to tighten them around my wrists. I flex my neck side to side and up and down, feeling as it clicks and crunches. The tight knots in my back and shoulders scream at me as I start punching the bag, hard and fast, not bothering to warm up my muscles. I still feel weak and dizzy from the bump on my head, but I ignore it.

I envision the bag as Peter, standing there with a smug grin. Then it turns into Frank, my so-called *father*. I punch so hard the bag swings back and then towards me. I duck to avoid it, turn slightly and continue my assault, imagining Frank's face in front of me. It changes again. This time the bag is me. I grit my teeth and throw all my strength into my punches as I attack, over and over and over until I cannot lift my arms up any longer. My vision begins to blur and I stop, wobbling on the spot slightly. I bend over at the waist to catch my breath, but it is no good. I feel as if I am about to faint so I bend one leg and kneel on the floor. Nausea washes over me, but I manage to compose myself within a few seconds.

Are you okay?

I thought you were supposed to be taking some time out?

But you seem a bit ... unstable. I'm worried.

I have just found out I was abused as a child and that I have a mental disorder where I have envisioned my identical twin sister as a personality in my head for years ... Of course I am *unstable*.

You're angry Alicia and we all know what happens when you get angry. You lose your composure and usually you end up killing someone.

Well, luckily there is no one here to kill right now.

I stand up straight, shrug off the dizziness and continue my attack on the bag.

Half an hour later I am drenched in sweat, breathing excessively heavily and beyond exhausted, but I feel good, strong, powerful. I have expelled the tension that has been building up over the past couple of days, but even while I stand in the shower with the water cascading down on my face I can feel it beginning to creep up again; a white hot rage that threatens to constantly overflow like burning lava from a volcano. I slowly breathe in the warm steam and close my eyes against the streaming water. It is then I suddenly feel the dizziness return and I stumble against the tiles before I lose my balance. Something is not right. A searing pain shoots through my head like a directly focussed laser beam.

Have you noticed that you've been getting a lot of headaches lately?

It is just from stress and lack of sleep.

I think it's me.

What is you?

I think I'm being to ... fade away. I can feel it. I don't really know how else to explain it, but I can feel an overwhelming pull and I'm fighting against it all the time. I think maybe I'm making you weaker as your body is fighting me. Now we know what I truly am ... you're trying to break through ... the real you.

I am not doing it on purpose.

I know, but you always did tell me that eventually I'd fade away.

That was when I believed you to be a remnant of the tumour I had removed. I assumed you would fade away when my body absorbed what was left of you, but now we know you are a split personality it means there is a chance you will not fade away. Maybe you will stay forever.

But what about what Frank said on the phone? It makes so much sense now. He said ... and I quote ... 'I know you do not remember our time together, but maybe one day that wall you have built up will fall down.' That's what he called me ... a wall. What's going to happen when it finally comes down and you start to remember what happened to you? Maybe you'll turn into a raging, murdering psychopath ... I mean, like ... even worse than you were before ...

I inhale deeply and let it out slowly as I switch off the shower and reach for a towel.

I thought we were not going to focus on this until we deal with Frank?

It's kind of hard not to focus on it ...

I begin to dry myself while I mull my thoughts over.

Despite the fact I would kill for five minutes of peace and quiet once in a while the thought of being completely alone in this body fills me with ... dread. Josslyn and I have coexisted for a long time now and I believe we have finally come to a mutual understanding and respect for one another. If what Josslyn says is true and she really is beginning to fade away what will happen when the metaphorical *wall* comes crashing down? If Josslyn really is a barrier I have created in my mind, then what dark and sinister things will I find in there when she no longer exists? Will I become someone different again ... Will I remember everything my father put me through as a child? From the things my mother mentioned on the tape it does not bear thinking about ...

The majority of the day is spent perusing the internet in search of Charlotte Murray, but my brain does not appear to be working correctly and the pain in my head is a constant distraction. I take some painkillers, but they barely scratch the surface. Looking at a computer screen is physically causing me to feel nauseous so later that evening I switch on the television and listen to the news with my eyes closed in an attempt to quell the queasiness. I despise this ritual, but I know I need to keep up to date on what is happening with regards to Josslyn's situation. I also keep an ear out for any possible mention of The Hooded Man or a similar sighting because it may give me an idea as to where Frank is hiding. I hope to not hear another woman has been stalked or raped or murdered, but unfortunately it happens far more than anyone likes to mention. I expect most instances do not even make headline news; a sad and depressing fact.

The BBC News headlines begin at six and I get the all too familiar sense of anxiety and dry mouth as I hear Josslyn's name. I flick my eyes open, ignoring the pain for now and focus on Josslyn's face as she appears on the screen.

Oh shit ... now what's happened?

Chapter Ten
Alicia

I stare at the screen for the duration of the broadcast, both my hands gripping the edges of the armchair as I lean forwards, scarcely able to believe my own ears.

A young, attractive news presenter is reading the news, probably very inexperienced because she keeps glancing down at some papers in front of her and appears to be sweating, as if speaking about this situation is making her severely uncomfortable.

'A new development has come to light in the search for Josslyn Reynolds, the ex-girlfriend of Daniel Russell who was found dead in a rubbish tip in the outskirts of Cambridge just over a month ago. Josslyn has been wanted for questioning by the police since blood belonging to Daniel Russell was found in her flat above her vet practice where she worked up until a year and a half ago.

'Doctor Jacobson, who works at Addenbrooke's Hospital in Cambridge, has contacted the local police with further information on Josslyn Reynolds, which has now shone a whole new light on her activity and state of mind. In November 2019 she was admitted to the hospital in an unconscious state. Peter Phillips, her friend who was with her at the time, told the hospital staff she was suffering from severe abdominal and head pain.

'Peter Phillips is known in the local Cambridge community as the History Buff and has won Teacher of the Year at Lampton Boarding School for Boys on numerous occasions. He is also the adopted brother of Alicia Phillips who supposedly committed suicide just over seven years ago. Peter is now wanted for questioning about the whereabouts of Josslyn, however he appears to be missing as well. His parents have stated that they haven't heard from him in over a month. His house has been searched, but it was found empty. More on Peter's disappearance later because we actually have further detailed information about Josslyn Reynolds, a seemingly average young woman who appears to have a fascinating history.

'Doctor Jacobson has released Josslyn's medical records to the police stating she not only has psychopathic tendencies, but she also has a very rare condition known as a foetus in fetu. He is with us now via live video link to explain this in more detail ...'

She turns to a nearby screen where a familiar face stares back at me.

'Doctor, thank you for joining us today. So what you're saying is that Josslyn Reynolds is a deranged psychopath and she has a rare medical condition. Please can you expand on this for us?'

'Hello. Thank you for having me. The case of Josslyn Reynolds is quite fascinating, but I'm afraid I'm not exactly calling her a deranged psychopath, as you put it. Her condition is far more complicated than that.'

The young news presenter blushes slightly as the doctor continues.

'Her medical condition is unlike anything I've ever seen before, or will probably ever see again, but first let me explain about her unorthodox brain activity. When she was admitted into my care she was unconscious and I couldn't figure out why, so I conducted numerous scans, including a brain scan and on it I found she had many of the anomalies that one would associate with being a psychopath. I won't go into the technical jargon now, but when I spoke to her she appeared not to realise she had these psychopathic tendencies. She appeared perfectly normal on the outside. Let me explain this in a little more detail …

'Psychopaths are renowned for being manipulative and can often be seen by others as charming, normal individuals and can lead perfectly ordinary lives. However, a sociopath can usually be seen as more erratic and prone to rage and therefore unable to lead as much of a normal life. It's my understanding that sociopaths are often created by severe trauma and physical or emotional abuse experienced at a young age, whereas psychopaths are usually prepositioned. To put the matter simply … sociopaths are made and psychopaths are born. Now, I'm not sure about Josslyn's childhood or what may or may not have happened to her, so I cannot state with certainty whether she's a psychopath or a sociopath—'

'So basically what you're saying is Josslyn Reynolds is dangerous and could very well have murdered Daniel Russell?'

'No, I'm not saying that explicitly … and here's why … Despite what is widely assumed by a large proportion of the population … not all psychopaths are bad people. Their brain chemistry is different from the average person, but it doesn't necessarily make them *evil*. It just means they find it harder to manage in everyday situations and struggle to adapt to normal, civilised behaviour. Thanks to movies and books these so-called *psychopaths* are always portrayed as the bad guy, but this isn't always the case. They are merely different.'

The newswoman looks confused for several seconds and frowns. 'But then …' she continues, '… you don't actually know if Josslyn is a good or bad psychopath. She could just be a very good actress.'

'Indeed, that's very true. If she is a true psychopath or sociopath then she is more than capable of killing someone and feeling no remorse at all.'

The newswoman looks pleased with herself, clearly having finally convinced the doctor to say what she had wanted him to say.

'Okay … and what about this rare medical condition she has … this foetus in fetu? Can you explain exactly what that is and how it could affect her?'

'Yes, of course. A foetus in fetu is an extremely rare condition where a malformed foetus is found within the body of their twin. Usually it's only ever seen in young babies, but on very rare occasions the foetus can go unnoticed for years and be found in a full grown adult. I believe Josslyn is possibly only the second adult woman to have this condition. I've only ever come across it in medical journals.'

'Wow ... that's fascinating, so what's this foetus got to do with Josslyn being a psychopath or a sociopath?' continues the newswoman.

Doctor Jacobson shakes his head. 'Absolutely nothing, however, she did ask me a very interesting question when I spoke to her and I remember it very well because it had seemed so odd at the time. She asked me ... and I quote ... "would it be possible for it to be alive inside me and speak to me, like a real person?" Now, even I know that is physically impossible, because the malformed foetus is nothing more than cells and tissue, but it could be that *she* believes it. It is possible she has further mental disorders we're unaware of, including Dissociative Identity Disorder. I did try and persuade her to be studied and tested, but she declined. I am also aware that she later had the foetus removed at another hospital. Her condition was kept quiet due to doctor–patient confidentiality, but since she is now wanted for murder I believe it's important for the police and the local community to know who we're dealing with. If Josslyn Reynolds does indeed have Dissociative Identity Disorder then we could be dealing with a very unstable and confused individual.'

The newswoman nods her head and smiles. 'Thank you Doctor Jacobson for explaining those fascinating details ... And now, on to other news, which is also connected to Josslyn Reynolds ... The body of Alicia Phillips has finally been found after she supposedly committed suicide seven years ago. She was found buried under a large tree in the New Forest near the childhood home of Josslyn Reynolds. Her body is now being removed and examined, but due to Josslyn's previous contact with Alicia's brother, Peter Phillips, she is also wanted for questioning regarding her death as well as Peter's disappearance.

'The police are treating Josslyn Reynolds as extremely dangerous and after what Doctor Jacobson has just revealed we must ask ourselves this ... could we have a psychotic female serial killer on our hands?'

Chapter Eleven
Alicia

I switch off the television, feeling as if my eyeballs are about to burst from their sockets, and sit in silence as I attempt to comprehend what has just happened. This was never supposed to happen. None of it. Everything is unravelling at an alarming speed and gaining momentum and there is nothing I can do to stop it.

I had a plan. I am not saying it was perfect, but it was a solid plan and up until five minutes ago it had been going in roughly the right direction, but now everything is fucked ... fucked!

Alicia Phillips was never supposed to be found, not yet anyway. She was supposed to rot in the ground for a few more years until all this shit had died down and then I would have made an anonymous call out of the blue and informed the authorities that a body was buried under the old tree. The only person who knew about her burial location was Peter and he is dead ... so he must have told someone between the time I told him and the time Josslyn slit his throat open.

Doctor Jacobson was never supposed to break doctor–patient confidentiality and tell the whole world Josslyn Reynolds is a dangerous psychopath who is possibly mentally unstable because she thinks that the foetus in fetu inside her is talking to her ...

Josslyn is wanted for two murders ... possibly three (if they eventually come to the conclusion that Peter is dead, although it is highly unlikely his remains will ever be found because they are nothing more than ash spread across several different recycling centres). She (or more appropriately I) will never be able to live a normal life again. There is no way out of this. Three murders ... No, wait, four ... Michael, my attempted rapist ... fuck. God only knows what Peter did with his body ... probably put it in a random location which will be discovered any day now ...

And that fucking newswoman making out I am a psychotic serial killer going on some random killing spree. I wish I could squeeze the life from her pathetic body, wiping that smug smirk off her face ...

Okay, Alicia ... before you completely lose it and go mental and kill someone just take a breath.

I stand up and begin pacing the room like a caged animal. I cannot breathe in this house. I can only blame myself. I should have been more careful, but I acted irrationally and just killed without thinking about the repercussions ... about how this would affect me down the line. I used to always think I was in control of everything, that I had everything planned down to the letter, but this has now proven to me that I have been deluding myself all these years.

We can get through this. Let's just focus on one thing at a time.

Charlotte Murray.

Right. We need to find her first so we can find Rebecca so we can find Frank …

I let out a sarcastic laugh.

'It is a never-ending game of catch,' I say out loud. 'We may as well be going around in circles.'

Just listen to me, okay? Josslyn Reynolds, technically, no longer exists. Her life ended nearly two years ago. One day soon I'll disappear forever and you'll be left to pick up the shattered pieces of our lives, so it's you we have to focus on right now, not me. Let them accuse me of all these murders, I don't care. You can still get out of this. You changed your name to Alexis Grey, right? But you aren't really her. Technically, Alicia, you don't exist. No one knows about you except me and Ben and he won't say anything, I can promise you that … And Frank. I doubt he'll send the cops after you because he wants you for something else. That doctor may think he knows about you, but he doesn't, not really. He's barely scratched the surface. Let everyone think Josslyn is mentally unstable and a psychopath. Let them chase after a ghost. They can focus on me while you focus on Frank Master.

I ponder her words for a moment, realising almost immediately that she is correct. I cannot spend my time worrying about Josslyn because she no longer exists in the outside world. Alexis Grey exists. I did not change my name officially of course. I used Josslyn's passport to fly to Tuscany and back to the United Kingdom. Alexis Grey is merely an alias, but no one is looking for her, not yet anyway. I can still use her name to get around. There is still hope ...

I need to think about myself and, for once, I am not being selfish.

Thank you, Josslyn, for making me think clearly.

Hey, that's what sisters are for, right?

You are not my sister.

Technicalities.

I smile as I retrieve the laptop from the table.

It is time to put a new plan in place.

What have you got in mind?

We wait for Benjamin to respond, but in the meantime ... we do some preparation.

Preparation?

I type a few words into Google.

You're going to buy a fake ID?

Preparation.

Chapter Twelve
Alicia

Two days later.

It has been a very productive couple of days. There has been no contact from Benjamin as yet, although I do secretly hope he calls with news soon because I am beginning to get impatient again. I have been keeping busy honing my boxing skills as well as conducting further research on Charlotte Murray. I ordered a fake ID online (which was surprisingly easy to accomplish once I discovered someone local in the area who agreed to do it for me … for a price, but since Benjamin left me his credit card that was no issue).

I am now *officially* known as Alexis Grey, with no links back to Josslyn Reynolds whatsoever. I should be able to step outside into the world now without the fear of being caught. There is still the possibility someone could recognise me, but that will not stop me from carrying out my plan. I must continue to keep my head down as much as possible and try not to draw too much attention to myself.

The news around Josslyn has begun to slowly die down somewhat, as do most headlines eventually. It is still there in the background, but there has been no new information as yet. Alicia's body is still being examined and her parents are begging the community to be on the lookout for Peter, but otherwise it is old news. I find myself feeling sorry for Mr and Mrs Phillips over the fact they have lost both their daughter and their son, but then again … their son was a mentally sick and perverted asshole so the feeling quickly passes. If they knew who he had truly been … well, they say parents will always love their children no matter what awful things they do, but I find it hard to believe they could still love him if they ever found out what he did to his own sister and all the other women over the years.

Josslyn has been more and more absent as the days have gone by so I have been spending a lot of time alone with my thoughts. I suppose I should be preparing myself for the inevitable – that at some point Josslyn will disappear forever. Josslyn appears to have accepted her fate, but I am full of trepidation (an emotion I do not enjoy) about the thought of being by myself forever. It has always been the two of us. I do not remember a time without her (apart from the brief stint in Tuscany) and, by the sounds of it, it is best I do not remember …

I am about to make a ham and cheese sandwich when my phone rings. I answer without even looking at the screen. I know who it is.

'Benjamin.'

'Alicia, it's so good to hear your voice! I'm sorry I haven't called. It's been a long few days.'

'You could say that.'

'Are you okay? Is Josslyn okay? I've just seen a news bulletin about her ... I had no idea it would get this bad ... is she okay?'

'She is fine.'

'Are you okay? I mean ... what the doctor said about you ... the media is making you out to be dangerous.'

'I am dangerous.'

'Right, but ... yeah, I guess you're right.'

There is an awkward silence.

'Do you have news?' I ask finally.

'Sorry, yes, but it's not good news.'

'Tell me.'

'Laura's dead.'

I let a few seconds pass, fully aware I must attempt to say something comforting to Benjamin, but as you know I have never been good at consoling people.

'I am sorry for your loss.'

Another few seconds pass.

'Thanks. I must admit a part of me already knew that she was dead, but I always had hope, you know, that I'd find her alive.'

His sentence makes no sense to me at all, but I allow him to continue.

'I spoke to the woman. It's a long story, but Laura left me something, a note, which I've read ... and Alicia ... it's not good. I swear to God if Phil was still alive I'd fucking murder the guy myself.' He sighs loudly. 'I'm coming home. That's what I called to say because I can't tell you all this over the phone. It's too much to explain and process. I want to see you.'

'You mean you want to see Josslyn,' I correct.

'I ... I didn't mean. I mean ... of course I want to see you too, Alicia.'

'How long will it take for you to arrive here?'

'I'll be home in the next couple of hours. I've just stopped to fill up the car and grab a bite to eat, but I won't be long.'

'Okay, I shall see you soon, but does the note help us at all? Does it say who was after her ... who could have possibly killed her?'

'That's the thing ... I don't think she was killed ... I think she killed herself.'

I nod, even though I know Benjamin cannot see me.

'And there is nothing else in the note?' I ask.

'You'll see when you read it.'

We say our goodbyes and I hang up.

Did you get any of that, Josslyn?

Yeah ... just ... I really hope there's more in the note than that.

As do I. Are you up to taking over for a while so you can greet Benjamin? I get the feeling he has missed you and he does not want to see me.

Of course he wants to see you, but thank you. Yes, I think I'm strong enough.

Chapter Thirteen
Josslyn

I wait like an excited dog by the front door for the next two hours expecting Ben to walk in at any moment. I can't wait to see him, to touch him, to feel him. I've missed him so much and after everything that's recently happened (finding out I'm a split personality and not a real person ... you know ... *that*) I really need a goddamn hug. You know me ... I'm not a naturally huggy type of person, never have been (and Alicia is about as huggable as a rabies-infested bear), but lately I've wanted and needed a hug. Whenever I used to get these urges I'd always go to my mum because she gave free hugs willingly and never asked why, but now she's gone and there's no one left to hug ... except Ben.

My mum always told me I'd fall in love one day and I'd just know when I found the right person. I, of course, would roll my eyes at her and say something sarcastic back, but she was right (and it physically pains me to say that). There's not a doubt in my mind Ben is the right man for me. Why couldn't I have met him years ago back when I had a real life? It all seems like such a waste now I know it can't last forever, that sooner or later I'll be gone and this will all end. Then what will happen? What will happen to him and Alicia? Will they stay together as friends or—

Do not concern yourself with me. I can take care of myself.

91

No offence, but it's not really you I'm worried about. You'll stay with Ben though, right? You'll look after him for me? You have feelings for him, I know you do and he loves you too. You can stay together and work something out, I'm sure of it.

I do not believe that will be possible.

Why not?

I do not love him.

But—

Do not question me.

But you do care about him. With me gone you two will be the only people who know the truth about me and what's happened.

Maybe we can remain ... friends.

Friends?

I do not wish to spend the remainder of my life attached to another human being. I will finally be free from you ... no offence—

Some taken.

—And I shall use my new found freedom to begin a new life, like I attempted to do last time, but this time shall be different. Peter is gone and soon Frank will be gone too, then you shall go and then I will be alone. It will be how it always should have been.

But Ben—

Benjamin shall adapt.

I bite my lip to stop myself from arguing.

Jesus Christ my sister can be so stubborn.

No … wait … I forgot … she's not really my sister. I keep forgetting I'm actually a split personality and not a real person. I've lived for so long thinking I know one thing and now I've found out it's actually not true. It's going to take some time to adjust.

Let's address this right now … I know being a living person thanks to the foetus in fetu made absolutely no sense and it was physically impossible, but I honestly and truly believed I was real … in some form or another. I was in control of this body for over twenty years. My parents … shit … my parents. I wish they were still alive so I could shout at them till I was hoarse because they lied to me *again*, but also to hug them and tell them I love them and to thank them for everything they did for me. They gave me a life, a good life and now it's all fucked up.

I don't know how this is all going to work itself out, but I do know that eventually Alicia will be on her own and, despite what she says, she needs my help to sort her life out so she can at least attempt to be happy—

The front door opens. My breath catches in my throat as Ben steps over the threshold. God, he looks like shit; like he hasn't slept since he's been away. Has he even changed his clothes? His hair is shaggy and tangled, his beard is pretty impressive too and his shoulders are hunched as if it's an effort to remain standing.

We don't say anything. We step forward into each other's arms (he knows it's me) and hug. Then I start crying big, fat tears. Dear God, not again. I'm so bloody emotional. Ben manages to close the door with his foot without breaking our hug and then he kisses the top of my head and lets me cry. All my pent up emotion pours out of me as I realise that at some point I have to tell him he was right all along about me. I am merely a personality and not a real person. Will he stop loving me when I tell him? I can't even begin to comprehend it all so I push the feelings aside and focus on the present. His warm body wrapped around mine is exactly what I need right now and I breathe in his musty scent (okay, he definitely needs a shower), but he smells like home.

Finally Ben breaks our hug, kisses me and then leads me into the lounge. His bags are left in the hallway while he makes us both of cup of tea (such a British thing to do, right?). I mean, I could do with something stronger, but I've sworn off alcohol for a while, mainly because Alicia wants us to stay focussed and not have our minds blurry and foggy, but also because I've come to realise I may be a little too dependent on it. I'm not saying I'm a raging alcoholic and I can't get through a day without it, but there is an issue I know I need to deal with, so that's what I'm doing ... I'm dealing with it.

Oh God, I could really do with a drink.

With a steaming cup of tea in my hand I relax against Ben as he takes a seat on the sofa. I snuggle into his warm body and instantly feel better.

'So,' he says, 'did you miss me?'

'Meh.'

'Meh?'

My face breaks into a wide grin, unable to keep up the charade for a moment longer. 'I missed you more than I ever thought was possible.'

'Me too.' He kisses me.

I run my fingers through his mop of hair and then stroke his beard and laugh. 'What's with the caveman look?'

Ben laughs. 'I've been too busy to even notice.'

'I like it.'

'Really?' he chuckles.

'I mean the hair could do with a trim, but the beard can stay.'

'Okay, I'll keep the beard ... just for you.'

There's a weird silence while we realise we've made enough small talk now and it's time for the serious stuff. Sigh ... I hate serious stuff.

'So, how's it been here?'

I shrug nonchalantly. 'It's been okay.'

He raises his eyebrows at me. 'Okay? I find that hard to believe. How's it *really* been? Come on, Josslyn ... tell me the truth, what's been going on?'

I struggle to hold back tears as the words tumble out of my mouth in a torrent. 'It's been fucking shit! Rebecca appears to have disappeared off the face of the earth, so I gave up searching for her and went to my old house to get the box from the attic—'

'Wait, you did what?'

'Can I finish my story first?' I snap.

'Sure, go ahead.'

'So I get the box from the attic and I find a notebook that's full of newspaper clippings about women who got attacked and raped over thirty years ago, one of whom I figured out was Rebecca's mother, so I've been searching for her, but she's somewhere in Scotland and I can't narrow it down anymore than that. I'm scared to walk out of the door after the news broke that I'm a psychotic serial killer and I'm wanted for so many murders I've lost count. Alicia is on some rampage and spends a lot of time beating the shit out of the punch bag so I ache all over … and also …' Oh God, I can't say it. My voice catches in my throat and I feel physically sick. I know I should tell him about the recording and everything my mum told me, but I can't bring myself to drag all that up again. Not now.

'Also what?'

I swallow, my throat dry. 'Also … I've really missed you.'

Ben looks at me in a way that tells me he knows I've got more to say, but he doesn't push it. 'And you didn't think to tell me any of this while I was away?'

'Well, you had your own shit to deal with and I didn't want you to worry. Plus you know how Alicia is. She never tells anyone anything.'

'Okay, fair enough. So you went to visit your old house even though we discussed that it was risky because someone could recognise you?'

'If it makes you feel any better it wasn't my idea.'

'Shocking … never would've guessed, so how'd you get there?'

'Alicia drove.'

'But I didn't leave you the car.'

'She improvised.' Ben raises his eyebrows at me again. 'Don't give me that look,' I say quickly. 'She returned the car in its original condition, minus a few hundred miles, to the exact location where she found it.'

'Right.'

I show Ben the notebook full of clippings and I spend the next hour filling him in on the information I've come up with based on what we already know (leaving out the tape recording). I have to be so careful about what I tell him because he still has no idea Frank Master is our biological dad (I mean Alicia's dad ... cos, you know, I'm not real). Fuck! I forgot again. How did things get so complicated? Can't I just rewind a couple of years and go back to before I found the bloody box in the attic? I can't help but imagine what would've happened if I'd said no to helping my parents clear out their crap. What if I'd been too tired to go over for dinner and they'd tidied the attic themselves? They would have left the box there I imagine because it contained my baby things (except as it turns out they weren't *my* baby things) and Mum especially was always very sentimental ... except ... she never knew me as a baby, did she? She never held me, fed me, sung me to sleep ...

I sit back as I watch Ben looking through the notebook. He's saying something because his mouth is moving, but I don't hear a single word.

Shit. It's suddenly all hit me at once ... the reality of all *this*. Would I have found the box eventually or would I still be living in that tiny flat above my vet practice with Oscar? Peter would most likely still be stalking me and other women and Frank and his cronies would still be murdering, raping and torturing women for fun ... so maybe it was for the best I started off on this journey ... or maybe not.

'Penny for your thoughts?'

I smile up at Ben, blinking back tears that are threatening to overwhelm me again. 'Sorry, I was miles away.'

'I know ... I'm just glad you came back to me.'

'I'll always come back to you,' I say softly and then add silently *until I leave forever.*

'So ... about my sister ...' says Ben after we've finished discussing Rebecca and Charlotte.

I shuffle in my seat and face him directly. 'Yes, tell me everything. Can I see the letter?'

Ben walks over to his bag, takes out a crumpled envelope and hands it to me. He then pours himself a glass of wine and is about to pour a glass for me, but I raise my hand.

'None for me, thanks.'

That's when he stares at me as if I've just spoken a different language.

'Are you sure you're okay? I've never known you to turn down a drink before.'

I smile and shrug. 'I'm trying to be healthy ... healthy body, healthy mind and all that.'

'Uh-huh ...' He frowns while he takes a sip from his glass and watches me intently as I open the envelope and pull out a piece of dull white paper covered in black squiggly writing.

Ben,

I don't even know where to begin with this letter. There's so much I want to say, but I can't. I'm so sorry I haven't been in contact. I've always wanted to reach out, but I couldn't. It's been too dangerous for me and I can't let you get wrapped up in all this mess, which I've caused myself. You're my big brother. I know you've always looked out for me and taken care of me and I've never appreciated that, so it's time I sort this out on my own ... the only way I know how.

I want you to know that this isn't your fault. You tried to help me and I threw it back in your face. I got messed up with the wrong people, the wrong man ...

This is going to be hard for you to hear, but you must know that your friend, Peter Phillips, is not who he appears to be. He's not a good guy, Ben. I should have told you sooner, but I was afraid you wouldn't believe me cos I was so fucked up at the time. Please promise me you'll stay away from him. We slept together once and ever since then he's been obsessed with me and has been following me.

I've been leaving fake trails everywhere to try and hide from him. I was never in India, but he thought I was and he sent someone to follow me. His name is Gerald. He's one of *them*. He's about six foot three, has blonde hair, is quite well-built and has a tattoo of a cross on his left bicep. The woman who I paid to pretend to be me told me that he was following her and she managed to get a good description. I hope she'll be okay.

I can't hide any longer. I'm tired of running. I just want this to be over. I'm scared and I don't know what else to do. I can't live with myself any longer so I'm going to end it once and for all. It's the only way I know that I'll be safe from him … from them.

I can't tell you any more. Please promise me you'll leave me in peace. I'm sorry I'm leaving you, but it's what I want. You may never find this letter. I'm leaving it with Joanne, but if you do it means that you've tried to find me, but this is where it ends. I'm gone, Ben.

Just stay away from Peter.

I love you. Always.

Your little sister,

Laura xx

I look up at Ben who has already finished his glass and is pouring another.

'I'm so sorry—' I begin.

This time it's Ben who puts his hand up to stop me. 'It's fine … a part of me already knew the truth. I just had to find out for myself. I needed closure.'

'Did you find her … her …'

'Body? No, but I found and spoke to Joanne. She wouldn't tell me much. She said she didn't want anything to do with Laura ever again, but she gave me the letter and some of Laura's belongings.'

'So she could still be alive? I mean … if there's no body then …' There's a hint of hope in my voice, but I know Ben doesn't want to hear it, so I trail off. I can't even begin to imagine how he must be feeling. All this time thinking his sister was alive somewhere just living her best life and now he finds out his best friend was after her all along and probably did awful things to her.

'No, she's dead Josslyn. She's dead. I don't need to see her body to know that.'

I nod, understanding. 'This man … this man with the cross tattoo on his bicep … Gerald … could he be one of Frank's henchmen?'

'We're calling them henchmen now?'

'For want of a better word.'

'Possibly, but we still have nothing to go on. There was nothing else in her belongings that could be of any use.'

I may have something.

What is it, Alicia?

I think I may know who the man with the cross tattoo is.

Chapter Fourteen
Alicia

Josslyn agrees it would be easier and quicker if I spoke directly to Benjamin, so within a few seconds I am myself again. I also concur with Josslyn regarding her decision to keep the fact she is a different personality a secret for now, despite Benjamin originally believing that was exactly the case, but I get the impression, if he found out the truth now, it might hurt him. I think even he believes Josslyn is real. He has such a strong connection with her and I cannot bear to break it. He can remain in the dark for a little while longer.

'Benjamin,' I say quietly.

'Alicia … it's … good to see you.'

I raise one eyebrow at him and he smiles back at me.

'I am glad to see you have arrived back safely,' I add.

'T-Thank you. I'm sorry things have been so crap here, but about stealing a car …'

'What about it?' My voice deepens slightly, ready to argue.

'I'm impressed.'

I do not respond, but I do shuffle further away from him on the sofa. He allows me my space. I study his face; Josslyn is correct – the beard does suit him.

'So ... who's Gerald, the guy with the tattoo?' he asks.

'I did not know that was his name until just now, but I recognise the description of the tattoo. I have seen it in a newspaper article ...' Without explaining any further I grab the notebook and flip through the pages, my head bowed, ignoring Benjamin's stare.

I know I saw it somewhere ...

There. That is him.

The familiar grainy black and white photo stares up at me from the page. It was taken back in 1988; the quality is extremely bad, but the black tattoo is clearly visible. The man in the photo is wearing a tight-fitting vest, which enables his biceps and shoulders to be on display, showing off the black cross tattoo on his left bulging bicep. He is a large man and towers over the tiny woman to his right, his arm around her. The woman's face has been blurred out in the photo (I assume for security reasons). They are both facing the camera, but now I look closer I can tell the woman's body language is forced and stiff, as if she is trying to shrink away from him, disgusted by his touch.

The woman in the photo is Charlotte Murray. The man standing next to her is her brother, Gerald Murray.

I point at the photo and allow Benjamin to look at it and read the small article underneath even though he read it earlier. It says Charlotte Murray was raped by a man in a dark hood and was found by a group of school boys and was then taken to Scotland to be looked after by her brother. I had previously assumed the man in the photo with her was her brother, but I had never imagined he was part of Frank's evil cohort. I should have paid more attention, but at the time I had maybe been too distracted by other factors.

'This is it,' says Benjamin, jabbing his finger at the page. 'We find this guy then we find Charlotte … and if we find Charlotte then we find Rebecca.'

Doesn't it feel as if we're going on a wild goose chase to find one person? Now we have to find someone else!

Yes, but all these people are connected. Gerald Murray is one of Frank's—

Henchmen.

Are we seriously going with *henchmen?*

It works, right?

I purse my lips together and Benjamin notices.

'What?' he asks.

'Nothing. Give me the laptop.'

Benjamin hands it over while I settle myself cross-legged on the sofa. I bring up the search engine and begin …

'I'm going to go and take a shower. Do you want another cup of tea before I go up?'

'No.'

'You know … saying please and thank you once and a while would really help your social skills, Alicia.'

I ignore him. I do not have time for niceties or inflating male egos. I have work to do. Benjamin sighs loudly before he leaves the room.

Thirty minutes later, after scouring the internet, I have found twelve Gerald Murrays living in Scotland and slowly but surely I disregard all but three of them due to them either being too young, too old or dead. I have brought up all of their Facebook profiles, as well as any mention of them in online articles or other social media apps. The online newspaper article from 1988 appears in my search, but it does not really help me any further with identifying the exact individual.

You know, I reckon you could actually be a private investigator.

Hardly. My skills with searching online only reach as far as Google and social media will allow.

Can you please say something to Ben? He's been sitting in silence staring at you for the past ten minutes.

It is true. He arrived downstairs after his shower, freshly washed, his hair trimmed and his beard tidied and had taken up residence in the armchair opposite me. I have been vaguely aware he has been staring at me.

I do not care if I hurt his feelings.

Yes, you do.

No, I do not.

Just humour him, please?

I grind my teeth and roll my eyes as I look up at Benjamin, annoyed I have to now attend to his needs.

'Benjamin ... can I have a cup of tea ... please.'

He stares at me without blinking for several seconds.

Uhhh … he looks a little scary right now. You may have just made it worse and pissed him off.

You were the one who told me to be nice to him.

Yeah, but when you try and be nice to people you end up making them feel uncomfortable or you make it sound sarcastic, like you don't really mean it.

That is because the majority of the time I do not mean it.

You're impossible!

Eventually Benjamin stands up without a word and walks into the kitchen, muttering something incoherent under his breath.

I return to my search, clicking on each Facebook profile in turn, as I read their *About* information section. Two of the men have open profiles, which allows me to see all their pictures, where they went to school, where they work and who their siblings are (none of whom are called Charlotte). The third profile is set to private, only enabling me to see his name, where he lives (Edinburgh) and his profile picture. The picture is a close-up of a man in his fifties; grey hair, grey beard, lots of age lines around his brown eyes. I stare at him for a few seconds before bringing up the picture of Gerald and Charlotte Murray from 1988. I align them next to each other, studying the contours of his face.

I will not lie … due to the large age gap and the bad quality of the newspaper photo it is difficult to confirm whether it is definitely the same man. The profile picture does not allow me to see his arms, so I cannot ascertain whether or not he has a tattoo.

What do you think, Josslyn? Could it be him?

Hard to say ... I mean ... it sort of looks like him, right?

At that moment Benjamin returns with a steaming cup and places it down next to me on the little side table. He then returns to his chair.

'Thank you,' I say after a few beats of silence.

I can see his mouth twitching, as if he is fighting back an amused smile. He wants to stay angry at me, but clearly he does not have it in him to hold a grudge.

'You're welcome.'

'Will you take a look at these pictures for me ... please?' I ask as I carry the laptop over to him and place it in his hands. I perch on the armrest of the chair he is in, our bodies precariously close, while he studies the two photos. I see him flinch slightly as the skin on our arms touches briefly.

'Is this him?' he asks.

'You tell me. Do they look like the same man to you?'

Benjamin takes a few moments before he answers. 'I'd say they look very similar. It could definitely be him ... is this all you've been able to find on him – a locked profile page and this article?'

'Yes. He appears to be keeping a low profile online, but this is the best lead I have found.'

'Then I'd say that's suspicious. Everyone's online these days ... well, apart from Phil, who never set up a Facebook account and now I know why.'

'But he did mention once he set up a fake account in order to spy on me.'

I grab the laptop back off Benjamin without asking and quickly scroll through a few of Gerald's friends, the ones that are visible without full access. I come across a man called Phillip Baxter.

It is him.

Holy crap, that's Peter! We've found him!

'There,' I say, showing Benjamin the screen.

'Fuck ... we've found him ... now what?'

I sigh in utter relief. I am exhausted, but finally we have found something tangible to go on.

'Now we are going on a road trip to Edinburgh.'

Chapter Fifteen
Josslyn

The next morning Ben and I are up bright and early (having enjoyed some late night activities ... and early morning activities too) and are on the road by nine. Ben keeps glancing over at me and smiling coyly, probably remembering what we got up to last night. In the end I tell him to cut it out and focus on the road because otherwise we'll end up in a deadly car crash before we even get there.

So as it turns out Edinburgh is a fucking long way! I mean ... yes, I've been to Tuscany, but I woke up there and then we flew back to England (in what I can only describe as the most terrifying experience of my life ... seriously, what sane person actually enjoys flying?). Alicia and I drove to Cambridge which was pretty far, but Edinburgh? It's like three hundred and fifty miles away (which is double the distance to Cambridge) and it's going to take us at least six and a half hours and everyone knows I hate sitting still for long periods of time. It makes my skin crawl with anxiety.

Already I'm getting that nervous feeling I always get before I travel. I've never really liked travelling too far from my home comforts, having spent the majority of my life living in a twenty-mile bubble of my parents' house. Ben has kindly offered to drive the whole way, which is great, but that means I have a lot of time to think about stuff and that's never a good thing. Obviously, I intend to talk to my boyfriend during the trip, but I also plan on doing more basic internet research on Gerald Murray and Charlotte. Now I know the rough location of Charlotte (I'm assuming she lives near her brother) I can try and narrow down the search even more. We need a little more information about where they actually live in Edinburgh. We can't very well just turn up and start asking around because it's a pretty big city and we don't have that sort of time to play with.

Alicia has been quiet since we swapped places last night after she and Ben finished their discussion. She said she didn't want to be around when he and I … you know … reacquainted. I can't say I blame her. I know she's having a hard time lately even if she refuses to admit it. I'm having a hard time too, but a part of me feels … satisfied … is that the right word? Content—

Satisfied and content mean the same thing.

Ah, there you are. Good morning.

Good morning. How are you feeling?

I'm okay. I mean … considering everything, I'm doing … okay. How are you?

I am fine … You appear to be taking all of this surprisingly well.

Is that so hard for you to believe?

I always had myself pegged as the strong one and you as the weak one.

You're not being weak Alicia … and thanks for the insult by the way … you've been through a lot. I'm just protecting you for as long as I can. I don't know what will happen when I disappear forever. You've come such a long

110

way. You're so different from the person you were two years ago. You're no longer a psychopath … you're …

I am quite possibly a sociopath and mentally ill.

Well … yes, but … you're also a good person deep down. The only reason you are the way you are is because you've had some very bad things happen to you. It's not your fault. You know that, right?

Alicia doesn't respond. I'll just leave her alone for a while.

I turn to Ben.

'So while we were on our road trip to my old home town Alicia took me to visit my parents' graves,' I say by way of starting up a conversation. The silence in the car is making my anxiety grow by the minute.

Ben raises his eyebrows in slight surprise, possibly because my statement was fairly random and out of the blue.

'That's nice,' he says, somewhat awkwardly. 'What happened to them, if you don't mind me asking? I don't think you've ever told me the whole story.'

'My mum died in the pandemic early on and my dad … well, he died later in a freak car accident. The police didn't suspect foul play. He was old and driving in the dark and lost concentration and hit a tree. That's what Alicia told me the family lawyer said anyway.'

'I'm sorry. That must have been difficult, especially with you being in a different country at the time.'

'Well, at the time I wasn't even around. Alicia was living in Tuscany, so I wasn't here when it all …' I stop and gulp back a massive lump in my throat. My bottom lip begins to tremble. Oh God … it's happening again. I haven't properly thought about my parents' deaths for so long and now I'm being hit with a wave of guilt even though it wasn't my fault I wasn't there. It was—

My fault.

Ben reaches over and places his left hand on my knee, giving it a light squeeze. 'I'm sure your parents understood why you went away.'

'T-They didn't. They didn't know anything. I never told them about Alicia being in my head so they must have found it so out of the ordinary when Alicia just upped and left them. She didn't care about them.'

'That must be very difficult to accept. Do you forgive her for what she did?'

I stare at the road ahead. It's just a boring motorway and I can see traffic building in the distance. 'I … I'm not sure. I want to forgive her, but knowing what I know now …'

'What do you know now?'

Shit.

'Nothing … just … you know, she's a psychopath, that's who she is and I've finally accepted that.' I cross my arms over my chest and lean my head against the headrest, blinking back tears that are threatening to spill.

Ben and I sit in silence for a while. I feel the weird tension hovering in the air like a bad smell. The words are trying to form on the tip of my tongue and I'm having to physically restrain myself from saying them.

Maybe it is time we told him the truth about what you and I really are.

We agreed we'd wait until the right time.

Maybe this is the right time. You clearly want him to know the truth. I can feel that the lies are eating you up inside. Tell him, Josslyn.

He won't love me anymore. I'll lose him.

I disagree. Give Benjamin a little more credit than that.

Can you tell him for me … please? I feel … the wall is crumbling and I'm struggling to keep it up. I think I'm fading …

As you wish.

'Everything okay, Josslyn?' Ben asks me. He has a worried frown on his face.

'Yes,' I reply with a smile. 'I just have to go away for a while.'

'You'll come back to me though, right?'

Tears fill my eyes as I choke back another sob. 'Yes … always,' I lie.

Chapter Sixteen
Alicia

I turn and look at Benjamin.

'We need to talk,' I say bluntly.

'Um ... should I maybe pull over for this or—'

'Just drive and listen,' I snap back. 'I have always wanted to keep things from you, Benjamin. I have never wanted to tell you the truth, mainly because I feel I cannot trust anyone and also because I have wanted to keep you safe. I have always believed the less you know the better, but I also believe you deserve to know the truth about Josslyn, especially since you two are, for all intents and purposes, dating. She loves you and I believe you love her.' I stop and look out the window, watching as the traffic begins to slow ahead, letting the frigid silence fill the entire space inside the car.

'Wait ... she loves me? She told you that, like out loud ... with words?'

'Yes.'

'But she's never said it to me.'

'She is afraid to say the words because there is no long-term future for the two of you and she knows that, as I am sure you do too.'

Benjamin nods slowly. 'Yeah, we've talked about the fact one day she might not be around, but ... Alicia, you're actually scaring me right now. What is it about

114

Josslyn I don't already know? What have you been keeping from me?'

'You were right.'

'I'm sorry?'

'You were right about us from the start.'

'You're going to have to explain in more detail.'

'When Josslyn told you about who we were back while we were prisoners in Peter's torture chamber you didn't believe her at first, did you? You said there had to be a more rational explanation as to why there are two people in this body. You were right. There is. Josslyn is not a real person. She is a different personality I invented when I was around six years old to shield myself from the abuse I suffered at the hands of my biological father ... who I have recently come to discover is ... Frank Master.'

Benjamin continues to stare ahead at the road. We have now drawn to a complete standstill due to the build-up of traffic. He is gripping the steering wheel so tight his knuckles are turning white and I can see him trembling. He slowly turns his head towards me and we stare at each other for several long seconds, neither one of us blinking.

Then the cars start to pull away in front, but Benjamin does not move. We stay rooted to the spot in the middle of the motorway as horns start blaring and loud voices start yelling from the other cars. I will not be the one to speak first.

Finally, he opens his mouth, but no words come out. Instead, he closes it, turns to look at the road and slowly pulls away into the flow of traffic. We sit in silence for at least five minutes before he finally decides to speak.

'How long have you known all of this?'

'I found out about Frank Master being my father when he called me on the phone before you left and I found out about Josslyn when I found the box in the attic. There was a cassette tape in it and on it my biological mother explained how my father abused both her and myself, but she managed to help me escape. I do not know exactly how everything unfolded after that, but the only thing I remember is appearing to Josslyn one day out of the blue. She was a seemingly happy child, if a bit lonely, and she assumed I was her imaginary friend, but in reality she was the one who was made up to protect me. I do not have all the answers, that is all I know. Josslyn has been protecting me all these years. I do not know how long she has left, but as I am starting to put together the pieces of my past she is beginning to weaken.'

'So the whole thing about the foetus in fetu was a lie?'

'No, it was true. I did have a collection of cells and tissue inside of me that would have been my identical twin sister had she developed properly. I believe Josslyn and I used that knowledge as a way to try and explain our existence. She was real to me and I was real to her. I never, not even for a moment, believed she was merely a split personality, but that is exactly what she is.'

'And what will happen when she disappears forever?'

I shake my head. 'I do not know, but currently she is holding back a metaphorical wall inside my mind and when it falls down ... I do not know what is behind it, but I can only imagine it will not be pleasant.'

The silence builds again while we watch the traffic ebb and flow in front of us. I glance at Benjamin out of the corner of my eye and see he is crying silently. I feel so helpless. What do normal people do to comfort those in need? Then I remember what he did for Josslyn only moments ago, so I slowly reach out my right hand and place it gently on his upper thigh and squeeze it lightly. He carefully lifts his left hand off the steering wheel and takes my hand in his. This feels extremely strange, but I allow him to continue to hold my hand, something I have never experienced in my entire life.

'I know this sounds crazy,' he says eventually. 'But I still love her. I know she's not real, but she's real to me. I hope she knows that.'

'She is real to me too. Thank you.'

In this moment my respect for Benjamin deepens and I feel a surge of ... affection for him. I cannot say it is an altogether terrible feeling; in fact, it is quite pleasant. However, the fear begins to grow inside of me as I realise I cannot afford to lose Benjamin as well as Josslyn. I must find a way to protect him at any cost.

Benjamin nods. I promptly remove my hand from his grasp as he returns to focussing on the traffic.

'So,' he says, his tone of voice changing to one slightly more forceful, 'about the fact you declined to mention that the man who is after us is actually your father. Why the hell would neither of you tell me? I thought we were in this whole thing together.'

'I did not feel like it was necessary for you to know. It does not change the fact I am still planning on killing him.'

'Really?'

'Yes, really.'

'But he's your father.'

'No, he is an evil man who raped my mother, tortured her and allowed other men to abuse me … he is not my father.'

Benjamin coughs violently, clasping a hand over his mouth as if to refrain himself from vomiting. He takes deep breaths to calm himself down and glances at me. I can tell he wants to ask me further questions about what I remember as a child, so I put his mind at ease.

'I do not remember anything,' I say slowly. 'I have blocked it out.'

'Good … I mean … I think when this is all over you should see a therapist. Josslyn did agree to that once.'

'She did say that, yes, but she did not mean it.'

'You don't think you need to see a therapist?'

'No.'

Benjamin raises his eyebrows, but says nothing else on the matter.

Chapter Seventeen
Alicia

I spend the next two hours on the laptop researching Gerald and Charlotte Murray using all the information I have available. It is like putting together a thousand-piece jigsaw puzzle made of only black shapes, but I eventually find a Charlie Murray listed on The University of Edinburgh's staff page under the Human Resources section. Due to the fact her face is blurred in the 1988 newspaper article it is difficult to decipher if she bears a resemblance to the woman from thirty years ago. She has no Facebook page either and I have been unable to find any further information on Gerald Murray. I make a fake profile using an image of an attractive woman I found on the internet and send him a friend request, but I highly doubt he will accept it. If he does it will enable me to see his entire profile, including if he has any siblings.

We stop off for a bite to eat around the halfway mark (although I remain by the car and keep as far away from people as possible). I walk several laps around the car, stretching my legs, and that is when I hear a ping from the laptop. I bend down and check it.

Gerald Murray has accepted your friend request.

Bingo.

Clearly he cannot resist a pretty face.

I open his profile and check his family history. He has a sister called Charlie Murray. She does not have a profile, but it is good enough for me.

While en route I book us a Travelodge to use as our base while we travel around the city. It is nearing the end of the working day when Benjamin and I finally arrive in Edinburgh, but instead of heading straight to the hotel we drive to the university campus. I want to attempt to find Charlotte today, hoping she will still be at work.

The University of Edinburgh is quite vast and spread out over several campuses, which means it takes us far longer than I have the patience for to find the Human Resources building, by which time it is nearly six in the evening, but we are here now so I take the chance.

I tell Benjamin to let me do the talking, which he reluctantly agrees to do, but still feels the need to tell me to try and be polite.

Josslyn has not said a word since she disappeared several hours ago before I told Benjamin the truth, which sets me a little on edge. I wonder if she heard our conversation. I do not like it when she disappears completely.

Benjamin stays behind me while I approach the main desk at reception. The corridors are empty bar a few stray students and staff, causing the massive building to emit a strange echo as I walk across the floor. There is a young man behind the desk who looks as if he is exhausted and ready to head home for a glass or two of wine after a busy week. His hair is dishevelled, his glasses perched right on the edge of his nose, threatening to fall off at any second. He stands as he sees me approaching and switches off his computer, clearly on his way out.

'I'm sorry,' he says without even looking at me, 'but we're closed now. You'll have to come back tomorrow. We open at eight.'

'I wish to speak to Charlotte Murray. Is she here?'

The man looks up at me and frowns, peering over the thin rims of his glasses. 'Who?'

'Charlotte Murray.'

Another frown. 'Do you mean Charlie?'

'Yes.'

'You'll have to come back tomorrow. We're about to close.'

'Is she still here?'

'Yeah, she's just grabbing her coat, but—'

'Then I wish to see her now.'

The man glances past me at Benjamin as if he is evoking some sort of guy code to get him to help him out, but Benjamin merely shrugs and sighs. I am glad to see he is keeping to his part of the deal and staying silent.

'Fine … wait here … what did you say your name was?'

'I did not tell you my name.'

'Then what is it?'

'Alexis Grey … and this is Benjamin Willis.'

'Fine … wait here.'

The man disappears through a door behind the desk, slamming it slightly harder than is deemed appropriate.

'Your people skills could still do with a bit of work,' says Benjamin.

I do not respond.

A few minutes later the man returns. 'She's just coming,' he grunts.

Silence.

Benjamin loudly clears his throat. I quickly understand the hint.

'Thank you,' I say reluctantly. 'I hope you have a pleasant weekend.'

Josslyn is indeed correct … I do sound sarcastic when I attempt to be polite. Of course I do not care if he has a pleasant weekend or not; I could not care less.

The man narrows his eyes at me as he pushes his glasses further up his nose. He and Benjamin share a look as he walks out of the room. Benjamin is about to open his mouth to speak, but he is interrupted by a woman entering the room, a white jacket slung over her left shoulder and a black bag clutched in her hand.

'Can I help you?' she asks, checking her bag for something, not giving either of us any eye contact.

I stare at Charlotte Murray, taking in her thin frame, her ageing but flawless skin and her strikingly blue eyes. She looks like she has recently stepped off a magazine shoot, not a hair out of place, her red lipstick flawlessly applied despite the lateness of the day. Her grey hair is styled immaculately in a short bob.

'Charlotte Murray?' I enquire.

She freezes at the mention of her real name, looking up at me slowly and locking eyes. 'Yes ... but I haven't been known by that name in years. My name's Charlie Murray now.'

'My mistake.'

She shrugs her arms into her jacket and does up the top button. 'How do you know my name was Charlotte anyway? Only my close friends and family knew me by that name.'

'It is a long story.'

'I'm afraid I don't have time for a long story. I've arranged to meet some friends for drinks. I'm sure whatever this is about can wait. Can we make an appointment to see each other tomorrow morning first thing?'

'This cannot wait. This is regarding your brother Gerald and your daughter Rebecca.'

The sparkle fades from her eyes and she stumbles against the desk, steadying herself by clutching the back of the chair.

'Oh,' she whimpers.

Chapter Eighteen
Alicia

Charlotte leads us into her office, which looks as if an entire ecosystem has made itself at home. Dozens and dozens of plant pots adorn the shelves, the desk and any spare space that is available. As we enter I cannot help but notice the warm and musty aroma of damp earth. I am momentarily taken aback by the amount of greenery and I somehow manage to stop myself before I say something offensive.

What the fuck?

Ah, there you are. Where have you been for the past six hours?

Somewhere dark. I kept calling your name, but you wouldn't answer.

I did not hear you.

That's what I was afraid of … Anyway … how did Ben take the news?

Did you not hear anything we spoke about?

No, I just vanished when you took over. It does happen from time to time but never for that long. What's happened? Why the hell are we in a jungle?

This is Charlotte Murray's office.

Right …

And to answer your question, Benjamin took the news very well and still loves you. I may have also let it slip that you love him too.

Wait ... you did what!

Granted, it was a mistake, but—

Wait ... let me get this straight. The first time my boyfriend hears the words 'I love you' from me ... it comes from you?

I did not exactly say 'I love you, Benjamin'. I merely said you loved him, but you were afraid to tell him because you know the relationship will not last for much longer.

For fuck's sake, Alicia. Bravo for making things fucking awkward—

'Excuse me? Alexis ... is it?'

I blink several times as I return to reality, suddenly aware that Charlotte has been talking to me. 'I apologise,' I say. 'The plants threw me for a second.'

Charlotte chuckles slightly. 'Yes, most people are quite shocked. It's a hobby of mine, you see. Would you like a drink?'

'No ... thank you.'

Wow ... you actually made that sound somewhat genuine.

Benjamin shakes his head. 'No, thank you,' he replies.

Charlotte smiles, looking slightly relieved that she does not have to make beverages for us. She gestures at the two chairs in front of her desk so Benjamin and I slowly take our seats. I glance around at the vast array of potted plants, attempting to not convey my surprise and confusion as to why a person would need so many plants in their office, whether it be a hobby or not.

It must take her forever to water them.

'So,' says Charlotte, taking her seat and folding her hands politely in her lap, 'you have piqued my interest … how exactly do you know about my daughter?'

'I do not know a great deal. Only that she may be in danger and I need to speak with her as soon as possible. She may hold information I need. I have attempted to find her for weeks, but she appears to have vanished.'

Charlotte narrows her eyes at me, her calm and kind exterior beginning to fade. Her maternal instinct to protect her daughter is abundantly obvious.

'Who *are* you, exactly?'

'Like I said … it is a long story.'

'Well, it looks like I won't be making the after-work drinks with the girls now, so … feel free to tell me.'

I nod curtly. If she wants the whole story, then she will get it and I do not intend to beat around the bush either.

'Very well. As I said, my name is Alexis Grey. My biological mother was called Jane Daniels and she was raped by a serial rapist who has lately come to be known as The Hooded Man. You may have seen him in the news. In fact, I believe he was the man who assaulted and raped you back in 1988 and that Rebecca is the product of that rape, which means she and I are potentially half-sisters. The Hooded Man appears to be the leader of an underground cult who tortures, stalks, rapes and murders innocent women for their own amusement. I believe Rebecca is in danger because he and his followers are after her, as well

126

as myself. I am attempting to put an end to his reign of tyranny, but I cannot find him. He is as elusive as a ghost. Rebecca may be the key to finding him as she was also stalked by one of his followers. She may have information that I do not.'

After my speech a deathly silence falls upon the room, during which Charlotte stares at me without blinking. I lock eyes with her, showing her I mean serious business. Those once sparkling blue eyes are now full of fear and tears and there is a vein in her forehead that looks as if it is about to burst. Her hands are still folded neatly in her lap, but they are visibly trembling and she is doing her best to stop them. She opens her mouth, but only a low whimper comes out.

'There is no point in trying to deny any of this, Charlotte. I need your help. I need you to tell me where your daughter is.'

Charlotte continues to stare at me as she battles with her emotions. Eventually, she lets out a long sigh and slumps back against the chair, covering her face with her hands. She bursts into tears, her prim and proper facade finally crumbling into pieces.

'Oh God,' she cries. 'It's finally happened.'

I glance at Benjamin for backup because he knows I am not good with shows of emotion. Benjamin immediately stands up, grabs a box of tissues from a nearby shelf and offers it to Charlotte. He places a gentle hand on her shoulder as she takes a tissue with a smile and blows her nose.

'I'm so sorry we've had to bring this up. I can only imagine how painful this must be for you,' he says.

Charlotte sniffs loudly. 'Not as painful as keeping it to myself all these years, believe me … Thank you.' She nods at Benjamin, clearly grateful for his kind gesture and then locks her eyes on me. I have not moved a muscle. Benjamin sits back down again in his chair.

'I've been hoping and praying that someone would figure all this out one day. You're right, of course, about everything you just said.'

'Why have you not told the authorities about it? If you have known who these men are this whole time … I do not understand why you would keep it to yourself.'

Charlotte smiles sweetly at me. 'You're not a mother, are you?'

'No.'

'Then you have no idea the lengths a mother will go to in order to protect her child.'

I think back to the tape recording my mother made for me.

'That cannot be the only reason you have stayed silent all these years.'

Charlotte's voice raises a few octaves. 'Of course it's not. These men are dangerous. Not only was Rebecca's life at risk, but so was mine.'

'What about the dozens of other women's lives they have taken or ruined in the past thirty years? Did you ever think of them?'

I hear Benjamin inhale sharply behind me, but he does not speak.

Alicia, you might want to tone it down … We're supposed to be getting information out of her and she won't tell us if you're being a bitch.

Trust me … she will tell us.

Charlotte begins to cry again.

'Your brother … he is one of them,' I state.

Charlotte nods. 'I thought I was protecting my family. That's all I cared about, but all Gerald ever cared about was The Collective.'

My breath catches in my throat. 'The Collective? Is that the name they are known by?'

Charlotte nods, her bottom lip quivering. 'Yes.'

'Do you know who else is part of it other than your brother and The Hooded Man? Do you know his name … the man who raped you?'

'No, I don't know the name of Rebecca's father. I had to put *unknown* on her birth certificate, but there are dozens of men in The Collective and they're always recruiting. I'm not sure how much more Rebecca can tell you other than what I've just told you.'

'I need to at least try. Where is she?'

'That's just it … I've hidden her. Three years ago she begged me to keep her safe from The Collective. I had some help, but basically I erased her existence. Not even Gerald knows where she is, which is why he keeps such close tabs on me these days. Only I know where she is and if I tell you then I'm endangering her life. She won't be safe

129

anymore and I'll be breaking a promise I made to her three years ago.'

'If you do not tell me then you are endangering many other young women's lives also. The Collective has to end and I am going to be the one to stop it once and for all … *that* is my promise to you.'

Charlotte blinks several times as she stares down at her shaking hands. She closes her eyes and keeps her head bowed as she speaks.

'Rebecca is in a high-security mental health facility on the outskirts of Edinburgh called Wickham Mental Health Hospital. She's staying there under the name Hannah Baker. No one there even knows her real name. She won't talk to you though.'

'Why not?'

'Because she's mute.'

Chapter Nineteen
Alicia

I stare at Charlotte for several long seconds, attempting to understand what she actually means. It is not that I am shocked by the revelation, but it does put a dampener on my plan to speak with Rebecca. Benjamin clears his throat beside me and shuffles in his chair.

'I'm sorry,' he says, 'but what do you mean exactly?'

Charlotte takes a few seconds to compose herself. 'My daughter has Selective Mutism caused by severe psychological issues. The doctors at the hospital believe it came about due to a traumatic experience. They don't know what that was of course, but I know what The Collective did to her, what they put her through. I was raped once by a man thirty years ago, but that's nothing compared to what she's been through. I didn't believe her at first. Before it happened she kept telling me she didn't feel safe, as if someone was watching her all the time. She kept saying she wasn't safe ... and I ... I didn't believe her. I told her she was being silly and paranoid, but then—'

'She disappeared,' I add.

'Yes, she disappeared for nearly two weeks. Her social media went quiet, none of her friends knew where she was and hadn't heard from her either. I'd assumed she'd ran away with the person she was seeing, but then ...'

Charlotte clamps a hand over her mouth, stifling yet another sob.

I refrain from rolling my eyes. I have never had much patience when it comes to crying people. Even when Josslyn cries I find it tedious and unnecessary.

Says the unemotional one.

'Please … take your time,' says Benjamin softly. 'We're sorry to have to bring all this up again, but it really is important we know as much as possible.'

I glance at him, silently thanking him for saying the right thing when he knows how incapable I am when it comes to being tactful.

Charlotte sniffs loudly and blows her nose before regaining her composure. 'I'm sorry … it's just … this is all very traumatic for me. I've been keeping all this a secret for so long and I'm afraid that he'll … that he'll … come after me again.'

'I have already assured you I will not let that happen,' I say quite sternly. 'What happened after Rebecca disappeared?'

Charlotte sobs loudly again, grabbing her throat and rubbing her eyes with her fingers.

'I asked my brother to help me find her and he said if I ever wanted to see her alive again then I'd keep my mouth shut about the fact she'd disappeared. He told me not to tell the police and that she'd be home soon, so that's what I did … I waited. A week later she came home, but she wasn't the same. She couldn't speak. When I asked her what had happened she stared at me blankly. There were cuts all over her body, which was black and blue, and she had two broken ribs. I decided then and there I'd had enough, so I did the only thing I could think of that would keep her safe. I asked a friend of hers to help me delete all of her social media pages and close down her bank accounts … and then I sent her to the mental health hospital under a fake name. I told them to keep her in the high-security section and on constant watch because I was afraid she'd be suicidal. Rebecca didn't argue with me and went gladly, but has never said a word since. A year or so ago she seemed to be making progress. The therapists there have been teaching her sign language and she has been communicating in that way and even writing a few notes down on paper, but only to answer yes or no. She won't speak about what happened. I don't think she'll ever recover.'

Yeesh … poor girl.

It appears she and I have a lot in common.

Yeah … The Collective fucked you both up and now you're mentally ill.

I roll my shoulders back, suddenly aware they are heavy and stiff. 'Do you have regular contact with Rebecca?' I ask finally.

'Yes, I visit her once a month when Gerald is away.'

'Where does Gerald go?'

'I don't know. I don't ask.'

I grind my teeth together, silently frustrated at this woman's naivety. Surely she must realise Gerald is leaving to go and hunt with The Collective, destroying women's lives in the process.

'I shall visit Rebecca tomorrow,' I say.

Charlotte shakes her head. 'They won't let you in. I'm the only person who is designated to visit her.'

'Then I suggest you come along and convince the staff to let us in to see her.'

'Haven't you been listening? She won't talk to you … and she certainly won't trust you. She barely trusts me … and I don't mean to sound rude, but you're not exactly very approachable or friendly. Your tone of voice puts me on edge.'

I cross my arms over my chest and sigh in annoyance. 'She and I have something in common,' I say as calmly as I can muster.

'Which is?' asks Charlotte, her perfectly plucked eyebrows raised.

'I also have a psychological disorder.'

At this statement Charlotte noticeably relaxes and nods, seeming to understand. 'I suppose that explains a lot.' She sniffs again, rises to her feet and straightens her jacket. 'Very well. I can't promise you'll get any information out of her, but you're welcome to try. Be there at eight sharp outside the gates of the hospital.'

'Thank you, we'll see you tomorrow,' says Benjamin as he gets to his feet, but I remain seated.

There is one more thing I wish to ask Charlotte Murray and I am convinced she will not like it.

'Where can I find your brother?' I ask, narrowing my eyes at her.

Charlotte gulps and shakes her head. 'No, I can't tell you. I've told you enough already.'

'Why are you still trying to protect him?'

'He's my brother.'

'He's a fucking rapist,' I shout slightly louder than I intended. The words echo around the room, filling the space with a sense of tension and fear. We are left in silence. Benjamin has frozen halfway out of the room.

Charlotte's entire body starts to tremble. 'He's my brother,' she whispers.

I slowly stand up and lean over the desk towards her, my face deadpan and only a few inches from her own.

'I have a sister and I have done a lot of bad things to protect her and I am willing to do many more ... but there is a difference between doing bad things out of love and doing bad things out of hate. You clearly love your brother,' I say through gritted teeth, 'but he takes pleasure in hurting and defiling women. He does not care about you or your daughter. He may have even hurt Rebecca himself and if you are so unbelievably naive and weak as to defend him ... then you deserve the same treatment as he'll get from me.'

Charlotte trembles as fresh tears stream down her cheeks. She begins to shake her head, but then appears to think better of it and lowers her head so she cannot look me in the eyes. I have not stopped glaring at her across the desk the entire time. Clearly I am making her uncomfortable, but I do not care.

'He works as a bouncer at a nightclub in the city centre called The Range. He'll be there tonight. It's where he scopes out his victims ... Please ... please ... you have to stop him. If you don't ... and he finds out what I've told you then he'll come after me and Rebecca.'

I nod and smile as I step away from the desk. 'It is done. See you tomorrow morning.'

Chapter Twenty
Alicia

I step through the door of the hotel room and my heart immediately performs a backwards somersault when I see they have provided us with a double room instead of a twin room. Benjamin appears to sense my uneasiness.

'I can ask them if they have any other rooms available if you like?'

I drop my backpack on the floor with a sigh. 'No, this will suffice.' With any luck Josslyn will resurface and take over when it is time to go to bed. She has disappeared yet again and I have not heard her voice since before we left Charlotte's office. I fear she may have gone to the dark place once more … wherever or whatever *that* is.

'Okay … I'll put the kettle on.'

I perch on the edge of the bed and watch Benjamin as he makes us a cup of tea using the ridiculously miniscule amount of items the hotel appears to think is sufficient. He hands me a tiny pack of biscuits. I take them willingly, my stomach grumbling.

'So … I take it you have a plan of action for tonight?'

'Attend the club and kill Gerald Murray.'

'Right … but … I mean *how* are you going to kill him exactly?'

I inhale deeply through my nose and out through my mouth. 'My feminine charm.'

Benjamin resists the urge to laugh. 'Was that a joke, Alicia? Did you just attempt to make a joke?'

'I do not know what you are talking about,' I say as I raise my eyebrows, the corner of my mouth twitching slightly. 'The point is Charlotte told us that this club is where he picks out his victims, so I intend to lure him into a trap ... and then drug him and kill him.'

At this Benjamin frowns. 'Drug him with what?'

I reach into my bag and pull out a small vile containing a clear liquid. 'This.'

'What the hell is that and, more importantly, where the hell did you get it?'

'This is Rohypnol ... and while you were away I kept myself busy.'

'Stealing cars and buying fake IDs and date rape drugs.'

'Amongst other things.'

'Amongst other things? What does *that* mean exactly?'

'Do you *really* want to know the details?'

There is a beat of silence.

'On second thoughts ... maybe not.'

'A wise choice.'

I decide to try and get some sleep before tonight's showdown so I set an alarm on my phone, roll onto my side, bring my knees up to my chest and close my eyes, leaving my cup of tea to grow cold. I dream of a black room. I cannot find my way out and Josslyn is not there this time.

I am jolted awake by the alarm. It startles me, as if I have just fallen off a cliff. I must have been in a deep sleep, my body drained of energy and in desperate need of recharging. I sit up on the bed and see Benjamin has fallen asleep beside me. He has been careful not to lay too close to me, but during his slumber his left hand has drifted close to my back. I stare down at his sleeping form, noticing how his wispy hair falls across his eyes and his eyelids flicker ever so slightly. I slowly reach out my hand and go to brush his hair out of his eyes, but then recoil before I do so …

No … stop …

I ignore the stirring of feelings within me, get off the bed and head into the en-suite for a shower. I spend the next hour attempting to transform myself into an attractive enough woman who would entice Gerald. I am aware it is possible he knows who I am and what I look like, but if I know one thing about rapists and perverts it is that they can never resist an opportunity when it happens to fall directly into their laps.

I did not bring many beauty items with me, nor any revealing clothes, but in the end I make do with a pair of tight denim jeans and a black vest top, which I tie in a knot at my waist, revealing my bare, toned midriff. I wash and dry my hair and then attempt to put some volume in it by backcombing it to within an inch of its life. My foundation is minimal, but I intentionally overdo the black eyeliner and mascara, then plump up my lips with some red lipstick. I am pretty sure I look like I belong in the 1990s, but it is the best I can do, given the situation.

Benjamin is laying on the bed watching a random game show as I exit the bathroom. I see his eyes flick over me several times, up and down. I am perfectly aware he finds me sexually attractive because I am technically his girlfriend … Speaking of which …

Josslyn, are you there?

Silence.

I listen as closely as I can, but I cannot hear her. I remember her saying earlier she had had a hard time getting back to me from the dark place and had been shouting for me to hear her. The thought is very disconcerting. I hope she finds her way back soon. I could really use her help tonight.

'Well?' I say. 'Will this do?'

Benjamin swallows hard and slowly nods. 'You look … nice.'

'Nice?'

'That's the word I'm going with for now. Is Josslyn around by any chance?'

'No. She is not.' I do not mention she is struggling to return to me now. We both know the end is drawing closer so I think it best not to dwell on the situation by speaking about it.

Benjamin gets back to watching his show. 'I guess I should shower and change in a bit,' he says.

'There is no need. You are not accompanying me tonight.'

At this revelation Benjamin sits bolt upright. 'Excuse me?'

'You heard me,' I snap.

'I heard you, but I don't understand you. Why wouldn't you want my help?'

'Having a male companion with me defeats the object of luring Gerald. He is not going to take the bait if you are hovering nearby.'

'Okay, so I'll just stand in a corner and keep an eye on you.'

'No.'

'Why not?'

'Because I do not need your help.'

'Let me just remind you, Alicia, that the last time I let you roam the streets at night by yourself you were attacked by one of Frank's henchmen.'

'You do not need to remind me. I remember the incident quite well, thank you.' In fact I often think about how I had bludgeoned that boy to death with a brick after he had attempted to pull my jeans down and rape me. I cannot help but wonder where his rotting body is now ...

Benjamin grinds his teeth, his jaw clenched, his eyes focussed directly on me. 'Why are you such a fucking bitch sometimes? There are times when I think you're actually starting to turn into a normal person and then you go and remind me that actually you're a cold-hearted, evil bitch.'

I raise my eyebrows, slightly taken aback by his tone of voice and language. If he wants to play … then let us play.

'Why are you such an asshole?' I retort.

'Seriously? We're going to do this right now … we're going to spit insults at each other? Why can't you ever just listen to me and accept what I'm saying actually has some relevance? How would you feel if you were in my position? Can't you, for one fucking minute, stop being a raging psycho and accept the fact someone cares about you and wants to keep you safe? I'm not going to sit here and twiddle my thumbs and wait while you go out and risk your life and kill someone. I'm in on this, I have been for a long fucking time and I think I deserve some fucking respect for putting up with you and sticking by you for as long as I have.'

I allow his words to fill the room. There are many things I wish to say back to him, but I hold my tongue, not because he is right, but because I know even if I told him to stay here he would not do it and he would follow me anyway. That is just the type of man Benjamin is.

'Fine,' I say finally.

'Fine,' he snaps back.

I can see he is shaking slightly as he gets off the bed and goes to walk past me to the bathroom. He stops next to me and we look into each other's eyes, heat radiating from our bodies after our verbal altercation. I cannot even begin to describe the emotions and physical sensations rippling through my body right now. I would like nothing more than to shove him down on the bed and straddle him. I can only assume the same thought is running through his head too, but neither one of us makes any movement to carry out our deepest desires.

Benjamin runs his eyes once more over my body. 'I'm sorry I called you a cold-hearted, evil bitch. I didn't mean it.'

'Yes, you did, but your apology is accepted.'

'Are you going to say sorry for calling me an asshole?'

I raise my eyebrows. 'What do you think?' I answer with a slight hint of playfulness in my tone.

Benjamin rolls his eyes at me. 'You're infuriating. I'm going to take a ... cold shower.'

As Benjamin closes the bathroom door and turns on the water I tilt my head up to the ceiling and close my eyes in frustration, fully aware it would be all too easy to join him.

Where the hell are you, Josslyn? I need you.

Chapter Twenty-One
Josslyn

Alicia ... can you hear me? I'm here!

I've been screaming her name for what seems like days, but it's probably not been more than a few hours. The last thing I remember is being in Charlotte Murray's office and Alicia convincing her to tell her where Gerald was. I'm assuming Alicia is now doing what she does best, but I wish I was there with her. I'm sure she can handle herself (let's face it, she's *always* been able to handle herself), but it feels weird not being there to help.

I'm in the dark place again. I can't hear or see anything that's going on. I don't know where I am exactly or what Alicia is doing. I'm sort of ... floating. No, that's not right ... *hovering*. Maybe I'm hovering, but I don't have a body. I'm just nothing and invisible, like the wind. Everything is black, completely black, not a speck of light anywhere. I'm obviously in Alicia's mind (where else would I be?) and I guess I've always assumed it would be black, a lot of darkness and confusion and that's exactly what it's like; a dark space of emptiness and I can't find my way out.

Previously, I've been able to come and go as I please, but lately it's becoming more and more difficult to escape back into the real world. Is this what it's like to be dead? Am I dead? Is this what will happen to me when I eventually fade away? I'll just stay in here forever and never be able to escape or will I literally cease to exist entirely? With all this free time so many questions zoom around my head (except I don't have a head) and I'm getting myself more and more worked up.

I scream and shout, but it's no use.

Alicia must be going crazy without me. I wonder if she's worried about me. I wonder if she's told Ben I've been staying away for longer lately. I know my time will come eventually, but I'm not ready to let go yet. I still have things to do and I need to help Alicia. I wish I could figure out a way to find my way back to her.

I *hover* around the darkness for a while. I think I'm moving forwards, but it's really hard to tell what direction I'm going in. For all I know I'm just wandering around in circles.

But that's when I see something ahead ...

It's a faint speck of light ... except it's not really light ... it's grey ...

I *hover* towards it and watch as the darkness around me begins to slowly fade from the blackest of black shades to a light grey.

Weird.

Okay, so now everything's grey, which makes no sense, but there we have it.

Alicia! Can you hear me?

Nothing.

I try shouting her name again, over and over, but eventually I stop when I feel the space around me start to shudder.

Oh shit … what have I done?

The entire grey atmosphere is shaking, almost as if …

The wall … maybe it's starting to crack …

I'm here, Alicia. Please don't give up on me yet. I'm still here. I'm trying to get back to you, I promise … I'm not letting go yet … not yet.

Chapter Twenty-Two
Alicia

Nightclubs should be banned. Does anyone even go to them anymore after the whole pandemic issue? Surely no sane, sober person above the age of twenty-five should be tempted to set foot inside one. It is nothing but sweaty, writhing, half-naked bodies attempting to attract another person in the hopes of initiating intercourse. It is a barbaric and ancient ritual, no doubt left over from our primitive need to copulate with the most attractive and dominant member of the species. Okay, so I am aware I sound bitter and old, but seriously ... I can think of many other more enjoyable and less ... messy ... ways of giving yourself an endorphin rush, such as jumping out of an airplane, or exercise ... or murdering someone.

The ridiculous rhythm of the music (which is almost unrecognisable as an actual song) is penetrating my very soul and not in a good way. It is so loud I can feel the vibrations radiating through my body, making my insides shudder. I wish nothing more than to leave this place as swiftly as possible, but I have a job to do and right now that is to attempt to locate my prey who is somewhere in this swarm of sweaty, adolescent bodies. At my age I feel like a complete outsider.

I take up residence on a small platform overlooking the dance floor, facing the entrance. I have not spotted Gerald yet, but I have a plan ... I always have a plan.

Benjamin is nowhere to be seen, but I assume he is keeping an eye on me and scoping the place out. He knows the plan. Or maybe he is becoming distracted and is attempting to find another girlfriend who is not crazy. Either way he has his job to do and I have mine. I have to wait for his signal, so while I kill time I scan the area whilst attempting to not touch a single thing with any part of my body.

A sweaty male of no more than twenty is hovering dangerously close to me, trying but failing to appear casual. I keep an eye on him from the corner of my right eye. My phone vibrates in my pocket so I check the text message from Benjamin.

Done.

Time to get to work.

The sweaty man/boy is inching closer and closer and has even found the nerve to gently brush his hand against my ass as if by complete accident (yeah, right). I wait for him to do it a second time—

I clench my jaw as I feel his hand on me, this time gently squeezing my butt cheek. I react instinctively and with one swift movement grab his right hand and twist it into an uncomfortable angle. He shouts in pain as I lean close to his ear so that he can hear me over the loud, pulsing music.

'Are you right-handed?' I ask, a sweet yet stern tone to my voice.

His confused expression tells me he is exceptionally drunk, but that is no excuse for violating my personal space.

'Um ... yeah,' he shouts. 'Why?'

'Because if you touch me again I shall break every bone in your right hand in such a way that it will never fully recover and you shall spend the rest of your miserable life attempting to learn how to masturbate using your non-dominant hand ... Is that what you want?'

The pathetic male attempts to shrink away from me. He quickly shakes his head, so I let go of his hand and shove him away from me, disgusted I have touched him.

'Fuck me, you crazy bitch! You're not even worth it. Now I see you up close you ain't even that hot.'

I smile politely at him and then, using the heel of my hand, thrust it upwards into his nose and follow it up with a kick to his precious groin.

I hear a few shrieks as people attempt to flee the area while my victim howls in pain at my feet, clutching both his nose and his private parts, clearly at a loss about which one to complain about more. He writhes around on the dirty, sticky floor, whimpering.

My phone vibrates in my back pocket again so I retrieve it and glance at the screen.

Nice shot.

I smile proudly as I type my response.

Thanks.

Another message appears from Benjamin merely seconds later.

Inbound.

I smile once more, returning the phone to my pocket, acting as innocent and nonchalant as I can.

I do not flinch as a heavy hand lands on my shoulder. I glance over and look into the eyes of Gerald Murray. He is wearing a black t-shirt that looks as if it is painted on with the words *Security* across the front in large white letters. He squeezes my shoulder quite hard as he turns me around.

'Excuse me, Miss … but you need to come with—' He stops as recognition dawns on his face. He narrows his eyes at me and his whole body tenses. Clearly he had not been expecting me.

I smile at him. 'I was hoping you would turn up.'

'Come with me.' His voice is sharp and deep.

As he leads me away from the dance floor the crowds part like the Red Sea. I feel my phone buzz again in my pocket, but I do not attempt to read the text message. I have no doubt Benjamin is keeping an eye on my movements, but he also knows to stay back until I need him. As it turns out having him here tonight was indeed the correct decision, although I would never admit that to him.

Gerald keeps an exceptionally tight grip on my shoulder while he steers me towards the back door of the club, past the grubby, stinking toilets and through a black door marked *Exit*. We end up outside in a tiny alley squeezed between two tall, brick buildings. At one end of the alley is a dead end where there are numerous piles of bin bags overflowing with rubbish, which fills my nostrils with a putrid stench. The other end of the alley exits out onto a larger road, which eventually leads to the main street. I know this because Benjamin and I performed some reconnaissance earlier in the evening, ensuring we knew all of our escape routes.

Gerald shuts the back door of the club with a loud slam and turns to me. 'It's good to finally meet you in person, Alicia. I've heard a lot about you.'

'All bad things, I hope.'

'What the hell are you doing here? I thought The Master told you to back off? Did you not get the message?'

'I chose not to listen.'

'So what are you doing here?'

'Righting some wrongs.'

Gerald raises one eyebrow, doing an exceptionally good imitation of Dwayne Johnson. 'You're pretty confident for a woman who has a target on her back.'

'I hear that confidence is key.'

He narrows his eyes at me. 'Have you spoken to my sister?'

I shrug my shoulders. 'I have no idea what you are talking about. I did not know you had a sister.'

Gerald stares at me, scanning me from top to bottom. 'You're lying.'

'Am I?'

'What did that bitch tell you?'

I remain silent, locking eyes with him, not blinking.

151

Gerald takes a step towards me, but I do not move a muscle. He grins at me. 'You've got some balls, I'll give you that. I can see why Peter was fascinated by you. You're … unique.' He is now within touching distance so he reaches out and strokes his fingers down the side of my face, down the front of my chest and then lingers at the top button of my jeans. 'Maybe I should take you for a test ride before I kill you,' he whispers in my ear.

'And maybe … you should think twice before taking a known murderer into a dark alley without telling anyone.'

'I'd like to see you try and kill me, little girl … I've heard stories about you, I've seen the pictures and the videos of what they did to you. I'm sorry I never got a chance to do it myself … I just …' Gerald stops and frowns. I watch as he attempts to focus his vision. He takes a step back, stumbling ever so slightly.

I silently watch him.

'W-What's happening? What the hell … what have you done to me?'

'I take it you are feeling a little dizzy at the moment?'

Gerald leans his hand against the wall and grunts. 'You bitch! I'll fucking kill you!'

'Well, I suggest you do it soon because in about five minutes you shall be unconscious and not long after that you will be dead. I had a friend of mine slip some Rohypnol into your drink when you were not looking. You must be familiar with the effects of that particular drug. It is what you use on your victims, is it not?'

Gerald blinks several times and then launches himself directly at me. I dodge out of the way as he trips over thin air and collapses onto the ground, covering himself in dirt and the contents of a nearby rubbish bag. He attempts to steady himself and climb to his feet, but he fails as he falls sideways. He begins to crawl across the ground towards me, but I merely keep stepping out of his way. This is too fucking easy ... I have forgotten how exhilarating it is to actually meticulously plan and kill someone. The few times when I have had to kill out of self-defence had been messy and awkward, but this ... this is pure symmetry in motion ... utterly perfect.

'If there is anything you wish to get off your chest, now is the time to do it. I shall be the last person you ever speak to or see ... so ... I will happily listen to anything you have to say for the next ... five minutes.'

Gerald begins to shake his head and slumps further down onto the floor. 'I ... I don't ...' He fumbles for his mobile phone, which I easily snatch out of his grasp. I also relieve him of his earpiece and walkie-talkie, which I assume enables him to communicate with the other security guards.

He is near to being completely unconscious. He does not have much time. I stand over him as he feebly attempts to grab my ankle and pull me off balance.

'I take it there is nothing you wish to say?' I ask.

Gerald mumbles something incoherent and growls like a dog. I guess I shall have to take that as a *no*. He then slips into unconsciousness. I stare at the helpless creature on the ground. He will never hurt anyone ever again and that fills me with such a satisfied and happy feeling, I actually smile.

I quickly text Benjamin the all-clear message and several seconds later he emerges at the end of the alley. He glances past me at the crumpled, drooling heap.

'Is he dead?'

'Not yet.'

'So what now?'

'Phase two.'

'Right ...'

Phase two involves carrying Gerald's limp body through the alley and manhandling him into the boot of a rental car that Benjamin procured earlier (we did not use the car we had driven up in for obvious reasons). We then drive a few miles to a completely secluded section of the Water of Leith, the large river that flows through the middle of the city, and drag him down to the edge. We place him face down in the river and watch until he takes his final breath. There is no need to hold him down because the dose of Rohypnol had been so large there is no chance he will wake up, even though he is drowning. It is a quiet, peaceful and painless death ... and it is more than he deserves. All of my kills have been bloody and violent in the past, but this one ... is different. Maybe I am growing as a person, as a killer.

Benjamin and I stand on the bank of the river staring down at the floating body of Gerald Murray as the current begins to take him away.

'Um … should we say something?' asks Benjamin awkwardly. It is clear he is not enjoying this experience as much as I am.

'Good riddance,' I say.

Benjamin and I head back to the hotel in silence. It is gone 2 a.m. and I can feel the overwhelming need to sleep closing in. I take a shower (because I refuse to get into a clean bed smelling like a nightclub) then he does too. When he emerges wearing nothing but a pair of loose trousers I am already in bed. He is drying his hair with a towel as he sits on the edge of the bed, his shoulders hunched.

'I don't think I'll ever get used to this,' he says quietly. 'Killing someone,' he adds.

'It gets easier.'

'It shouldn't,' he snaps.

We remain silent as he climbs under the sheets and lays his head against the pillow. He lets out a long sigh and then turns his head to look at me, a longing in his eyes.

'Do you not feel anything after what we've just done?'

'I feel relief.'

'You enjoyed it, didn't you?'

I turn to look at him. 'Yes.'

A sadness appears over Benjamin's face. He then shuffles his body so he is facing away from me and is as far away as physically possible whilst still remaining on the bed.

'Goodnight, Alicia,' he grunts.

I clench my teeth together, feeling extremely sexually frustrated. I am not saying killing someone turns me on. I am not like the monsters I am hunting, but being in such close proximity to Benjamin is certainly causing my senses to come alive. I would never act on my feelings of course because Josslyn loves him and it would mean betraying her, so I settle down under the covers and pull them up to my chin.

'Goodnight, Benjamin.'

Chapter Twenty-Three
Josslyn

I'm warm and comfortable; it feels nice. My eyes flicker open briefly, but I don't recognise the room. I assume it's a hotel room from the obvious tell-tale signs (small TV, random comfy chair that no one ever sits in, kettle and two white cups), but I can't remember how I got here. I have a momentary flashback of my university days when I would often wake up in strange places with no memory of how I arrived ... and in strange beds. Come on ... we've all done it at least once.

My head hurts as I gingerly lift it off the pillow and glance around, hoping I'll see something that will spark a memory of why I'm here. That's when I feel a warm body next to me, so I turn and come face to face with Ben, who has his eyes closed, breathing softly. His hair is sticking up all over the place and he has a hand outstretched towards me as if he's been spooning me during the night.

I smile as I watch him sleeping. I've missed him so much ... wait ... why is Ben in bed spooning with Alicia? What the fuck is going on?

Calm down ... nothing happened. Neither of us fancied sleeping on the floor.

I didn't say anything ...

No, but you were thinking it.

Sorry ... well, I just ... I know he loves you too and I thought maybe you two had ...

I would never betray your trust like that ... again.

Yeah, I guess technically you did sleep with him first.

Nice to have you back by the way. Where have you been?

I was in the dark place again, but this time it turned grey, which was really weird. I'm sorry I've been away so long. It's getting harder and harder to come back. Did I miss anything good?

Only the murder of Gerald Murray.

Aww man! I hope you made him suffer.

I decided to be gracious and let him go quietly and peacefully. He is currently floating face down in a river.

I'm sorry I wasn't there to help.

Benjamin was adequate help.

We stay silent for a few moments, knowing the end is drawing ever closer, but neither of us is willing to say the final goodbye yet. Maybe if we don't ever say it, it will never need to be said. Maybe we don't have to say goodbye ...

Alicia tells me she is going to disappear for a while to give me and Ben some privacy. I wish I could come and go as I please. I'm not sure where she goes exactly, but maybe she goes to the grey place too ... or maybe she goes somewhere else. You know ... I've never asked her.

Ben's eyelids start to flutter so I nestle down close to him, my face only inches from his. His eyes slowly open and he jumps.

'Good morning, boyfriend,' I say happily.

'Good morning, girlfriend,' he replies with a sleepy smile.

He leans over, grabs the back of my head and pulls me into his body, kissing me deeply. There is something urgent and animalistic about the way he kisses me and starts pulling at the t-shirt I'm wearing. I can feel him hard against me, which makes me go tingly all over.

'Is everything okay?' I ask in-between heavy kisses.

'Of course,' he replies as he removes my t-shirt. 'I've just missed you.'

'What happened last night?'

Ben stops what he's doing. 'With Gerald Murray?'

'With Alicia,' I reply. 'I woke up just now and you were practically spooning her.'

Ben gulps and flushes slightly. 'It was an accident, nothing happened … Wait … are you jealous?'

I laugh sarcastically. 'Ha ha. No, of course I'm not jealous. If I was it'd be ridiculous because I'm not really real, I'm just a personality of hers …' I stop myself and look away, suddenly realising this is the first time we've spoken since he found out the truth about me.

'Alicia told me,' says Ben, stroking my face gently, 'and it doesn't change a thing. I still love you. I'll always love you.'

'Do you still love her?'

Ben doesn't answer straight away. He avoids my gaze, suddenly finding my right nipple extremely interesting to look at. I smile as I lift his chin with my fingers so he has no choice but to look at me. He grins stupidly, knowing full well how adorably cute he is right now.

'I'm sorry ... okay, but yes ... yes, I do love her and I can't for the life of me understand why because she's a fucking raging, emotionless psycho who is so goddamn infuriating I want to rip my own hair out sometimes.'

I raise my eyebrows at his angry tone. 'Wow ... you really do love her.'

Ben sighs in frustration. 'I know it's weird and it's wrong and I feel like I'm cheating on you or something, but—'

'Let me stop you right there, Mister ... I'm not a real person so you can't cheat on me because otherwise you're basically cheating on me with myself ... Wait, no, that's not right ... what I mean to say is—'

Ben doesn't give me a chance to finish; he pins me down on the bed and kisses me again as he runs his hands down my naked body and down between my legs ...

Hmm ... what was I saying?

Never mind.

Eventually we manage to tear ourselves away from each other and get dressed (no time to shower because it's nearly time to meet Charlotte ... oops).

'So,' I say as I step into my jeans. 'I hear I missed out on some fun last night.'

Ben frowns at me as he fishes his jeans from the chair. 'I thought I told you nothing happened.'

I chuckle. 'No, not with Alicia ... I meant with Gerald Murray.'

Ben pulls his t-shirt over his head and straightens it out. 'I'd hardly call murdering someone ... *fun*.' By his tone of voice I can tell I've annoyed him. Maybe fun had been the wrong word to use in front of him. I forget he's not like us ... me ... Alicia ... whatever.

'It was just a figure of speech,' I reply.

'Was it? Or are you actually enjoying this the same as Alicia?'

I face him square on, my hands on my hips. 'These men are getting what they deserve,' I point out harshly. Honestly, does he not get it at all?

Ben rolls his eyes. 'Fuck sake, you sound just like Alicia. The Josslyn I know would never—'

'You've never really known me, Ben. You don't know what I'm capable of, the things I've done, the things that ...' I trail off because I've run out of examples.

'I think I know you pretty damn well, Josslyn. I mean ... I don't know why you do that thing with your feet before you get out of bed in the morning, but I do know you don't really enjoy killing people, not the way Alicia does. You're not a psychopath.'

'But neither is she,' I respond quickly. 'She's mentally ill because of the trauma she suffered as a child and I'm the one who's been protecting her all these years. She's not a psychopath ... she's not a sociopath ... she's just

... a bit broken.' Tears fill my eyes as I finish getting dressed. I turn away from Ben so he can't see how upset I am.

Ben comes over, turns me around and wraps his arms around me as he kisses the top of my head.

'I'm sorry. I'll never call her a psychopath ever again.'

'Thank you ... just try and give her a break, okay?'

'Fine, but can you tell her to stop being so difficult?'

'I'll try.'

Chapter Twenty-Four
Josslyn

We arrive outside Wickham Mental Health Hospital at precisely eight o'clock and pull up into one of the empty visitor parking spaces. Charlotte hasn't arrived yet.

I can't help but stare at the enormous building in front of me with awe and general uneasiness. It sends a shiver up my spine, as if cold fingers are gently tickling the back of my neck causing all the hair on my body to stand to attention. You've seen horror movies with abandoned mental asylums in them, right? Well, that's pretty much what this place reminds me of, but it's clearly still occupied and active as there are cars in the car park and lights on in the windows. However, that doesn't mean it still doesn't look abandoned. Clearly it needs some funding to bring it into the twenty-first century. The building is four storeys high (five if you include the basement which I'm assuming it has because ... well ... all creepy buildings have basements).

I think your imagination might be running away with you.

Ah, it appears Alicia has surfaced.

Are we looking at the same building? It's got to be haunted and full of ghosts and have a basement with chains and hooks hanging from the beams, and maybe a random locked door with noises coming from behind it.

It just looks like an old building to me.

That's because you have no imagination. If I see one weird thing happening or something moves on its own ... I'm out of here.

I continue to study the building for several more minutes while we wait for Charlotte. I can see a few people walking in front of the windows dressed in white coats and holding clipboards. The red stone bricks on the outside clearly lost their new sheen years ago and look dirty and dull; some of the tiles on the roof haven fallen off, no doubt rotting on the ground somewhere, leaving ugly gaps.

'You okay?'

I'm startled by Ben's voice as he comes and stands next to me. 'Yes ... just ... thinking.'

'What about?'

I make an immediate decision to not tell him what I'm thinking, which is that if I'd told people I had a voice in my head years ago I'd probably have been locked up in one of these buildings and would most likely still be in one. Maybe this is where I belong ... or where Alicia belongs.

'Nothing,' I answer with a forced smile.

I wonder what would've happened if I'd told Mum and Dad about the voice in my head. Would they have sent me to therapy? If I'd have gone would I have been healed eventually (can you even heal from this type of mental illness?) and would I have disappeared years ago?

Urggh ... too many questions to even think about. Let's not go down that road right now.

At that moment a car pulls up next to ours and Charlotte gets out. She's dressed in a sharp, light pink suit, impeccably over-dressed for visiting such a run-down crap hole. She looks me up and down, taking note of my dull attire. She sniffs and raises her nose, clearly ashamed to even be standing close to me. Who the hell does she think she is, looking down at me like that? Snooty bitch.

'How did it go last night?' she asks as she straightens her jacket, sounding calm and measured, as if she's asking after a date night and not the murder of her brother.

'Fine,' I reply. 'It's all taken care of.'

Ben filled me in on the details in the car this morning. Not that there was much to say on the subject of Gerald's death. He's dead ... that's all that really matters ... currently rotting and bloating somewhere in the Water of Leith.

'He's ... he's ... gone?' she asks timidly.

'Yep. You might want to prepare yourself for a phone call from the police when they eventually find his body ... you know, make sure you act like the grieving sister and all.'

Charlotte glowers at me. 'I *will* be the grieving sister ... he may be–have been–a bad man, but he was still my brother.'

I nod my head, but then turn and roll my eyes so she can't see me.

Charlotte suddenly grabs my arm and squeezes it tightly. 'T-Thank you,' she whispers, her voice breaking ever so slightly.

I must admit I'm taken aback by her words, but I acknowledge them with a smile.

'He can't hurt you or Rebecca anymore.'

Charlotte nods curtly. 'Remember … in here her name's Hannah.'

'Got it.'

Ben and I follow her wordlessly through the front door of the hospital and approach the reception desk. It smells like a mixture of rot and suffering in here. I hate hospitals even when they don't potentially house crazy ghosts.

I follow Charlotte's lead and we sign in using the pen and paper (both Ben and I use fake names, but no one seems to bat an eyelid or ask for any form of ID). Great security they have … I'm surprised Rebecca's been able to hide here for so long and remain undetected. The receptionist is surprised to see Charlotte again so soon, but doesn't question her motives for visiting her daughter again, nor does she question why two strangers wish to see her.

The three of us take a seat in the meeting area where there are a few tables and chairs set out. I feel like I'm visiting someone in jail. There's already a family here talking to a patient who looks and sounds perfectly normal. In fact, he doesn't look sick at all, but then again the people who are in here don't all have visible illnesses. Just because they're invisible it doesn't make them any less real. I'm a perfect example.

'Hannah will be out in a moment,' says one of the staff members who shows us to our seats.

'Thank you,' replies Charlotte, setting her handbag down on the floor beside her.

There's an awkward silence while we wait. Charlotte eventually leans towards me.

'Please try not to upset her. She's been doing well lately, as I said she's been learning sign language and communicating a bit in that way and I wouldn't want her to be set back in her recovery.'

'I understand, but there's no way to tiptoe around this subject. I'm going to need to speak to her about what she went through, to see if she remembers anything, anything at all that could help us find The Collective and her father, but I'll be as diplomatic as I can.'

Charlotte frowns at me. 'You seem different today,' she says. 'You're actually pleasant.'

I grin. 'Thanks.'

I guess that means she thinks you're unpleasant, Alicia.

I could not care less.

I turn to Charlotte. 'So do you know sign language too?'

'A little bit. I've been learning it ready for when she actually speaks to me. Obviously she can hear me when I speak to her, but so far I haven't had to use it.'

It suddenly dawns on me I'm about to meet my half-sister ... an actual blood relative who has been through a similar experience as I have (as Alicia has). What if all of this is a complete waste of time and she knows nothing, or worst of all, that she refuses to even speak to me? I'm not expecting her to make a full recovery and start blabbing her deepest, darkest secrets to the whole room, but I hope she'll at least give me something to work with ... anything.

Oh God ... now I'm nervous ...

Chapter Twenty-Five
Josslyn

I look up from fiddling with my fingernails at the sound of a door buzzing and see a bedraggled, skinny woman shuffling into the room, a notebook and pen clutched tightly to her chest. She's wearing a matching cream tracksuit that's swamping her tiny frame and is in desperate need of a wash (huh, I always thought people in these places wore white nightgowns or maybe I've seen too many horror movies) and fluffy panda bear slippers, which causes me to do a double take and crack a smile. The whole ensemble makes her look like a young teenager, but I know for a fact she's closer to my age. Her black hair is limp and lifeless, hanging down like curtains on either side of her face and her lips are squeezed shut, as if she's afraid to even open her mouth.

My own mouth goes dry and I take a gulp as she shuffles towards us, barely lifting her feet off the floor, and sits down gently without making a sound. She's staring down at the floor, not making eye contact with anyone, not even her own mother. She's startling to look at with her pale white face and dark, dead eyes.

'Hi darling ... I know you're probably surprised to see me again so soon, but I've brought some people to see you. This is Alexis Grey and Benjamin Willis. They're here to ask you a few questions about ... about ... what happened to you.' Charlotte whispers the final few words like they're dirty and she's ashamed to say them.

At this Rebecca snaps her head up and glares at me ... only me. I jump a little in my seat.

Oh God ... she's freaking me out. Her eyes are empty of life. There's no spark, no flicker of energy or anything and she's staring at me as if she wants to leap out of her seat and kill me.

'Um ... hi,' I squeak. 'Nice to meet you. Love the slippers by the way.'

Rebecca twitches her nose and goes back to staring down at her lap where she's still clutching her notebook.

'What's in your notebook?' I ask, attempting to sound like I want to start a general conversation.

'It's what she uses to write in sometimes,' says Charlotte. 'Sometimes she'll use sign language and sometimes she'll write a word or two in there.'

I nod my understanding and try again. 'Um ... have you been outside lately? The weather's quite lovely.'

Seriously? You are talking to her about the weather?

Shut up. I'm trying to bond with her.

By talking about the weather?

Shut up.

Rebecca slowly lifts her head and frowns at me, tilting her head to one side, as if ... no, that's impossible. She couldn't have heard ...

Without breaking eye contact Rebecca lays her notebook on the table and writes something on it. I hear a gasp from Charlotte. Then she turns it around so I can read what she's written.

Who said that?

No ... fucking ... way.

I'm speechless, like properly speechless. I glance at Ben for some backup, but he looks about as confused as I am. I turn back to Rebecca.

'What do you mean?' I ask her.

Rebecca turns to Charlotte and does some sign language. Charlotte immediately stands up.

'I'm afraid she wants me to leave so she can speak to you alone. I'll wait for you outside. I'll see you at our regular appointment, Rebecca darling.' With that she leaves the room.

Regular appointment? She is her daughter, not a scheduled doctor's meeting.

Rebecca is performing more sign language at me, so I shake my head.

'I'm really sorry, but I don't understand sign language.'

Rebecca grabs the notebook again and scribbles more words.

He can leave too.

I glance at Ben and shrug my shoulders.

Ben sighs as he stands up. 'Text me if you need me.' And he leaves too.

Now it's just me and Rebecca ... who still won't stop looking at me with that vacant expression.

'You can trust him, you know … Ben's a good guy,' I say.

I don't trust men.

I like her already.

Who is that?

'Can you really hear her?'

Rebecca slowly shakes her head.

No, but I can sense … something.

What does that mean?

Why are you asking me?

I smile at Rebecca, aware I haven't answered her yet. To be honest I don't know what to even say to her, but at least she's talking to me. I open my mouth to speak, but she's writing again.

You look like him.

My heart drops into my stomach and I feel it banging around down there, making me feel nauseous.

Oh shit … she knows exactly who I am without me even explaining it. Is it that obvious? Then it hits me … the truth about what she actually means. She must know what *he* looks like. Oh my God, this is it! We're finally getting somewhere.

'I … I do?' I say awkwardly because I still have no idea what to actually say.

Rebecca nods, finally turning her head to look out of the window next to us. From where I'm sitting I can see a few trees and some gravel paths, so I assume they have some sort of garden here where the patients can go for fresh air and exercise. It still feels like a prison somehow, but from looking around at the patients they all seem relatively happy. Maybe this is their safe space. They aren't judged by the outside world in here.

We sit in silence for a few moments. I don't feel as if I need to rush her. I want her to feel safe with me and I want her to *want* to open up on her own terms. We're related after all … well … I guess she's not related to me. She's related to Alicia.

Maybe you should be the one to talk to her. You're always better with words than I am.

Not yet. I do not wish to scare her. I will take over if need be.

Whatever I end up saying will most likely scare her anyway. There's no easy way to ask her about what happened.

Just tread carefully.

Rebecca takes her notebook and scribbles again.

You're like some of the other people here, aren't you?

I look around at some of the other patients.

'Yes,' I answer truthfully. 'I'm a bit … broken too.'

Rebecca smiles, showing a few uneven but fairly clean teeth.

That's a good way of putting it. The doctors here say we're all sick. I'm not sick.

I nod. 'I know. You had something bad happen to you and now you can't talk. I had something bad happen to me as well and I … well, my brain sort of … broke into two.'

173

At this Rebecca tilts her head, which still really creeps me out, but now she doesn't look quite so scary like the woman in the horror film *The Ring*.

You have a split personality, don't you?

I'm literally lost for words right now, so I merely nod as she continues to scribble frantically.

What's her name?

'Her name is Alicia … and my name is Josslyn.'

I thought your name was Alexis.

'That's just a fake name Alicia came up with a while ago. We're trying to hide from the law for reasons I won't bore you with right now.'

Rebecca smiles, but she actually looks as if she's trying to hold back a laugh. Her eyes have changed since I first saw her merely minutes ago. They are twinkling under the bright lights of the room and even her body language has changed: she's now sitting up a little straighter. I can see a doctor in the corner of the room glancing over at us and making notes on her pad. I expect they'll want to talk to her afterwards, amazed at her sudden breakthrough.

'Listen,' I say as I shift uneasily in my seat. 'There's no easy way to say this. I'm so sorry about what happened to you and please believe me when I say that I can only imagine how painful it must have been. Alicia and I went through a similar experience not long ago, but we had each other. I know you didn't have anyone. The last thing I want is to scare you or bring back horrible memories, but Alicia and I really need your help. We're taking them down … The Collective … we're taking them *all* down, but it's proving to be rather difficult to find them. We're hoping you might know something that could help us.

'We need to find him … Frank Master … The Hooded Man … whatever you want to call him. I know you know who I am … he's my father and he's yours too. We need to take him out. Peter is dead. Gerald, your uncle, is dead. We need to finish what we've started. We can't have them hurting or killing any more women. I know you and your mother are scared, but I promise that Alicia and I won't let anything happen to you. Anything you can tell us, anything at all, will be helpful.'

There … I said it. I said all of it. I just hope she doesn't get up and run for the door, but something tells me she won't. There's a horrible silence and for a second I wonder if she's gone back into her shell and now won't talk to me.

She just stares at me, lightly tapping her pen on the table.

Tap, tap, tap.

Tap, tap, tap.

Who took you?

I feel a rush of relief at the fact she's still willing to talk to me. I decide to be completely honest because, let's face it, I have nothing to hide from her. She's clearly appreciating my honesty. I keep my voice low as I speak.

'Peter took me. Alicia and I were tortured for two days, but we managed to escape and we killed him. He stalked us for years without us knowing. I know he stalked you as well because I've seen the pictures. I'm so sorry. I know he tricked you into falling for him because he did the same thing to me. He was a horrible, sick man, but he's gone now.'

Did he suffer?

'Yes.'

You're wrong about one thing.

'What's that?'

Rebecca spends a few minutes writing.

He didn't trick me into falling for him. We never dated. I never fancied him in that way. We became good friends, but then he started to change and he became controlling. He'd turn up randomly at my door and act jealous when I went out with other friends. I started pushing him away because he was getting clingy, but one day he went too far and he raped me.

I'm momentarily stunned as I think back to the naked photos of Rebecca sleeping on Peter's wall. The photos of them smiling together. I'd just assumed … but clearly I was wrong.

'I … I'm sorry … I thought, I mean, from the photos and notes he had on you I thought you were in a relationship at some point.'

I've never been in a relationship with a man. I'm gay.

I lean back in my chair, expelling the air in my mouth. Shit … all this time I'd believed Peter had never raped a woman, that he had merely wooed them with his charm and good looks. He'd told me he'd never raped them, that he was different to the other men in the group, but he wasn't, was he? He was exactly the same. It's no wonder Rebecca doesn't trust men!

'I didn't realise you're gay. I'm sorry, I shouldn't have assumed,' I say. God, I feel like a right pompous bitch now.

Rebecca begins writing again.

Peter took me out for drinks one night after I'd had an argument with my girlfriend and he drugged me. I woke up in a sealed room which was covered in pictures of other women and myself. I now recognise you as one of them, but at the time I had no idea who you were. Peter raped me multiple times in front of a live web cam. He then invited other men into the room and they took it in turns to abuse me, torture me, rape me, but there was always one who never touched me. He just watched quietly and never said a word.

My breath catches in my throat. 'Frank Master.'

Rebecca nods and scribbles.

His real name is Henry Smith.

Chapter Twenty-Six
Josslyn

My mind reels with this sudden revelation. His name ... it's the one thing we've needed this whole time and here it is, in black and white, scribbled on a piece of paper in front of me. I stare at it for several seconds, the letters searing themselves into my brain. I've seen it before ... that name ...

Henry Smith.

Henry ... Smith ... Henry ...

Why does his name sound so familiar? I've definitely heard or seen it somewhere before, I know I have, but I can't remember where or when. The answer is staring me in the face, but I can't pluck the memory from my tired and confused brain.

Alicia, any ideas?

I am thinking.

I turn back to Rebecca. 'Thank you. Thank you so much for telling us his name. Is there anything else you can tell us about him ... what does he look like, his age, hair colour, that sort of thing?'

Rebecca nods and drags the paper back towards her.

Fifties. Dark hair with flecks of grey. Brown eyes. Clean cut. Smart. Well spoken.

I remember now.

You do?

The black-tie ball we attended with Peter and Benjamin. Henry Smith was the Head Master of the school who introduced Peter to the audience. He was also photographed with Peter in the paper in the online articles I found while I was stalking him.

Holy shit!

Alicia's right. The memory pops into my head as clear as day. Henry Smith had been wearing a black tuxedo, a beaming smile and had shaken hands with Peter on the make-shift stage before Peter had given his speech. They'd both acted so casual, so ... normal, but behind their cool exteriors they'd been hiding a dark, dark secret.

Henry must have seen me that night, must have known who I was. Peter had kissed me in front of everyone and caused a huge scene. It had all been a massive ploy. I'm so angry at myself for not seeing it, but then how could I? At the time all I'd been focussed on was destroying Peter. I'd not taken any notice of people around me.

I take a deep breath, aware I haven't responded to Rebecca.

'I've seen him before,' I say. 'He's the Head Master of the boarding school where Peter used to work. Peter told me he groomed a young student from the school too. His name was Michael and he tried to rape Alicia after Peter told him to.'

I think for a moment. Oh my God ... I have an idea ... just go with me on this ...

I lean forwards towards Rebecca and lower my voice. 'Maybe all of the men in The Collective work or study at the school. Maybe it's like a whole big ... organisation and the school is just the cover.'

Rebecca doesn't attempt to write anything, but she nods in agreement at me.

That is a certainly a very real possibility. Well done, Josslyn.

I continue enthusiastically, my thoughts and ideas gaining momentum as I speak. 'We need to look into all the men who work there and all the students. Oh my God, there could be dozens ... there's no way we can kill them all, it would cause too much suspicion. We need a new plan ...' I lean back in my chair and run my hands through my hair. It's suddenly dawning on me how massive a job this really is. 'We have to reveal them somehow, but we need proof first ...' I stop and sigh heavily.

I have an idea.

Good, because I've just run out of them.

Let me talk with Rebecca.

'Alicia would like to speak with you,' I say to Rebecca quietly.

At this she looks genuinely excited and enthusiastically nods her head.

Yeesh ... I've never known anyone to be so excited to talk to you.

I have a feeling she and I will get along quite well.

Let me warn her first.

'There's something about Alicia you should know,' I say. 'She's the real person here. I'm actually her split personality that evolved years ago to keep her safe from the trauma she endured. She's not like me ... she's ... different.'

Rebecca nods her understanding. There's so much more I should probably tell her, but now's not the time.

Chapter Twenty-Seven
Alicia

I slowly open my eyes and take in my surroundings, scratching the back of my neck, stretching it to the side until it clicks. The chair I am sitting on is rock hard and I can smell ... something that is vaguely familiar and pleasant. Benjamin. I can only assume while I was gone earlier Josslyn and Benjamin spent some ... time together.

Okay, look, I didn't have time to shower this morning ... and since when do you know what Ben smells like?

I roll my eyes, declining to answer.

I lock eyes with Rebecca, who is staring at me in the same way I often stare at people. Josslyn is correct ... it is slightly unnerving, but I do not feel nervous or awkward. In fact, I feel ... I am not sure of the exact emotion ... or if it is even an emotion I am feeling, but something inside me is calm and at peace as I sit with my half-sister.

'Hello, Rebecca,' I say in my usual tone, but quietly so as not to be overheard.

She flinches ever so slightly at the change in my voice as she grabs her notebook.

Hello, Alicia. This is weird.

I nod in agreement.

So ... you're my real half-sister.

'It appears so.'

Josslyn is nice.

I purse my lips together before speaking. 'She is pleasant enough, although slightly annoying at times.'

Gee ... thanks.

I always wanted a sister.

I do not reply, but merely take a deep breath. 'I am afraid I do not have time for general pleasantries or to swap sister stories. There will be time for that later on down the line. I need you to answer a few more questions for me.'

Surprisingly, Rebecca does not recoil at my harsh tone or look disappointed. She nods enthusiastically, so I continue.

'First of all, I need your permission to release all the photos Peter took of you to the authorities. Some of them are very revealing and derogatory, but eventually I will have to release them.'

Rebecca blinks and then slowly nods.

'Secondly, I need you to tell me, in as much detail as you can remember, exactly what you recall when Peter took you and everything you can about the other men who abused you. I need their descriptions, any names, tone of voice, age, anything that can help me and Josslyn recognise these men. There are hundreds of men working and studying at that school and I need help to narrow them down.'

Rebecca nods again and begins to scribble, but I lean forwards and place my hand over hers to stop her.

'And third ... I need you to tell me why you have kept the fact you have known who Henry Smith is this entire time and have not revealed his identity. I need to know why you have locked yourself up in this prison ... the real reason. I know you are unable to speak, but I believe there is more to it than what you and your mother have told us. I need you to tell me the truth about why you are here.'

Rebecca reacts exactly as I thought she would – she does not react at all. She glances down at my hand covering hers, blinks several times and then pulls her hands out from under mine, relaxing back into her chair. She retrieves her paper and pen and begins to write. It takes several long minutes, during which I do not take my eyes off her. She is hiding something ... and I have a fairly good idea what it is.

What's she hiding?

You shall see.

Oh, come on ... don't make me guess.

I want her to tell me herself.

Rebecca finally finishes writing. She pushes the notebook towards me and then proceeds to lean back in her chair and stare out of the window. I pick up the notebook and read.

Peter told me Henry was my dad. He seemed to know everything and enjoyed the fact he knew something Henry didn't. Peter must have done his own research and discovered my identity and kept it a secret from Henry. I get the feeling Peter wanted to use his knowledge against him somehow. I think he was Henry's number one guy and wanted to take over from him as The Master one day.

While I was being held captive they made me do horrible things ... things that make me sick to even

think about. By the time they were finished with me Peter said I wasn't in any state to return to the outside world. I'd seen who they all were and I'd seen who Henry was. They said they couldn't trust me not to tell anyone even though I promised I wouldn't tell a soul. I think they planned to kill me, but then Peter told Henry who I really was and Henry lost it. He was angry at Peter and eventually he refused to accept it and basically denied it. He said he already had a daughter and didn't need another one.

Henry told me if I revealed his identity my mum would die, my friends would die and anyone who ever knew me would die. I knew my own life was on the line too. They told me I had to prove my devotion to them, prove that I would never tell anyone, so they made me kill a young boy, one of their own. I stabbed him over and over. Then they said if I ever told anyone they'd release the body and have me arrested for murder.

I didn't return home. I was broken and beaten, so I returned to Edinburgh, the place I grew up. Mum still lived down south. I was homeless for several weeks and I almost walked into a police station on several occasions to tell them what had happened, but Gerald, my uncle, found me. He followed me. I knew I had to disappear because I didn't feel safe. I eventually called my mum and told her what had happened, but she didn't believe me, not at first. She had lived in denial for so long, ever since she was raped all those years ago. She was also under the control of The Collective.

Not long after that I lost my voice and she finally believed me. She decided to hide me away so I'd be safe. I didn't want to live in the real world anymore. She never reported me missing so no one ever came looking for me. My mum never spoke about me again to anyone. I'm safe here … protected. And now I've told you all of this we're both in extreme danger.

I lower the paper and set it down on the table in front of me. I stare at Rebecca for several seconds; she stares right back, neither one of us blinking. It is a tense moment.

'You killed someone to keep your family and friends safe,' I say solemnly.

Rebecca nods, not showing a single drop of remorse or any sort of emotion.

She does a good imitation of you.

'I have done the same … several times.'

Another nod; we have an understanding.

'Why tell me all of this now? You could have just remained silent.'

Rebecca begins writing again. It does not take her long to finish.

I trust you.

We hold eye contact and then both smile in unison.

'One more question,' I say, raising my voice slightly. Rebecca stares blankly at me for a few seconds. 'Do you know how to access the online site The Collective use where they showcase their … work?'

Rebecca shakes her head as she writes.

No, but I know someone who can help you.

'I am wary about bringing in an outside informant,' I say quietly.

I trust you, so now it's your turn to trust me. She can help you. She's my ex-girlfriend. She knows all about the dark web, computers and online stuff. She can get you fake IDs, a licence to own a gun and even high-tech camera equipment.

I look up from the page and raise one eyebrow.

'I take it none of this is technically legal?'

Rebecca does the so-so gesture with her hand, then writes.

She's the one who helped my mum when she needed me to disappear. She erased my identity. Trust me … she can help you bring down The Collective. I never told her the real reason why I had to go into hiding. She knows nothing about Henry or The Collective. If she did then she'd probably have tried to take them down herself by now.

'What is her name?'

I can't tell you. She has to fly under the radar. She uses the codename 'Web Ninja'. I'll give you her email address, but she'll want you to use a codename too.

What are we … spies now?

'Web Ninja?' I say with a hint of sarcasm in my voice.

Rebecca smiles.

She'll tell you her real name when she trusts you.

'And you think she will help me?'

Tell her I sent you. Tell her I still love her and that I'll come back to her when this is all over, I promise.

'Okay … thank you for your help.'

While I wait for Rebecca to finish writing down the contact details I casually glance around the room, taking note of the other patients and their visitors again. One family is deep in conversation while the other is sitting in complete silence, the patient not even lifting his head to acknowledge his parents (I assume they are his parents). There is one doctor in the room, standing in the corner with a clipboard. She is staring at me with a confused look on her face. I am not sure if she has been watching us this entire time.

She was definitely watching us earlier too. Does she recognise me from the news? Shit …

I stand up abruptly, the chair making a screeching noise on the hard floor as I push it backwards.

'It is time I left.'

Rebecca looks up at me, stands and then rips a page out of her notebook and hands it to me. She grasps both of my hands and squeezes them before enveloping me in a tight hug. I am momentarily stunned as I do not think I have ever been properly hugged before, not as myself anyway. I do not return the hug, but merely stand awkwardly while she hugs me, finally pulling away. She smiles at me and then swiftly leaves the room, never looking back. I see the doctor make a note on her clipboard, frowning as she does so.

That can't be good.

Chapter Twenty-Eight
Alicia

Benjamin is waiting for me in the reception area, but Charlotte is nowhere to be seen. I can only assume she got tired of waiting. He stands up from slouching in a hard, plastic chair when he sees me, a hopeful look across his face.

'How did it go? Did she start talking?' He reaches out to embrace me (thinking I am still Josslyn), but I stop him by holding my hand up.

'I do not require a hug … I just received one and that is quite enough human contact for one day.'

Benjamin looks taken aback for a second, but then smiles. 'She hugged you?'

'Indeed.'

'I'll take that as a sign it went well then?'

'Yes, it went even better than I expected. She told me what we need to know. Frank Master's real name is Henry Smith and he is the Head Master of the school where Peter worked. Josslyn came up with the idea that all the men in The Collective either work there now or have worked there at one time or another. I also have a way of accessing the online site on the dark web where all the proof we need to reveal them will be.'

Benjamin lowers his voice as he leans closer to me. 'I thought you were going to kill them all?'

'There has been a change of plan. There are possibly far too many to take out one by one. I now intend to take them all down in one fell swoop. Henry Smith, however, will not be so lucky.'

Benjamin nods in understanding and stuffs both his hands into his pockets. 'So what's she like ... your real sister?'

'Half-sister,' I correct him.

'Right ... half-sister.'

'She is deeply troubled and broken ... but she is ...' – I stop and think about my words before I say them out loud – '... pleasant.'

'Pleasant?'

'Pleasant,' I repeat.

You used that word to describe me earlier too. It's a weird word to use to describe someone.

I roll my eyes and continue. 'She also severely distrusts men, and I cannot say I blame her, and she is a lesbian. In fact ...' I stop myself again. No – it is time I start withholding information from Benjamin. It will be for his own good, so I decline to mention Rebecca's ex-girlfriend and the fact she will be able to help us take down The Collective.

'In fact, what?'

'Nothing,' I say bluntly.

Benjamin frowns at me. 'Hang on ... I thought her and Peter were an item at one point?'

'No ... he raped her in front of a live web cam while she was drugged.'

Benjamin's face drains of all colour and he shudders and clutches his throat as he leans forwards over his knees, sucking in a few deep breaths.

'I can't believe I was ever best friends with that asshole,' he stutters. 'Fuck ... if he did that to her then what did he do to my sister?'

'It is not your fault. He fooled a lot of people.' I do not know what else to say to make him feel better, so I stand beside him while he gathers himself.

'S-Sorry,' he says when he finally stands upright, straightening his t-shirt. 'This is all a bit—'

'I get it.'

Benjamin says nothing further on the subject as we sign out and walk out of the building, but he does inform me that Charlotte had indeed got tired of waiting and left to go to work earlier.

We are just getting into the car when a female voice shouts from across the car park back the way we had just come.

'Wait! Hold on!'

The female doctor is jogging towards me; the one from the meeting room who had been watching us and taking notes.

Oh shit ...

Benjamin leaves his car door open as he approaches her. 'Can we help you?'

The doctor smiles as she stops jogging, bending over at the waist to catch her breath. 'Sorry,' she says. 'I'm not as fit as I used to be. I thought I'd missed you.'

The woman is in her late fifties, at least, a little soft around the waist, her white uniform slightly too tight under the armpits. Her hair is grey at the roots, indicating that she is behind on her box dye job. She has over-sized glasses perched on her nose and red lipstick on, which is smudged at the corners of her mouth. She finally stands up straight, ignores Benjamin completely and turns to me.

'I'm sorry to suddenly come running after you. I know this is highly unprofessional of me, but I saw you with Hannah Baker in the meeting room and I couldn't believe my eyes when she started communicating with you the way she's never communicated with anyone here, not even her own mother. I also ... I also had an overwhelming feeling I knew you from somewhere, but I couldn't for the life of me figure out where from, but as you were leaving it hit me.'

I've never seen her before in my life.

'I do not know you,' I reply bluntly.

She ignores my comment. 'I've worked all over the place you see, having only moved up to Scotland in the last few years with my husband. Before that I worked in Bournemouth at the Psychiatric Hospital for Children. I worked there for many years. I always pride myself on the fact I remember all my patients ... and I remember you, but as a child.'

I do not respond to her. Instead, I turn my head away and go to get into the car, but the woman lunges forwards and grabs my wrist tightly with her hand, scratching me with her fingernails as she does so.

'Alicia ... Alicia Reynolds,' she says.

I snap my head towards her and slowly turn my whole body to face her. She lets go of my wrist and takes a step back, clearly feeling threatened.

'How do you know my name?' I demand. I do not care if I sound rude. This woman knows who I am and if she is not careful she will find herself face down in the river like Gerald Murray. I cannot have anyone revealing my real identity when I am so close to completing my goal.

The doctor's eyes light up and she gasps loudly, clamping a hand over her mouth. 'Oh my God … it is you! It's you … it's … is Josslyn still—'

'How the fuck do you know about Josslyn? Answer me!' I take a large step towards her.

At this point Benjamin places a gentle hand on my shoulder and pulls me backwards slightly.

'Alicia … calm down. Let the doctor explain,' he says.

I glare at the doctor.

She stutters as she continues speaking. 'M-My name is Doctor Channing. I knew you when you were a little girl. Your parents brought you to see me after they adopted you and—'

'I have no parents,' I interject. 'You must be mistaken.'

'Ronald and Amanda Reynolds … they are your adopted parents, aren't they?'

What the fuck! Why would Mum and Dad take me to see a therapist? I don't remember that at all. What's she talking about?

I make no response while I contemplate my next move. The only other time I have seen the names *Alicia* and *Reynolds* together was on the envelope I found in the box in the attic, which I still have not read. Why does this stranger know me by that particular name? Unless ...

Benjamin interrupts my thoughts. 'Alicia ... maybe you should talk with Doctor Channing and sort all this out.'

'No!' I shout loudly as I point my finger at the doctor as if I am telling off a naughty child. 'I have nothing to say to you. I do not know you and neither does ... I do not know you. This is not about me. I have work to do. I will not let anyone get in my way.' I step closer to Doctor Channing, bringing my face within inches of hers, which is closer than I generally want to be to another human being, but I feel this situation warrants this particular threat. 'If you tell a single soul about who I am then I will hunt you down and slit your throat, do you understand?' The words come out much angrier and more threatening than I anticipated and for a second I am reminded of my old self, the one who would kill on a whim. I am not that person anymore, but I am desperate.

Doctor Channing takes a step backwards as she nods. 'Alicia ... Josslyn ... please believe me when I say that I'd never tell anyone, I promise. I don't believe what they're saying on the news ... that you're a serial killer—'

Clearly she doesn't know us that well then ...

'—But please ... when you're finished with whatever it is you have to do ... come back and see me and I'll tell you everything you need to know. I can help you get

195

better.' Doctor Channing rummages around in her uniform pockets and finds a scrap of paper. She lifts the pen which is tucked into her collar and scribbles a number on the paper before handing it to me with a shaking hand.

'I do not need your help,' I say as I step backwards, rejecting her offer. I get into the car and slam the door. I stare ahead as I wait for Benjamin to join me. Several seconds later he is sitting beside me in the driving seat. He sets the piece of paper down on the dashboard so I can see it.

We drive out of the city without a word and head back to Cambridge.

Chapter Twenty-Nine
Alicia

Benjamin drives in silence and I use the laptop and begin the tedious task of scrolling through the Lampton Boarding School for Boys' website, page by page, reading all the staff profiles and taking notes on each one. Who fits the profile for creepy stalker/rapist? And whose profile photo matches the descriptions Rebecca provided? Those are the questions I am asking myself as I scour each and every profile meticulously.

I notice Peter's profile has not been taken down yet, but there is a small note at the top next to his picture saying he is 'taking time off to travel and will return to teaching soon' – more like never. The note should read something along the lines of 'Peter is currently dead and has been burnt to ashes and scattered across local rubbish tips. He will not be returning to teaching … ever'. It does make me wonder who is in charge of designing and keeping the school's website up to date because the news channels are saying he has disappeared and is presumed dead. Maybe the school is attempting to keep their options open and staying positive … as if that will really help the situation.

Yes, I have still been keeping an eye on the news, but no, I do not care because I am so close to my end goal now. While on the drive, the radio annoyingly decides to remind me every hour of the manhunt (womanhunt) that is ongoing for Josslyn and the cases of Alicia Phillips, Daniel Russell and Peter Phillips, of which there are no new updates, so the news channels persevere with the tedious repetition of the same information. My face is still plastered across every channel too (the old me) and no one appears to have located me or seen me yet (which I am taking as a win, considering I have driven basically the entire length of the United Kingdom in the past few days). The authorities are searching in Tuscany as that is where *Josslyn* flew to just before the pandemic hit, but so far they have not located my villa, nor have they realised that Benjamin Willis is aiding me, nor is there any mention of Alexis Grey. So, for the time being, the search for Josslyn Reynolds has come to a slight standstill; a small victory.

After three hours of listening to the radio I switch it off and the remainder of the drive is spent in silence; the way I like it.

I click on the Head Master's profile and immediately my eyes are drawn to the beaming, happy, fifty-odd-year-old man. He is wearing an impressive, navy-blue, tailor-made suit, which fits him like a glove, highlighting his strong arms and thick torso. He has a slightly rounded stomach and his greying beard is neatly trimmed, as is his hair. He looks every inch the perfect, middle-aged, professional Head Master, but his eyes … they are no ordinary brown eyes. They are the eyes of a mad man, a sick and twisted, full-blown, crazy psychopath. There is a terrible darkness behind them, no sparkle, no happiness ... nothing. Only someone who already knows about his true darkness would recognise it in his eyes. Do I look like that? Do my eyes hold the same darkness when someone looks at me? Rebecca was right ... I do look like him. How did I not recognise him before?

I pull the car visor down and look at myself in the small mirror. The eyes; they are the same. I have never noticed that about myself before, but there is no happiness behind my eyes, no joy, no emotion, no ... anything.

I don't think that's true. You have that evil stare thing you do which freaks people out, but otherwise your eyes look fine. They look normal.

I appreciate you trying to make me feel better, but the truth is I am the daughter of a deranged serial rapist. I am the daughter of a monster; born from rape and abused.

But that doesn't make you a monster too.

I disagree.

Just look how far you've come, Alicia. You're a different person than you were nearly two years ago. Back then all you ever thought about was yourself and you killed people to please yourself, but now you're doing it to protect others. You're helping people. You're changing, whereas our dad has, quite clearly, never changed. He's the real monster, not you.

I fold the visor away and read Henry Smith's profile page.

"Henry Smith started working at Lampton Boarding School for Boys in 1999 as the English teacher. He quickly worked his way up the ranks and became Head Teacher in

2005. He prides himself on hiring only the very best teachers at his school and he has a very strict recruitment process. Henry works with several local charities and is a keen golfer, having won several golfing championships in his youth. He speaks several different languages and has even written a novel. Henry is single and has no children; however, he thrives on knowing that his school is the best and considers it a great honour to be part of the young boys' lives, knowing he is helping to turn them into well-educated, sophisticated men, ready to take on the world."

My breath catches in my throat at the mere thought of how many boys Henry Smith has twisted and ruined while he has been working there. The recruitment process comment is interesting, if not a little sick.

Yeah ... like they can only apply if they've killed or raped three women or more. Gross. Are there even any women teaching at the school?

Yes, several actually.

I wonder what they did to get the job.

Or what they had to endure.

Urggh ... I feel sick.

'Everything okay?' asks Benjamin.

We have not spoken for several hours now. I believe he may still be annoyed at me, but his voice is full of concern.

'Henry Smith is evil,' I say matter-of-factly.

'I kind of gathered that ... and I know what you're thinking.'

'Go on.'

'You're thinking that by being his daughter it makes you evil.'

'Do you not agree?'

'Of course not. I mean … I know you're not exactly … normal …' Benjamin gives me a sideways glance from the corner of his eye. '… But you're not evil.'

I sigh as I scratch my neck.

'What else have you found?' he asks, clearly determined to change the subject. It appears we are now breaking our silence and moving on from the awkwardness earlier; the whole situation regarding Doctor Channing.

Before you ask … no, I do not wish to talk about it.

I turn back to the laptop and click to another staff member's page.

'I have been making notes of several other staff members. I believe these men may be involved with The Collective.'

'You can tell that just from their staff profile page?'

'Call it a hunch. They also vaguely match the descriptions Rebecca gave to me.'

'Tell me.'

I click on the first one and read aloud.

'Dwight Pearson began working at the school in 2006. He teaches Mathematics and Geography. He has a wife and two children, enjoys running and fishing and collecting mementoes of his trips to different cities around Europe, which he displays in his school office.'

There is a long silence.

'Is that it? What makes you think he's one of The Collective? He sounds pretty normal to me.'

'He joined the school a year after Henry became Head Teacher. He enjoys running and fishing, both of which are usually solo activities, during which he could be doing anything, and he collects mementoes when he visits different countries and displays them in his office like some sort of trophy.'

'You think these *mementoes* have something to do with ...'

'Collecting women, yes.'

'Shit ... okay ... who's the next one?'

'Mark Craft is the current Science teacher and began his career at the school in 2004. He and Henry Smith were close friends for several years before he began working there. His hobbies include stamp collecting and singing karaoke on a Saturday night.'

I turn to Benjamin, awaiting his response.

'The fact he was friends with Henry is dodgy, but what's wrong with singing karaoke?'

'Everything.'

Benjamin attempts to hide a laugh behind a cough. 'Next.'

'Luke Johnson is a recent addition to the teaching team and is currently the assistant teacher to Peter Phillips. Luke hopes to one day teach History so he is shadowing Peter and learning the ropes. He enjoys keeping fit and taking his dog on long country walks.'

Benjamin nods. 'I think I remember Phil talking about him a few times. He always went off to meet Luke, leaving me behind. I never met him though, but they were good mates I think.'

I close the laptop and lean back in the car seat, attempting to take some of the pressure off my butt cheeks. I have never liked sitting still.

'Are those the only three?'

'For now. There may be more, but these three stand out the most.'

'So what's the plan when we get back home?'

'I plan on following them.'

'Okay ...' Benjamin pauses and glances at me. 'Like a stake-out?'

'Yes. I need to build up evidence to eventually show the police, but first—'

I cease talking and return my attention to the screen, checking my new email account, which I set up a few hours ago (mydarkself@gmail.com), for a reply. I had immediately contacted Web Ninja using the email address Rebecca provided me. The next phase of the plan cannot go ahead without her help. There has not been a response as yet, so I re-read my sent email.

Web Ninja,

You do not know me, but I know Rebecca. She told me to tell you she still loves you and that she will come back to you when this is all over, but in order for her to do that she needs you to help me.

What I am asking you to do is dangerous and illegal (something I am aware you have no issue with) and by helping me you will enable me to put an end to the suffering and abuse of many innocent women. Rebecca was one of those women, as was I. She kept the truth from you in order to protect you and you did as her mother asked and hid her away from the world, but now the truth must be revealed.

Will you help me?

My Dark Self

As soon as I finish reading, an incoming message appears in my inbox.

My Dark Self (love the name),

The fact you know Rebecca is … surprising. I thought only myself and her mum knew about her and where she is now, but if she gave you my contact details then I can only assume she trusts you and she needs help.

I miss her. I love her.

Of course I will help you.

Dangerous and illegal are my middle names.

Give me all the details you have and I'll get back to you within 24 hours.

Stay dark.

Web Ninja

Chapter Thirty
Alicia

It is nearly midnight by the time Benjamin pulls up in front of his house. He looks exhausted, but graciously did all the driving so that I could build my plan and conduct my research. I decline from telling him about Web Ninja because, unfortunately, the next phase of my plan does not involve him. It is time to cut him loose, something I am perfectly aware will anger and confuse him. Josslyn agrees with me, although she has been coming and going so sporadically lately I am not completely sure how much of the plan she is aware of, but she has not attempted to persuade me otherwise.

By the time we arrive home Web Ninja has acknowledged my email containing all of my requests and information regarding The Collective. She has also already emailed me back confirming the items I requested are waiting for me in the allocated location.

Now I just need to get rid of Benjamin ...

Benjamin sighs in relief as he enters his home. He immediately dumps his bag on the floor and heads for the stairs, no doubt intending to shower and sleep. He stops halfway up the stairs and turns to me.

'Is Josslyn around?' His voice is low and it sounds as if it is causing him an extreme amount of effort to speak.

'No.'

I watch as his face drops slightly, clearly disappointed. 'I – I need to tell her something.'

'What?'

He pauses.

'Whatever you tell her you are telling me,' I remind him.

Benjamin nods. 'I love you, girlfriend.' He turns slowly and walks up the stairs, closing the bedroom door gently behind him.

I stare at the door for several seconds, contemplating my thoughts. Josslyn does not respond in my head, but I can hear her words echoing anyway.

I love you too, boyfriend.

I lower my eyes, turn away and enter the kitchen to make myself a strong cup of coffee before returning to the sofa with the laptop. I still have work to accomplish. There is no time for sleep and rest.

Thanks to social media, and with a little help from Web Ninja, an hour and a half later I have been able to find out where all three of the men live, attend the gym, do their food shopping and where their favourite bar is located. I leave Henry Smith alone for the time being. His time will come soon enough. Besides, I have a feeling he will not be so easy to locate.

I see a little girl of no more than five huddled tightly in a dark corner. She is shaking uncontrollably and covered in dirt and what looks like dried blood. Her clothes are soiled and torn, her hair long and tangled, plastered to her tear-stained face. Her eyes … her eyes are empty of life, merely a dark void.

The girl screams as a man slowly walks towards her. He is so large he appears to fill the entire room; his face is indiscernible in the darkness. There is nowhere for her to run as the man kneels in front of her and grabs both of her ankles, his rough calloused hands squeezing tighter. He drags her towards him. She is screaming … screaming … screaming—

'Alicia! Wake up!'

I am being shaken with a great deal of force.

I immediately defend myself from my vicious attacker, drawing back my arm ready to strike with my tightly closed fist.

'Stop! Alicia, it's me! It's Ben!'

I am straddling Benjamin on the floor, my knees pinning his arms down on either side of him. My fist is still raised above my head, poised to come crashing down into his shocked face. Benjamin keeps repeating my name, but I barely hear him over the blood pumping in my ears. The room goes in and out of focus as I finally begin to return to reality. Both of our breathing rates are high. I am gasping for precious air as I lower my arm to my side. I slowly get off Benjamin and stand up, but the adrenaline in my body is keeping my muscles rigid and ready to fight.

'I heard you screaming,' says Benjamin. 'I'm sorry I scared you. I was just trying to wake you up. I've never seen you have a nightmare before.'

I open my mouth to apologise for attacking him, but then change my mind. After all, he was the one who knowingly woke me – an unstable woman – up.

I nod my thanks instead.

'I'll make some coffee,' says Benjamin, turning to enter the kitchen.

I glance at the clock. It is nearly five in the morning. I have been asleep a mere two hours. I had fought it for as long as I could, but even my body requires rest.

Benjamin makes the coffee and returns. We sit side by side on the sofa only inches apart. There is something inside of me that wishes to reach out and touch him for the last time, but I am fighting to hold it back. I cannot allow myself to become distracted; not now, not when I am so close to the end. I know Benjamin needs me – needs Josslyn – but this is not about him. I cannot know exactly what is going through his own head, but I know there may not be a way back for him, back to reality that is. Eventually he will be hunted down as an accessory to murder and then what? He will go to jail. All because of me and I feel ... I feel ... this is the point where Josslyn would usually butt in and tell me what I am supposed to be feeling, but she is not here. Again.

Benjamin stirs slightly beside me as he reaches over and takes the laptop from where it has fallen onto the floor.

'Did you find anything else?'

'I found enough.' I snatch it back off him.

It is time ...

I abruptly stand up and face him. 'Benjamin, I need to do this alone. I know you are probably going to argue with me, but you must hear me out.' Benjamin nods so I continue. 'I cannot allow you to become any further mixed up in all this. You have done enough, more than enough. I can never begin to express how much gratitude I feel, but ... the time has come for us to part ways. I no longer require your help, but what I do require is that you leave me alone to finish my plan. When it is over I shall find you, and you and Josslyn can say goodbye.'

Benjamin shakes his head. 'No way. Not going to happen.'

'I must insist ... and this is me asking nicely.'

'And I must insist that you go to hell.'

'If you do not agree to leave then I shall be forced to do something I would rather not do.'

Benjamin jumps up to standing, facing me square on. 'Let me guess ... you're going to kill me, right? That's your answer to everything, isn't it?'

I remain silent for a beat. He is too tall to be glaring at him face to face, so I stare up at him instead and speak very slowly.

'I would never kill you, Benjamin. You are forcing my hand. Please reconsider my offer.'

'Alicia, I'm not going anywhere.'

I inhale deeply. Fine. If that is the way he wants it.

'Then I must reveal the truth to you and you are not going to like it, but do not say I did not warn you and ask nicely. Josslyn and I have been lying to you from the start. Josslyn does not love you. I certainly do not love you, nor could I ever feel such things. Josslyn and I have been using you, lying to you, manipulating you into helping us all along. We did need help and as you began to get more involved we came up with a plan. You went along with it because you fell in love with us and we knew we could use that to our advantage. All this time ... we have been playing you ... and you fell for it. We no longer need you, so we are dropping you.'

I finish my speech and watch as Benjamin's face pales, his jaw clenches, and he trembles as he takes a step back from me.

'No ... n-no ... you're lying. That's a lie. Josslyn would never—'

'I admit I am an exceptionally skilled liar, so you are right in the fact that I could be lying to you right now, but I am not. Josslyn, as you are well aware, is a part of me. She is a different personality. She can also lie just as well as I can.'

Benjamin clenches his fists together at his sides. 'Stop it. Stop lying!' he shouts.

I remain still as Benjamin falls apart in front of me. His eyes fill with tears. He reaches out a hand towards me.

'Josslyn ... I want to speak to Josslyn.'

'Josslyn is gone,' I retort bluntly.

'W-What?'

'Josslyn is gone. She has disappeared forever. I am alone in this body.'

Benjamin frowns. 'W-When did she leave?'

'Several days ago.'

'You're lying! I woke up in bed next to her. We had … I mean … we …'

I smile. 'I did tell you I am an exceptional liar. I believe that was one of my finest moments.'

There is a long silence during which Benjamin and I continue to stare at each other. I hold my nerve and my gaze, but his is falling apart little by little.

'She's really … gone?'

'Yes.'

'She didn't even say goodbye.'

'She never loved you Benjamin, so she did not want to say goodbye. It is over. I suggest you come to terms with it quickly so that you can move on with your life. I also suggest you get out of the country, but I cannot tell you how to live your life. I shall pack my things now and leave.' I pick up the laptop (his laptop). 'I still require this … I shall destroy it when I am finished with it.'

Benjamin aggressively grabs my arm and squeezes hard. 'You really are a fucking psychopath, aren't you? I've always stood up for you, always believed you were a good person deep down, but you're not … you really are evil.'

'I did try and tell you, did I not? You have no one to blame but yourself. Now … remove your hand from my arm.' I shrug out of his grip, wincing at the slight pain.

'You'll regret this,' he says through clenched teeth.

I lock eyes with him. 'No, Benjamin … I will not.' I turn and walk out of the room, feeling his eyes searing a hole in the back of my head.

211

I close and lock the guest bedroom door and slowly sit down on the bed. I cannot deny hurting him in that way does not feel pleasant. In fact, I feel a hot, burning sensation deep down inside. I know it is for the best. It is for his own good and I am doing this to protect him. One day he will understand. I have pushed him away because I love him and if anything happened to him I would never forgive myself.

I told you I am an exceptionally skilled liar.

Chapter Thirty-One
Alicia

All of my possessions fit neatly into my black backpack which I have been carting around with me since day one. I glance around the downstairs area one last time and leave, closing the door quietly as I do so. Benjamin may hate me forever, but I can live with that as long as he is safe and, more importantly, alive.

I walk the mile-and-a-half to a run-down, one star Bed and Breakfast, which is definitely worth its twenty-pounds-a-night fee. As long as it has running water I am happy; I do not even care if it is cold. Web Ninja has set this all up for me. How she has managed to do it in such a short time frame is beyond me, but I am grateful as I push open the creaky door and spy a box on the single bed.

My phone vibrates, indicating a new email, so I open it up as I take a seat next to the box of goodies.

My Dark Self,
I hope everything is in order. In the box you'll find your new identity and the items you asked for. I've already sent you the locations of the men you mentioned, but Henry Smith is definitely elusive. I've managed to get on to the dark web and found their online site … It's … graphic, to say the least, but I've saved and downloaded all I can without being detected. They have a lot of firewalls up, which

prevent me from seeing a lot of it. In order to see the whole site I'd need to be a member and go through a strict vetting procedure by the looks of it.

These sickos are going down, mark my words, but you're right ... we need to be cautious. We need solid evidence, so that's where you come in. I believe Henry Smith must have some sort of safe house somewhere near here. You mentioned that Peter had sound-proofed one of his rooms. I think there's more to this. These men mainly work online, but I think a select few meet in person at a particular location. Once we find their safe house we can gather more evidence.

Anyway, once you're all set up I'll be notified.

Good luck.

Stay dark.

Web Ninja

(P.S. When this is all over I think you owe me a strong drink ... or two ... maybe three.)

I smile to myself as I begin to lift the items out of the box and lay them out on the bed one by one, inspecting them as I tick them off my mental inventory. There is a large hunting knife, a stun gun, a new mobile phone, a large wad of cash (at least two hundred pounds), a fresh supply of black clothes (including black boots), two days' worth of Army rations, binoculars, a range of camera equipment, the key to this room and, last but not least, a new form of ID (I am now Lucy Adler).

I pick up the knife and caress it as if it is the most important thing in my life, feeling the cool metal between my fingers. It is a thing of beauty, serrated on the top edge and viciously sharp on the bottom, the handle constructed of solid wood. If I am going to do this ... then I am going to do it properly. I do not question where on earth Web Ninja managed to procure all of these items in less than a day. Maybe I will ask her when we eventually meet. I glance at my new identity and smile. I have a vague recollection of Josslyn's veterinary nurse being called Lucy, so it is a somewhat familiar name. I have a plan and, with Web Ninja's help, I know I will be able to accomplish it.

I take a long, lukewarm shower, get dressed into the black clothes (jeans, a camisole top and a long-sleeved shirt over the top) and survey myself in the mirror. The knife is strapped to my side, hidden beneath the shirt and my backpack holds the remaining items.

You look bad ass right now.

I am momentarily taken aback by her voice, which sends a jolt through my body.

Hello, Josslyn.

What the hell's going on? Where are we? Where's Ben? Why do you look like Lara Croft?

Benjamin is safe, but he will not be joining us for the foreseeable future.

You cut him loose, didn't you?

I did what I had to do.

You didn't hurt him, did you?

215

He refused to accept my polite request so I had to be … ruthless.

I get it, I do, but at least he'll be safe, that's the main thing. The last thing I want is for him to be hurt or used against us like last time.

Indeed.

I wish it didn't have to end like that though. I didn't even get a chance to say goodbye.

I am sorry.

It's okay … now about that knife … it looks pretty fucking scary.

Web Ninja has been extremely sufficient and provided us with everything we shall need to bring down The Collective.

But I thought you weren't going to kill them all.

I am not.

Then what's with the knife?

Collateral.

Right. So … this is it. We're really doing this.

Yes.

No going back.

I hope you will stay with me for a while this time. I do not want to do this without you.

I'll try, but I can't make any promises. It was so hard to come back this time. I think this may be it … the last time.

Then let us make it count.

I begin with Luke Johnson. According to his Twitter account he is currently 'pumping iron' (his words, not mine … as if I would really use that godawful phrase) in the gym before work. I wait outside the gym for him to finish and then follow him to a local health food shop where he buys a green super-food smoothie. He appears to be in his late twenties, but he is extremely average-looking. His tight clothes indicate he is proud of his body, but from the looks of it he needs to put a little more *work* into his workouts. Something tells me that he spends most of his time in the gym taking selfies and updating his social media accounts rather than 'pumping iron'.

Unfortunately I am only able to follow him as far as the school. I do not wish to gain access this time because it would be like walking into the serpent's lair. I watch him enter, satisfied that he will most likely be teaching all day, and then check the location of my next target: Mark Craft.

He appears to have the day off work and I find him at his local pub, downing a pint (at ten in the morning). I position myself in a corner of the area, order a juice … and wait … and watch.

Two hours later.

Okay … stake-outs are so fucking boring! What are we even looking for?

I am attempting to gather information about them, learn their movements … eventually something will happen.

Wanna bet? This guy is three pints down on a Wednesday morning and has barely taken his eyes off the TV screen.

I do share Josslyn's frustration, so to pass the time I remind myself of my third target: Dwight Pearson. I scroll through his socials, but he is fairly quiet on them thanks to being a middle-aged man with a wife and kids. It appears he does not have a lot to share with his small number of friends and followers.

I look up from my phone as a loud shout booms across the room.

'Get in!' Mark jumps up from his chair, sending his beer flying and pumps his fists in what I can only assume is a gesture of happiness at the fact one of the football teams on the television have just scored a goal.

The game ends and Mark pays his tab, but he does not leave the pub. He continues to sit for a while, staring at his phone. He has a smug smile across his face as he is typing.

Wonder who he's texting?

Eventually Mark gets up, straightens his jacket and leaves the pub on wobbly legs. I follow him to his house, which is a semi-detached in the middle of a built-up area. I find myself an adequate hiding spot and watch the place for a while, but nothing happens, so I decide to focus my attention on victim number three.

Aren't you supposed to stay on one target at a time during a stake-out? What if we leave and something happens and we miss it?

I know where they all are for now. Luke is at work. Mark is probably sleeping off his buzz, so I'd like to check on Dwight.

I wait at his house for him to return from work. His wife is waiting for him and greets him at the door like it is the 1950s. He appears to be very ... normal, but there is something about him that does not sit right with me. His kids are teenagers, both of whom barely say a word to their parents during dinner. My binoculars come in handy because I can see the family as clear as day through their windows ... until it gets dark and they close the curtains.

Fuck.

Now what ... we go back and watch one of the others again?

No ... I am going to stay with Dwight for a bit longer. He kept checking his phone during dinner, did you notice? I think he is expecting a message from someone.

Several hours later my instincts appear to be correct. It is eleven at night and all the lights are off in his house, but then I see him coming out of the front door, dressed in black ... and he goes for a walk.

So I follow.

Chapter Thirty-Two
Alicia

Dwight circles his neighbourhood three times, dodging down back alleys and cutting through narrow paths, but always circling back around. It is easy to follow him after the first time because I know where he is going to end up.

What the fuck is he doing?

I have no idea.

Dwight checks his phone for the seventeenth time (yes, I counted), sighs and then positions himself with his back up against a brick wall down a narrow side alley, in-between two houses. It is very dark so it is almost impossible to make him out using just my eyes, but luckily the binoculars I have acquired are equipped with night-vision—

Of course they are.

—so I train them on my target and watch.

Several minutes pass, but then I spy a young woman wearing a short skirt approaching from another road over. She also circles around for a while, attempting to look nonchalant, but eventually winds up in the alley with Dwight. He is not an attractive man by any stretch of the imagination; he has a gut on him, rough stubble and too many wrinkles, which suggests too many late nights and not enough sleep. I find it hard to believe that he has charmed this young woman with his looks alone.

I begin to take photos with my camera, but due to the darkness they are not of good quality (unfortunately it does not have night-vision capability and obviously I cannot use the flash). I can just about make out their silhouettes, which are pressed very close together. They are talking in hushed whispers, but then …

Wait … what the fuck!

Dwight is stroking the woman's arm and then …

Oh my God! Ewww!

I watch in disgust as they start to partially undress each other enough to … well, you get the idea … gain access. They begin to awkwardly grind and bump against the brick wall of the house, grunting and moaning in what I can only describe as over-exaggerating eagerness.

I feel sick … urggh, my eyes …

Okay, so it appears Dwight Pearson is not such a boring family man after all, but I need proof he is more than just an adulterer. I need evidence … I need—

A shrill ringing interrupts their activities (which appear to be almost over anyway). It echoes around the otherwise silent street. Dwight swears loudly and pushes the woman off him, who staggers against the wall, and answers his phone whilst attempting to shove his now limp dick into his trousers. The woman stamps her foot angrily, but then stomps off as she stuffs her knickers into her pocket.

'Yes,' says Dwight, sounding slightly out of breath. 'Of course, I'm on my way. Call The Master.'

Bingo.

The woman is now approaching my hiding location, seemingly unaware that one of her breasts is popping out of her top. I step out from behind the shadows and she lets out a shriek.

'Do not scream, just listen,' I say as I hold my hand up to show I am defenceless and not a threat. 'Never contact that man again. Trust me. Your life depends on it.'

'What the fuck lady! Were you watching us, you pervert!' She attempts to cover her modesty. Her make-up is smudged and her brown eyes are cold and hard, a deep frown etched between them.

'Dwight Pearson is dangerous. Woman to woman … take my advice.'

She stares at me blankly for a few seconds. 'H-He told me his name was Kevin.' Then it seems to dawn on her. She lowers her eyes to the ground and nods. 'He wasn't a good shag anyway. Always finished first and never cared about making me happy.'

I watch as she scurries away.

I immediately give chase to Dwight who has ducked down another street. I hope I have not lost him, but I feel I owed it to the woman to at least warn her.

It takes several minutes of frantic searching, but I finally locate him. He is casually strolling down the main streets, looking pleased with himself. He is furiously texting while he is walking, often not looking where he is going, but always keeping a smug smile on his face.

Finally, after twenty minutes, he arrives at a semi-detached house. It appears perfectly ordinary. In fact, there is nothing I can say other than that. It is located in a fairly quiet part of town; a few other houses dotted around, a quiet cul-de-sac, not much noise or activity. He sends a text and waits outside the door, which opens within seconds and then he disappears behind it.

Shit.

It is not as if I can stick my face up against the window and peer inside. I stare at the house, the brick walls, the blue door, the steps leading up to it, the random potted plant at the front. The more I stare at it the more it feels … familiar. Have I been here before?

Any ideas, Josslyn?

I thought you were supposed to be the brains of this operation?

Sometimes I require a break.

There's nothing we can do really but wait and see if anyone else turns up and take notes. Use your fancy gadgets. Maybe check round the back. Take a photo of the front. Write down the address. We can stake out the place for a few days if we need to.

All perfectly reasonable and acceptable ideas.

Why, thank you.

I follow Josslyn's lead and slowly walk around to the back of the house, crouching behind a hedge before peering over it. There are blackout curtains drawn in every single window with bright, yellow light escaping from behind the cracks where they do not quite reach the edges. The garden is bland and empty, nothing of prominence apart from a partially broken drainpipe. There are empty beer bottles strewn by the back door, which also has some sort of black sheet hung across it on the inside.

There is something in that house they do not wish to be seen from the outside.

I take some photographs.

I circle back to the front and find a position on the other side of the street where I can watch the entrance to see if anyone else arrives. My stomach grumbles in protest and my eyelids become heavy.

When was the last time you ate or slept?

I had two hours' sleep on Benjamin's sofa this morning.

You can't keep this up.

Watch me.

Minute after boring minute ticks by and I am growing frustrated and bored. I finally succumb to my hunger and eat an energy bar from my backpack. My eyes start to close, so I quickly readjust my position. I cannot help but think that killing the whole lot of them would be far easier than this bullshit ...

An expensive black car pulls up outside the house and a man gets out, straightening his black cashmere jumper as he does so.

Oh my God.

The Master has arrived.

Chapter Thirty-Three
Alicia

A memory blasts its way into my brain, powerful and so real I could easily reach out and touch it.

I am slowly walking up the front steps of the house - my house - and open the front door. My small, weak body is sore and I am tired, my eyes stinging with the effort of keeping them open. My father greets me as I close the door. He envelops me in a warm hug which makes my skin crawl and my stomach lurch. I never really like getting hugs from him; he smells funny.

'I have a friend I would like you to meet,' he says, stroking my long, dark hair, which is tied into two pigtails.

'I don't want to meet them. I'm tired, Daddy. Can I go to sleep instead?'

'Of course, my child. You may sleep as long as you like. Here … drink this.' He hands me a glass of tepid milk which tastes funky. I smile and nod, happy that my belly is now full. 'Good girl. You are my good girl, Alicia. What are you?'

'I'm your good girl,' I respond.

I follow my father through the narrow corridors of the house and down into the basement where a man is waiting for me. He smells funny too and is sitting on a small cot bed.

'Here ... lay down and sleep,' the man says, patting the bed beside him.

I look up at my father for reassurance. 'Do I have to sleep here?'

'It is okay, my child. Trust me.'

I take the strange man's hand and lay down, slowly drifting into a dreamless sleep.

Reality hits me like a bucket of ice water to the face. I blink and see the house in front of me. The ordinary blue door, the blacked-out windows, the pot by the steps. I remember this house and what happened within its walls; not everything, just snippets, but I remember enough.

What happened? Are you okay?

I ... I am remembering. The wall is coming down.

I'm not sure how much longer I can hold it.

Try harder.

I don't know how!

I need to get inside the house. I am useless out here. The evidence I need to take down The Collective is behind that door and there is no way of getting inside without being detected.

It is time for Plan B.

I'll probably regret asking this, but ... what's Plan B?

I emerge from my hiding place, stomp up the front steps of the house and bang my fists against the door.

Ah ... Plan B.

There is no immediate answer, so I pound my fists against the door again.

Okay, I know you're a bit emotionally unstable right now, but think about this for a second, Alicia. You're putting yourself in very real danger. Let's just calm down and—

'If you do not open this door I am calling the police!' I shout.

Or not ...

The door creaks open, letting out a slither of yellow light. Henry Smith stares down at me with a completely emotionless expression on his face. Seeing him up close and personal sends a jolt of fear throughout my body, rattling me to my very core. He looks older than I remember ... but I can see his younger self so clearly in my mind now; his jet-black hair and how he used to stroke mine and call me ...

'My child ... you have come home.'

I open my mouth to speak, but my words have been stolen. My once perfect, unwavering demeanour is shattered in the space of a second.

Say something! You can do it. Don't let him scare you. He's just a man.

I inhale, feeling woozy, but finally my words are free. 'Hello, Henry.' They are not as strong and confident as I would like, but at least I can speak.

Henry smiles. 'You found out my real name.'

I nod.

'You have been a busy young lady.'

'Let me in.'

'I would not recommend that. For you see, there are several men inside who would delight in torturing you and making you bleed.'

'It never stopped you before.'

'Ah, so you do remember.'

'Not all of it, but I remember enough.'

'Then you may enter, but only if you agree to a search and hand over every single item you have on you.'

'Fine.'

Henry smiles and steps aside for me to walk past him and into the house. I pause for a moment on the threshold before taking small steps into the familiar building.

This is literally the worst idea you've ever had. Do you even have a plan?

Yes.

Really?

No.

Didn't think so.

Just hold it together a little while longer.

I'll try.

I watch Henry as he closes the door. He beckons me to follow him, which I do, but as I walk I am forced to block out sudden flashbacks of being in this house all those years ago. They are merely snapshots in time, all appearing out of order, but they begin hurtling into my mind so fast it causes me to stumble against the wall for a second. My stomach is in knots, my throat appears to be constricting itself and my palms are sweating. I have never been afraid before, not like this … but as much as it is unsettling me, I have also never felt more alive than I do at this very minute. The fear is making me stronger and I am enjoying the feeling.

As I walk into the main living room I see several men standing around a table. I attempt to recognise them, but several I have never seen before. I do spot Dwight Pearson. He narrows his eyes at me as I come to a stop in front of the table. I feel all their soulless, evil eyes boring into me, drinking me in. I can almost hear their wicked thoughts about what they wish to do to me echoing around the room.

'Gentlemen,' Henry says. 'Let me introduce you to my daughter, Alicia.'

A couple of the men inhale sharply, others grind their jaws or clench their fists. One man, roughly about the same age as Henry, licks his lips and takes a step towards me. A flicker of recognition ignites in my brain …

The man from my flashback just now … What did he do to me?

'Before anyone says anything please search her and remove everything apart from her clothes. Be as precise and thorough as you need to be, but you are not to hurt her.'

Henry steps aside while two men (including the one from my flashback) approach me. I glare at them, sending them a silent warning, but they merely smile.

'I'm gonna enjoy this,' whispers the man I recognise in my ear. The feel of his warm breath sends a cold shiver down my spine, setting alight all my senses. I am prepared to defend myself if it comes to that, but in order to proceed I know I must be searched.

The men slowly and carefully run their hands over my body, removing my backpack, phone, knife and, finally, my boots. The items are removed from the room. Henry then instructs the men that they are allowed to talk now.

'What's she doing here, Master—'

'You're risking everything by having her here—'

'She shouldn't be here—'

'She killed Gerald—'

A chorus of voices speak at once, but Henry silences them by holding up his hand.

'Gentlemen, Alicia is here of her own free will. She has come back to me, as I always hoped she would. You are not to lay a hand on her unless instructed ... is that clear? If you wish to touch her without my permission, then you will do so at your own risk.'

The men mumble and nod in unison, bowing their heads in surrender.

It is at that moment my voice finally decides to make a comeback. I take a step forwards, glancing briefly at the table, which is covered with pictures of women in various stages of undress.

'It is nice to meet you ... *gentlemen.*' I sound out the last word with as much sarcasm as I can muster and then pick up a random photo. 'More of your ... masterpieces, I presume?'

I hear one of the men actually growl at me like a dog.

'Down boy,' I say.

'Fucking bitch,' one answers back.

'You'll get what's coming to you,' another mumbles.

'As will you all,' I say calmly and with a smile. I turn to Henry. 'I suggest you take me somewhere where we can talk in private.' Henry nods in agreement. *'Gentlemen*,' I say again, before turning and following my father out of the room.

None of them have any idea they have been filmed by the tiny hidden camera that is attached to my clothing, which is currently live streaming to Web Ninja's computer.

I may have lied when I said I did not have a plan.

Chapter Thirty-Four
Alicia

Henry leads me down some creaky wooden stairs and into the basement, which appears to have had an upgrade since the last time I was here. It used to be a damp, dark hole in the ground, but now it looks like an exact replica of Peter's torture chamber. Dozens and dozens – hundreds even – of pictures of women adorn the walls. They are separated into different sections, such as *Active, Suspended* and *Future Prospects.* I do not recognise any of them, but I do not need to know who they are in order to want to save them. I scan every wall, aware that the camera is doing its thing, making sure I hover by the more gruesome images.

The room is cold with only the one door and has a low ceiling. There are a few beams and foundation structures, but otherwise it is completely empty apart from one table, which has nothing on it. The walls look as if they are padded (some sort of soundproofing I assume), but the photos cover the majority of them.

'I know what you are doing.'

I turn and look at Henry who is standing in front of the door, blocking my exit. 'And what is it you think I am doing?' I ask.

'You are here to try and gather evidence on us.'

I fold my arms across my chest and stare at my father. 'Fine … you got me. I have been outsmarted by my own father. What do you plan on doing with me now?'

'How about we just have a chat, catch up, reminisce …'

Is he actually being fucking serious right now?

'I am afraid I do not engage in general conversation with people. It is a skill I have not yet developed.'

Henry smiles. A man appears behind him carrying a tray holding two glass tumblers and a carafe of dark liquor. Henry takes it from the man who then backs out of the room and closes the door. It clicks shut, sealing me and my father inside.

I watch silently as he begins to pour the liquid into the tumblers. He holds one out to me.

'Drink?'

I hesitate briefly before reaching out and taking the glass; it is cold. 'How do I know you have not poisoned it?' I ask.

'Why on earth would I ruin a perfectly good whiskey by poisoning it?'

I do not respond.

'You have trust issues, my child.'

'Can you blame me … *Father*?'

Henry chuckles before knocking back his whiskey and pouring another. I do not take my eyes off him as I take a sip. The smoky liquid burns my throat as I swallow and I resist the urge to cough; it is not pleasant. We sip our drinks in silence for a few moments, both of us staring at the other, unwilling to make the first move.

'So ... where to begin?' he asks me finally.

I glance around the room. 'Where indeed ...'

'Why did you demand to be let in just now knowing you will most likely never leave this house again?' His words hit me like a punch to the stomach, but I hold my composure.

'I want answers.'

'Then ask away, my child, ask away.'

I take another disgusting sip, fighting the urge to cough again. 'My mother ... tell me about her. Tell me everything that happened. I want to hear your side of the story.'

'Do you mean to say you have heard her side of it already?'

'I have.'

'Interesting.' Henry frowns. Clearly he is not aware of the video tape she made me. 'Your mother ... was a remarkable woman. So powerful and independent and strong when I first met her. In fact, you remind me of her a great deal. You have the same fire inside. I loved her ... but ... she was not what I truly wanted or needed. I used her to get what I wanted ...'

'An offspring,' I added.

Henry nodded. 'Yes. Exactly.'

'Why?'

'I have lived my entire life surrounded by sick and sadistic men who would willingly follow me to the ends of the earth because they think I can give them something they all crave. They are all so pathetic really, their only mission in life is to inflict their own brand of torture on women. I, myself, am no different. I admit I am flawed and my primal instinct is to dominate and humiliate women, to use them for my own pleasure, but long ago I had an idea. It was quite inspired, actually. I became bored of teaching men who I had no connection with. I wanted to create my very own masterpiece, my very own ... sociopath.

'I did not want to teach any ordinary man, as I mentioned I had been doing that for years. No ... I wanted this person to be my own flesh and blood, so when I met Jane Daniels I knew she was the perfect specimen to carry my masterpiece. I raped her over and over until she fell pregnant. I ensured she received the best care possible, although I kept her locked up for her safety of course. I did not want my prodigy to come to harm.

'The day came when she went for her first scan ... and I found out that she had two lives growing inside of her. It was not part of my plan, but I knew aborting one child would look suspicious, so I allowed the pregnancy to continue, but when I found out that neither of you were male ... I admit I lost control and took my anger out on your mother.'

Henry stops to take a drink and glances at me with a hint of a smile across his lips. I squeeze my glass so tight I fear it may shatter as I step towards my father.

'Go on,' I say slowly.

Henry continues. 'When I eventually calmed down I realised that, actually, this was an opportunity to change my plan and create a whole new type of masterpiece. However, I only needed one of you. I could not put my full attention into creating two sociopaths, so I disposed of Josslyn, knowing that she would be cared for. I told your mother to put her up for adoption straight away. I could have killed her, of course, but I decided to show her mercy. She was of no interest to me.'

'Why me? How did you choose between the two of us?'

'I dropped your mother off at a hospital in Salisbury, far away from here so I was not there when you were born. I was not the one who chose you. Your mother did.'

I nod to signify my acceptance of his response.

'Now, I knew in order to create a sociopath one must endure physical and mental abuse as a child. I did my research. I knew it would not be pleasant for you and I could not perform the abuse myself. I had no interest in harming you or submitting you for my own sexual needs, so I passed you to my followers and they ensured the damage was done. I had no idea how long it would take before your mind broke, but I was willing to wait years if I had to because I knew you would be worth the wait … My own creation …

'Unfortunately, your mother betrayed me. She played me, telling me she was going along with my plan, but somehow she managed to get you out of the house without my knowing and I lost you. She paid for her betrayal with her life. I searched everywhere, but somehow a little girl of six was able to evade me.

'For over twenty years I mourned your loss, taking my rage out on women, disposing of them like soiled rags. I decided to not start over. I even looked for your sister, but to no avail. I gave up on my masterpiece ... until ... one of my followers showed me a picture of you, his latest victim. He told me this woman was special, that she had two very distinct personalities and that he had chosen you because he believed you had killed his sister.

'I knew it was you. I had no solid proof at the time, but I recognised your eyes, those soulless, dead eyes ... and I knew that at some point you had finally cracked and broken and you had been out there in the world, conducting your evil deeds without me. I was overcome with relief and I felt so proud of you that day, my child ... and now ... you are finally home ... and we can finally begin.'

I drop the glass and it shatters into thousands of tiny, sharp fragments, the amber liquid spilling across the floor. My legs collapse and I fall into the shards of glass, numb to the feeling of them embedding into my skin. I lunge forwards and vomit up the whiskey I swallowed earlier, feeling it burn all the way up my oesophagus.

I cannot breathe ... this is too much ... I cannot—

Chapter Thirty-Five
Josslyn

I immediately do what any normal sibling would do … I summon up what little strength I have and step in to protect my sister. I take over and allow her the time she needs to get herself together. I don't know how long that will take, but I know I can't stand by and watch her suffer any longer, so I do what I've been doing for the past twenty-odd years … I keep the wall up inside her mind for a little while longer, although I can feel her trying to push it down with all her might, whether she's aware of it or not. It's happening …

I spit the last bit of bile onto the floor and look up at the man in front of me. If you can even call him a man – he's a monster; he isn't even a human being. I used to think that Alicia was evil, that she had no soul, but now I know that's never been the case. How wrong I was about everything. This man created her … he's the evil one. He's staring down at me, a frown on his face. I know he knows about me, but I'm sure seeing the transformation for himself is quite something.

'Hi Henry … we've never officially met … I'm Josslyn.' My voice is calm and level. For once I'm the strong and controlled one and Alicia is falling apart inside of me. I watch as Henry attempts to cover his surprise.

'J-Josslyn ... my child, I did not expect you to come forwards. I thought you may have ... disappeared.'

I slowly get to my feet, doing my best to ignore the sharp, stabbing pain in my knee. I think a shard of glass is buried quite deep; I can feel warm blood trickling down my leg. I'm feeling slightly woozy thanks to Alicia's lack of sleep and food over the past few days.

'Sorry to disappoint you,' I mutter.

'So ... you are the one who has been keeping Alicia from living up to her full potential all these years. If it were not for you she would have returned to me years ago.'

I take a deep breath and fix my gaze on him. 'I've been protecting her from you, more like.'

Henry clenches his teeth together. 'I must admit you are ... different ... compared to how Peter spoke about you. He said you were weak and gullible and easily manipulated, but it appears he was mistaken.'

'I guess I've evolved over the years too,' I say with a casual shrug. 'I've learned a thing or two from Alicia.'

'Evidentially ...' Henry continues to stare at me, barely blinking. I wish he'd stop. It's giving me the creeps. 'You are fascinating, my child. The human mind really is an amazing work of art, is it not? The mind can crack, bend and break and conjure up completely different personalities in order to protect it from harm. Alicia created you to shield herself from me. Tell me, my child, what age was Alicia when you first took over?'

I have no idea where my feistiness (or bravery?) is coming from, but all I know is that I have to keep him

239

talking long enough to allow Alicia the time she needs. I know she's listening; I know she's there.

Hurry up, Alicia. I can't do this for much longer …

'I don't know exactly,' I say, standing up a little straighter. 'I don't remember actually taking her over. I know she appeared to me when I was seven.'

'Then it must have happened very soon after she escaped.'

I nod, just playing along, hoping he'll reveal a bit more. I wish I could remember, but all I remember is my childhood growing up on the small farm with my parents.

'Your parents … they helped you, yes? They helped you forget.'

'I don't know,' I reply honestly.

'But I think you do, Josslyn. I think you are more clever than you give yourself credit for. You are just choosing *not* to know in order to protect Alicia.'

I stop and think, but my mind is a haze of darkness and swirly shapes. I can't remember anything. My mind refuses to conjure up any sort of memory. All I know is that I grew up with a loving family on a farm, in the middle of nowhere, had lots of pets and was homeschooled … oh, and at the age of seven I began to see Alicia and thought at the time she was my imaginary friend. There's nothing at all before that and I guess the reason for that is because I didn't technically exist … Alicia did … the real Alicia; the one who was abused by this … this … vile creature who clearly looks like a human being, but isn't.

'Why did you even come forward, Josslyn?'

'Because you fucking broke her!' I scream. 'You broke her mind! She escaped, but it was too late. She was already too far gone and I protected her. I protected her from you!' Tears stream out of my eyes before I can stop them, but I don't care. I don't care if crying makes me look weak and pathetic; that's not how I feel. I feel strong and fucking angry, like I could take on this entire house full of freaks and win. I stomp up to Henry and shove him hard in the chest with as much strength as I can muster.

'You're a fucking sick, twisted psycho and I'm going to make sure you and all your goddamn followers get what they deserve whether it's the last thing I ever do!'

Henry stumbles back ever so slightly with a smug grin on his face. 'You know, Josslyn, I wish you had been the one that was born. You have strength and power in you that you do not realise is there. Is it true … about the unborn foetus? Peter told me about it. That was you?'

I sniff and wipe my eyes and nose with my sleeve, both of which are streaming. 'Yeah, that's true. I've always been a part of Alicia, but she had me cut out.'

'And how did that make you feel?'

'What are we … having a therapy session now?' I snap.

'Humour me.'

I sigh angrily and stare up at the ceiling where I see more pictures of tortured women. Jesus … he has them on the ceiling too? I close my eyes. I don't want to see them anymore.

'Yes, she used me and lied to me. She killed people, tried to frame me, alienated my parents, destroyed my life and was basically a bitch to me my whole life … but she's different now. She's changed. Your plan failed. She's not really a psychopath or a sociopath, or whatever it is you want to label her as. She's a human being and she's stronger and more resilient than you could ever understand. She's not like you. She may not cry or show any emotion, but deep down inside she's good, and decent, and you'll never touch her or hurt her, not ever again.'

I finish my speech and gasp for breath. My heart is thumping as if I've run a hundred metre sprint, but I've never felt stronger in my entire life. Maybe this is it. Maybe this is the end. I know I've always been considered the weak one. You've probably thought that yourself, right? Well, maybe it's true, but I like to think that now I've reached the end … I've redeemed myself somewhat … and I'm fucking proud of myself for that.

Henry is staring at me whilst sipping his drink. I have an overwhelming urge to grab a piece of shattered glass at my feet and shove it in his face.

'I am afraid, Josslyn, that our time is up. However, I would like to reiterate the fact that since you are close to leaving us forever, you will have no say on what Alicia does once you have gone. What will happen when the wall finally crumbles and the real Alicia is set free? That is the beauty of this little scenario … we just do … not … know.' His smile makes me want to throw up, but I hold my nerve.

'When I'm gone it won't matter anymore. Alicia won't change into some hideous monster like you, I can promise you that.'

'We shall see about that.'

Henry finishes his drink, sets the empty glass on the table and begins walking towards the exit.

'Wait!' I shout. 'What happens now?'

'Now we wait and see … Goodbye, Josslyn. It was nice meeting you, my child.' And with that Henry walks out of the door, slams it shut and the lights go off, plunging me into complete darkness.

Every fibre of my body wants to scream and cry and bang on the door for him to let me out, but I don't do that. I take a few deep breaths and allow my eyes to adjust to the black, but they don't. It's so dark I know that no matter how long I spend in here I'll never be able to see anything. A horrible thought crosses my mind: I wonder how many times Alicia was locked down here by herself … or with someone else? This basement was obviously used to keep her locked up; her mum too.

Alicia … are you there?

I am here.

Are you okay?

Yes. I am now. I do not know what happened. Thank you for taking over.

It's fine. What happens now? We're locked in here and I have a feeling we won't be getting out for a long time.

This was always the plan, Josslyn. Henry may think he has outsmarted us, but the camera has still been recording everything he has been saying. All the evidence we need is on camera.

But you might not get out of here alive. Can't you contact Web Ninja and have her send in the cops or something now that we have proof?

Not yet.

Why ... what are you waiting for?

Alicia doesn't answer me, but I don't need her to in order to know what she's thinking. She knows that only one of us is going to survive this ... and it's certainly not going to be me. I've been trying to fight it, trying to avoid this moment.

I think this is it ... I think it's time we say goodbye.

It's time the wall came down for good.

I slowly find my way over to a corner of the room, feeling around with my hands and sit with my back up against a wall. It's cool and somewhat refreshing.

I close my eyes ...

Chapter Thirty-Six
Josslyn

When I open them I'm standing in a completely white space. It's not a room because it doesn't have any corners; it appears to stretch out for eternity. The brightness is warm and comforting and I feel ... happy ... at peace. At least it's better than the dark place (or the grey place). My body doesn't ache and I don't feel sick anymore. I feel the best I've felt in forever.

I glance down at myself and find I'm wearing different clothes now: tight, light denim jeans and a white strappy top, but my body isn't the same. It's how it used to look; a bit rounder and softer at the edges, not as tight, but it makes me smile. I love this body because it's mine. I've missed it. I run my fingers lightly over the tattoos that are exposed. I stop when I reach the tiny paw print on my wrist ... Oscar. My Oscar. It's funny how at the end I think of my little companion, who had no idea that I wasn't actually a real person. He loved me for who I was. Hell, he even loved Alicia. I hope, wherever he is, that he's happy and warm like I am now ... Wait ... am I dead? I can't be ... it doesn't make sense.

That's when I see a faint speck of colour ahead of me. It's just a blob to start with, but it slowly gets bigger and bigger until I realise that it's human.

It's her ... and she's walking towards me.

Alicia.

She's so beautiful; her golden blonde hair shiny, healthy and bouncy. She is radiating with light and wearing the exact same outfit as me, showing off her toned arms and shoulders. Damn, she looks good. Our hair and bodies may be different, but we're the same in every other way, from the light scattering of freckles on our noses to the scars on our arms (thanks Peter!).

As she gets closer I realise she's smiling. Alicia stands in front of me. This is so surreal and weird ... I didn't even know she could smile, not like this anyway. It's lighting up her whole face and it doesn't look sarcastic, the way it usually does when she smiles. She looks genuinely happy.

'Hello, Josslyn.' Her voice is as smooth as butter and gives me goose bumps.

'Hi, Alicia. It's so nice to see you when neither of us are being tortured.'

She gives a little chuckle. 'Yes, that is a bonus, I will admit. You look ... nice.'

'Thank you ... so do you, by the way, but then you always did look better than me.'

Alicia reaches out and touches my longer, darker hair. 'You always did look better as a brunette,' she says. She takes her hand away and we stand in silence for a few moments.

I glance around the white space. 'Where are we exactly?'

'In my mind.'

'It used to be black and then it was grey, but I prefer the white.'

'As do I.'

We stop and stare at each other, holding eye contact. We both know what we're doing ... we're making random small talk, trying to stall the inevitable for as long as possible.

I gulp back a huge lump in my throat and my bottom lip wobbles. 'I don't want to go, Alicia.'

'I know, Josslyn.'

'I've tried to hold on for as long as I can.'

'I know.'

'But I feel like you don't need me anymore, that I'm holding you back.' Alicia doesn't say anything. Tears slowly leak from my eyes as I speak. 'I wanted to stay until the very end. I wanted to watch Henry die so I knew, without a doubt, that it was really over, but I can't. I now realise you need to do this by yourself, that I'm only getting in the way. This is your fight. It always has been. I'm scared, Alicia. What will happen to me? What happens to a personality when it goes away?'

Alicia smiles gently as she shakes her head. 'I believe they never really go away. You will always be a part of me, Josslyn. Always. But you are right. It is time I walk alone for the first time. You have made me strong. You have protected me, but now I must finish the fight by myself.'

I nod and stare down at the white floor, which looks like smoke, swirling around my feet. It's still so bright that both of us look as if we're glowing. It's emanating all around us and feels as if it's getting brighter by the minute; the warmth is increasing too.

'I feel like I have so much to say to you, but I can't seem to find the words,' I say with a slight laugh.

'I feel the same way.'

'If you ever see Ben again can you tell him I really did love him and that I'm sorry?'

'I shall.'

'And will you promise me that no matter how hard it gets, how hopeless the situation … you'll never give up? Promise me you'll kill Henry and take down The Collective no matter what the cost and you'll never be his captive ever again.'

Alicia nods. 'I promise I will do whatever it takes. I will not give up. I will have your strength and courage with me.'

My bottom lip quivers again.

Alicia and I look at each other and then she does something I never thought would happen, not in a million years … She steps forwards and hugs me.

The floodgates open and I sob into her shoulder, shaking uncontrollably, but they aren't sad tears. They are the happiest tears I've ever cried and the love I feel for my twin sister overwhelms so much I think I may burst. Alicia is gripping me so tight, but she's as steady as a rock, holding on to me for dear life, ensuring I do not collapse under the weight of my emotions. There are no tears in her eyes, but that doesn't matter. I'm crying for the both of us. The warmth of the light circles us and pulls us closer and I can honestly say that this is the happiest moment of my life.

I know she'll be okay. Of course she'll be okay … she's Alicia! She can do anything. She's always been the strong one.

I don't know how long we hug for, but it's not enough time. It will never be enough time. We pull apart … and finally, we are both at peace.

It's time.

We smile at each other and nod slowly in unison.

'Goodbye, Alicia. I love you.' Those three words are the easiest words I've ever had to say.

'I love you too. Goodbye, Josslyn … Thank you.'

We hold onto each other's hands for as long as we can, but then I slowly let go of her fingers as I turn and walk away. After a few steps I turn, glancing back over my shoulder once more. She nods. I take one last look at my twin sister, the voice in my head, my protector, my best friend … and I walk away from her for the very last time.

Chapter Thirty-Seven

My eyes remain closed. I know there is no point in opening them because the room will be dark and there is nothing I wish to see anyway. I do not know how I expected to feel when Josslyn finally left me, but I do not expect to feel ... nothing. The wall is down, laying in pieces in my mind, but I do not experience a sudden rush of bad memories, nor do I feel any pain. I feel ... nothing ... empty. I am alone – completely alone in my own body, in my own mind and I feel nothing.

Am I broken? Is this what it feels like? Am I still me?

Josslyn ...

Josslyn ... are you there?

Josslyn ...

I know she will not answer me, but I cannot sit in silence because it is terrifying. I continue to repeat her name for many minutes ... hours ... I cannot be sure.

She never answers me.

The darkness is surrounding me like a cold, wet blanket and I shiver against it. I want to go back inside my head, back into the warmth and the light ... back to where Josslyn is ... was ... I do not like it here in the shadows.

I finally peel my eyelids open, but the darkness is still there, haunting me. I am so cold I cannot control the shaking. I search around in my mind for some glimmer of light, of hope ... of Josslyn, but I cannot find her. I know this is what I wanted, what needed to happen, but now that it has I want to turn back time more than I want to draw my next breath.

Please come back, Josslyn. I was wrong. I still need you. I cannot do this alone.

Then I remember the promise I made her ...

Promise me no matter how hard it gets, how hopeless the situation ... you'll never give up.

Her words echo in my mind, urging me forwards. I grit my teeth together, using the wall for support as I stand up on shaking legs. Every movement feels like the hardest thing I have ever done. My body is weak and heavy and does not feel like my own.

Still shivering, I follow the wall all the way along until I find the door; not even a sliver of light is escaping through the cracks. It is still locked. I turn and lean my back up against it, sinking down to the floor once more, too exhausted to remain standing.

I must survive. I must.

Someone will come. Someone ...

Josslyn ... I do not like this ... please come back.

I close my eyes again and then it happens ... a tiny, salty tear escapes from my left eye and gradually trickles down my cheek, drying before it reaches my chin. It is the most comforting and the most frightening thing I have ever experienced, but it makes me smile because I know she is not really gone. She remains a part of me ... including her goddamn emotional side.

I laugh out loud. Not a small giggle, but a full-on happy and relieved laugh. I probably sound a bit sadistic, but I have never laughed like this before and I find it hard to stop.

Several hours later I am still leaning up against the door when the light comes on. It sears my eyes even though they are closed, temporarily rendering me incapable of doing anything other than attempting to shield them with my hands. As soon as my eyes adjust I immediately wish the darkness would return. I do not want to see hundreds of pictures of tortured women. I have been locked in here with them and I need to get out. That is when the rage begins to build, not because I have been held captive, but because I have had enough of ... everything.

I stand, stumbling slightly and bang my fists against the door, over and over and over.

'Open up you fucking goddamn asshole!' I scream. I continue to shout expletives until my throat is hoarse and my fists hurt.

Eventually sounds begin to emanate from behind the door, shuffling and mumbling – male voices. I press my ear up against it and listen.

'... Got him ... yeah ... he's ...'

'... Bring ... she'll be ... ready ...'

I take a few steps back just as the door swings open and Henry stands on the threshold holding a glass of water and a piece of bread. He hands them out for me.

'I am astounded you have lasted this long. I thought for a minute I might have lost you completely.'

I glare at him, but my body is unable to stand upright and I still cannot control the shaking.

'How long have I been down here?' I ask, my throat croaky from all the shouting.

'Almost three days.'

I gulp back a gasp. Three days?

'Here … eat … drink. You will need your strength. Do not worry … I have not poisoned it. I do not wish to kill you, Alicia.'

Despite my best efforts my stomach grumbles and my mouth feels and tastes like sandpaper. He is correct. I will need my strength for what is to come so I take the offering and eat and drink.

'I assume I can safely say that Josslyn is no longer with us?'

I shoot him one of my evil looks while I chew the stale bread before washing it down with the tepid water.

Henry smiles. 'There is my good girl.'

'Do not fucking call me that,' I mutter under my breath.

'I have been searching for you for so long, Alicia. You are now who you truly have always meant to be. How do you feel now that Josslyn is no longer holding the wall up?'

'Whatever your plan was … you have failed. I feel nothing. I remember nothing.'

Henry frowns. 'Such a shame ... it seems I may have to break you all over again.'

At this point three men appear in the doorway behind him carrying an array of weapons: knives, hammers, wrenches, a saw. I spy my own backpack and knife amongst the items. I do not take my eyes off Henry who allows the men to pass and set the weapons on the table. There is a tense silence which fills the room, but it does not appear to be making anyone nervous, myself included.

The men line up next to each other like pathetic sheep and stand with their hands clasped behind their backs, awaiting their next set of orders. They are clearly under strict instructions not to touch me unless they get the go-ahead.

I glance briefly at the open door, the bright light taunting me, beckoning me to sprint towards it as fast as my legs can take me. I could probably make it, but I am not stupid. They would have locked the doors to the outside and blocked my escape somehow. I highly doubt that these men are the only ones in the house. The more logical and safer option right now is for me to stay here and watch this play out. As far as I know the camera is still rolling and Web Ninja is fully aware of the plan. She will not make a move until I tell her, no matter what happens.

'So ... Father ... your plan is to break my mind so that I become like you.'

Henry smiles. 'That is all any father ever wants for their child ... to follow in their footsteps and learn from their mistakes.'

'You are a prime example of a man who should never be a father.'

I see the three men tense slightly. I assume because they have never dared to stand up for themselves and actually talk back to their leader, but, unlike them, I am not afraid of him.

Henry picks up my knife and begins to stroke it gently along the sharp edge and down the other jagged side. He walks towards me and stops. I can feel his warm breath on my face.

'I know you are different, Alicia. You have evolved into an extraordinary woman. I wish I could see inside your mind. Now that Josslyn has gone it is time to unleash your full potential – to become who you were always destined to become. A female serial killer and rapist is one of those rarities in life that are hardly ever spoken or heard about. You could become a legend. I am The Hooded Man ... I can teach you things, ways to torture people to bring you such realms of pleasure you would not even believe it were possible. All you need to do is let go of the woman you are ... and become the woman you were *designed* to be. If you resist ... then I will take away the last thing on this earth you care about ... and then I will allow these men to do unspeakable things to you. It is your choice, my child. Choose wisely.'

My body is still shaking, but I somehow force the repulsion I feel deep down and hold my head up high, determined not to falter.

'You are mistaken, Henry. I have already lost the one person I cared about. She has gone ... and I am still here. I will never join you.'

'Funny ... I assumed you felt some sort of connection towards someone else. Granted, I know you do not feel many emotions, if any, but I could have sworn you were attached to him.'

Him.

No ... No ... Not—

'Bring him in.'

Chapter Thirty-Eight

I thought I was being so careful, that I had been doing the right thing when I pushed Benjamin away from me, when I hurt him and lied to him and walked out on him like he meant nothing. I should have known better. I despise myself for letting it drag on for as long as it did. I should have told him to leave months ago. It is all my fault and now, here he is, bound and gagged, kneeling in front of me. He does not appear to be injured, but that does little to comfort me. This is what I have always been afraid of. Benjamin was my weakness last time when Peter threatened him, but back then the only thing he wanted was the location of his dead sister. Now ... now if I am to save Benjamin I must become a monster, like my father ... and I cannot allow that to happen.

Benjamin locks eyes with me and I see tears streaming down his cheeks. I cannot even begin to explain how much I wish he had never come into our lives. Another tear leaks out of the corner of my eye and Benjamin notices, frowning slightly. One of the last things I said to him was Josslyn was no longer with me, so I cannot blame him for his confusion.

'Choose now, Alicia. Either you join me ... or this man will die. I will not bother with torturing him. It will be a quick death. You get to choose. I will only ask once.'

I do not allow my eyes to leave his as I say, 'I am sorry ... Benjamin.'

Benjamin's eyes fill with more tears as he blinks and nods ever so slightly. It makes me hurt even more knowing he has accepted his fate and my decision.

Without a moment's hesitation Henry lunges forwards and plunges the knife directly into Benjamin's chest, burying it to the hilt. Benjamin emits a choking, gurgling sound before collapsing on the floor, but I get there before he does and catch his heavy body in my arms.

'You have five minutes,' says Henry, 'and then the real fun begins.' He and his three henchmen leave the room, slamming the door, making the entire room shudder.

I quickly turn Benjamin around so he can see my face, ripping the gag from his mouth and untying his hands. Blood is flowing out of his body at an alarming rate. I grab the handle of the knife and go to remove it, but Benjamin stops me.

'No!' he shouts. 'L-Leave it.'

I obey his wish.

'Benjamin … I am sorry. I never meant for this to happen. I hoped that by leaving you I would be able to protect you from further harm.'

I do my best to stop the bleeding by taking off my long-sleeved top and push it against the wound, but I know that it is a completely useless gesture. My black strap top I am wearing underneath is immediately soaked in blood, but luckily it remains invisible.

Benjamin smiles and coughs as blood fills his mouth and runs down his chin. 'I-I know. It's okay.'

I hang my head, unable to form the right words. I feel as helpless as I did when Oscar was dying in my arms.

'They are trying to use you against me. They are trying to break me. I cannot allow that to happen,' I say.

'B-Boy … are they m-messing with the wrong woman.'

We both smile at his feeble attempt at humour. In a situation such as this it is all we have to hold on to.

'C-Can I ask you for a favour?' he says with a pained stutter.

'Yes, of course … anything.'

'Can I speak to Josslyn for one last time? I know she didn't really disappear.'

I gulp back the sudden lump in my throat. I cannot do it. I cannot refuse his final, dying wish to speak to the woman he loves. I at least owe him his last request. I must lie … again, but this time it is to give him what he wants.

'Yes,' I say with a smile.

I close my eyes and when I open them I am Josslyn.

'Ben!' I gasp as I lean forwards and press my face against his in a hug. I run my fingers through his hair and smile at him, tears filling my eyes. 'I'm so sorry that Alicia said those things to you. They weren't true. I only went along with it to try and protect you. I'm so sorry.'

'J-Josslyn …' He reaches up and strokes the side of my face. 'I understand. I would have done the same thing to protect you. I-I love you so much, girlfriend.'

I slowly lean down and gently kiss him on the lips, not caring that he tastes of blood and tears. Our lips only touch briefly, but it is enough. I pull away slowly and we stare into each other's eyes.

'I love you too, boyfriend,' I say as tears run down my face.

There is a short silence.

Benjamin smiles at me. 'You've gotten a lot better at pretending to be Josslyn. I'm impressed.' He coughs up more blood.

I attempt to look startled, but then realise there is no point in continuing the charade. He has seen right through my feeble attempt.

'I tried,' I reply solemnly.

'I know. Thank you.'

'She really did love you. She told me to tell you if I ever saw you again. She has gone for good now, Benjamin. I am alone in this body.'

Benjamin nods. 'I'm sorry. I'm sorry you have to continue by yourself, Alicia. I know you and I have had our differences and I know you could never really love me, but I wish we'd had a chance, you know ... to try ...' He tails off, overcome with pain. His breathing is becoming very shallow and I know he does not have much time left. He reaches up and touches one of the teardrops on my face.

'This is new,' he says.

I smile through my tears. 'It is an annoyance already.'

Benjamin closes his eyes. The puddle of blood has grown while we have been huddled on the floor, spreading out in a large irregular pool. I feel his body growing heavier in my arms.

'I love you … Ben.' My words are quiet, barely even an audible whisper, but he hears them. His eyes open.

'I love you too … Alicia.'

Benjamin grows still as he takes his last breath. I slump further down to the floor, unable to hold my own weight any longer. He slips from my grasp, the blood making it almost impossible to keep a firm grip. I hang my head down to touch his forehead with my own, then gently plant a soft kiss on it.

Benjamin …

My Ben …

Chapter Thirty-Nine

The blood feels like ice against my skin as I remain kneeling in the puddle, the metallic odour tickling my nostrils, turning my stomach. The smell of blood has never offended or disturbed me … until today. I am not sure if it is because Josslyn has now gone or because the blood belongs to someone I care about … belongs to someone I love …

Benjamin is dead and so I must ensure his death is not in vain. He cannot have died for nothing; I will not allow it. Henry may be a deranged killer, but he is wrong. Killing Benjamin has not made me weak, it has not broken me … nor will it break me. His death has, in fact, made me stronger. I run my fingers through Benjamin's hair and whisper in his ear my final promise to him, to Josslyn … I will not give up.

I clench the handle of the knife buried in his chest and yank it out, more blood spurting from the wound, covering me. I look up at the table, complete with the assortment of weapons and my items. The Collective have been careless to leave me inside a room with them … Henry believes he will enter the room and find me cowering over the body of my ex-lover, weak and broken. He is mistaken.

I stand up with force, leaving Benjamin's body to slump onto the floor and grab my backpack, swinging it onto my shoulders. I then move my tongue around the inside my mouth, feeling for the small metal implant on top of the left back molar. I bite down hard and feel it break.

The small device I have just activated is linked to an alarm located on Web Ninja's computer. She has now been given the signal to … send in the troops, as it were. She has instructions to contact the local police and inform them of suspicious activity located at this address relating to The Hooded Man. It will not be long before this house is surrounded by law enforcement and Henry will need to make a decision – risk being caught or leave.

The door clicks open and Henry barges into the room, lunging towards me. The police cannot have arrived that fast so I can only assume he suspects I am up to something or has been watching me on a hidden camera. Like father like daughter. I suppose that is indeed where I get my trust issues from.

Henry reaches for the knife, but I am quicker and manage to dodge out of his way. His left foot stamps down in the pool of blood and he skids, losing his balance. I use the opportunity to sprint to the door, hurling myself into the hallway. My legs give out and I clatter to the floor, but I immediately right myself, struggling to get a grip on the laminate flooring due to my bare feet being drenched in blood.

I turn right when I reach the hallway and run directly into a behemoth of a man, who towers over me with rage. He is large and cumbersome and takes a swipe at me as if I am a plaything, but I duck down and take a swipe of my own, slicing the skin on his right arm. He yells, but I am already past him and running for the stairs at the very end of the hallway.

I clamber up them, crawling and dragging myself as fast as I can. I can hear the commotion behind me, Henry yelling to his men to grab me, but I block it all out and focus my attention on the door at the top of the stairs, which has been left open. At the top my breath comes in short, sharp gasps and I am struggling to catch it, but I continue through the house, dodging into an empty room when I hear approaching footsteps. I crouch down behind a bookcase for a breather, contemplating my next move. I cannot be here when the police arrive; I must escape.

Go upstairs.

I do not know where the idea comes from, but it forms as clear as day in my mind. I need to go upstairs ...

I have no idea how many men are hunting for me, but I know it will not be long until one of them finds me. I check to ensure the coast is clear and step out from my hiding place and begin creeping towards the main staircase.

'She's here!'

Fuck.

Run!

I clench the knife tighter in my fist as I propel myself forwards. I trip up the stairs, scrambling and fighting to get a grip on the wooden steps. Loud footsteps come from behind me as I reach the top and I freeze. I do not know which way to turn.

But then a vivid memory smashes its way into my mind and I can see a little girl looking up at the ceiling, so I follow her gaze.

A loft hatch.

I smile as I jump up and grab the handle. My weight pulls the hatch open and a metal ladder crashes down in front of me, catching me on my shoulder, slicing a chunk of skin off in the process. The pain is intense, but I ignore it as I clamber up the ladder, knowing my assailants are not far behind. Benjamin's blood is still making it difficult to get a grip on anything I touch, but my sheer will and determination is driving me forwards. I know where I am going now.

I remember.

This is how I escaped the last time.

I follow the little girl in my memory through the attic as I hear someone climbing the ladder behind me. I duck down behind a load of storage boxes. My hunter is in the attic with me and I know I cannot escape with him so close.

'Come out, come out wherever you are, little girl,' he coos.

Another flashback.

The little girl is hiding in the same place I am, shaking and crying with fear. She clamps a hand over her mouth to stop the terrified moans from escaping.

'Don't you remember me … Alicia. We used to have a lot of fun together.'

I close my eyes in an attempt to stop the memory, but it arrives anyway, pounding its way into my head.

The little girl tries to remain quiet, but she accidentally knocks a box over and the man finds her. She screams and bites and kicks, but he is too strong. He easily restrains her flaying arms and legs and pins her down against the floor.

'You're mine,' he growls.

She screams.

I return to reality and am about to lurch out from behind the boxes and bury the knife deep into his neck, but then ...

A dark shadow jumps out from the far corner, screaming and spitting. It jumps on my attacker's back, sending him off balance. He shouts as he attempts to shake it off, but it is clinging on for dear life. I use the opportunity to jump out and plunge the knife into the side of his neck. Blood spurts out in short, sharp jets as he gasps, clutching his throat as he sinks down to his knees, the dark shadow still clinging to his back.

'No,' I say, standing over him, staring him in the eyes. 'I belong to no one.'

I kick him hard in the face and he collapses forwards – dead.

There is a strange silence while the dark shadow and I contemplate whether we are enemies or allies, but then I realise it is not a shadow at all ...

It is a woman.

Chapter Forty

The woman and I stare at each other for what seems like hours, but in fact it is only a few seconds. I know we cannot waste time. She needs help. I cannot leave her here, although it would be easier. I had only expected to rescue myself, not another human being. She looks to be in a bad way. Her hair is matted, dirty and she is omitting a pungent smell, although that could also be due to her filthy, stained clothes. Her face is grimy, her eyes black like lumps of coal and her skin is ghostly pale behind the dirt. I do not recognise her. The poor thing is clearly another innocent woman, held captive in this hellhole.

'The police will be here soon. Either you come with me or stay here and they will take care of you,' I say. 'Choose quickly.'

'Y-You,' she croaks quietly.

I nod my acceptance. 'Follow me … and keep up.'

I turn and head towards the end of the attic, knowing exactly where I am going. I remember it as clear as day now; a little girl crawling quietly towards freedom all those years ago. I hear the woman following close behind me.

I reach the end of the attic just as I hear several cars pull up outside. The police. I hear loud, booming voices, but am unable to make out exactly what they say. I do not have time to listen. I crouch down and feel along the inside of the roof for a loose tile … I find it.

I hear shouts and bangs down below, both from inside and outside of the house. The police have broken down the door. I claw at the loose tile, breaking it away from the others, slowly creating a hole in the roof, but it is not easy and my fingers sting with pain as I rip my fingernails trying to get a grip.

Finally, the hole is big enough for me to fit through. I quickly turn to my follower.

'Keep quiet,' I order.

She nods and I see a flicker of light in her eyes; the hope of freedom.

I squeeze my sore body through the hole and inch my way out onto the roof. I am grateful it is night-time, but I have absolutely no idea what the time actually is or what day it is. The night air is crisp and I immediately feel light-headed as I breathe in, but once I have a stable footing on the tiled roof I turn and help the woman through the gap. She is weak, but her determination to escape is no doubt keeping her going.

Neither of us know each other's names, but I feel an immediate bond with this woman, almost as if I have known her in some other life. What I do know is that she needs my help. She grips my arm tight as we slowly creep across the roof under the cover of darkness, keeping as low as we can to avoid a silhouette against the moonlit sky.

There are blue flashing lights below us and several police cars lined up outside the house. I smile to myself as I reach a drainpipe on the back of the house away from the growing commotion; the same broken one I had seen earlier. I see the little girl again in my mind's eye climbing down the pipe to the ground, causing it to snap as she reaches the ground. There is no other way down from this roof and we cannot stay up here and wait for the police to leave because it could be days until they do.

I point to the drainpipe and help the woman as she lowers herself off the edge of the roof. I hold my breath as she cautiously makes her way to the ground. The pipe groans and she slips, but manages to grab on to a nearby windowsill. I sigh in relief as I watch her feet finally touch the damp earth below. She scurries to a nearby bush and hides, peering out at me, barely visible in the darkness.

My turn.

I grasp the pipe and begin to shimmy down an inch at a time.

Suddenly the back door is flung open and a beam of light illuminates the entire back garden. I freeze and pray that the woman has retreated further into the bush. I glance down and watch as a man attempts to flee out through the back garden, but a policeman rugby tackles him to the ground. They struggle, but the policeman eventually slaps a pair of cuffs on the man and leads him back into the house, slamming the door.

I immediately begin my descent again. I get to within eight feet of the ground when the pipe wobbles and cracks. My heart lurches into my throat. It breaks away from the building, sending me flying backwards. I land with an almighty thump on the grass below, severely winded but otherwise unhurt.

Move!

I obey the voice in my head and force myself to stand, quickly joining the woman inside the bush. We wait patiently for a few moments to ensure the coast is clear and that no one heard the loud crack when the pipe broke.

Then we slink off into the night, leaving the authorities to deal with the evil within the walls.

By the time the two of us arrive back at the hotel room dawn is breaking. I open the door and usher her inside. She is shivering uncontrollably and looks close to passing out. She stands in the middle of the room staring at me as tears fill her eyes and run down her cheeks, causing small lines to appear through the grime.

'T-Thank you,' she whispers.

'I did not expect to have to rescue anyone, but you are welcome. Come ... I will help you to shower and get dressed into some clean clothes, then you must sleep while I decide what to do next.'

The woman nods her thanks and turns to go towards the bathroom, but then stops. 'Who are you?' she asks. 'Why were you in the house?'

I do not reply straight away because I am unsure whether to tell her my real name or my newly acquired fake one.

'It does not matter who I am right now ... who are you?'

'L-Laura ... my name's Laura.'

Chapter Forty-One

I feel my heart skip a beat and my stomach drop the way it did when I fell from the drainpipe. I stare at the woman in front of me ... Laura. She barely looks human anymore. I had seen photographs of her in her wild youth and in various states of undress on the walls of Peter's torture chamber, but the woman standing before me looks nothing like her former self. The Collective have stolen her identity, her life, her existence.

'Laura Willis?' I ask, just to make sure.

She nods. 'Y-Yes ... do you know me?'

'I know your brother.'

Laura gasps and rushes towards me, her eyes suddenly full of hope, and a smile forms on her dry and crusty lips. 'Ben! Oh my God! Ben ... where is he? I told him in my letter to stop looking for me, but he didn't, did he? He kept looking. Where is he?'

I remain rooted to the spot. 'I am sorry ... but Benjamin is still inside the house.'

'You left him there?'

'He is dead. He was stabbed in front of me and died in my arms.' I gesture to the blood, which has now dried and is caked onto my skin. 'I could not save him.'

Laura makes a gargling sound like she is choking and then drops to her knees, burying her face in her hands. She does not attempt to hide her sobs as they take over her body.

'I told him to leave me alone!' she screams into the carpet.

I look down at the sobbing ball of mess falling to pieces on the floor. Usually, I despise it when people cry or show emotion in front of me. It annoys me, but not now … now I feel … empathy. Tears begin leaking from my eyes as I crouch on the floor beside Laura. I gently lay a hand on her back, something I would never usually do either.

'Benjamin thought you were dead, that you committed suicide. He was not in that house because of you. It is not your fault he is dead … it is mine. I take full responsibility.'

At this revelation Laura peels herself off the carpet and looks at me. 'You? Who the hell are you? How do you know my brother?'

'My name is Alicia. I have been working with your brother for the past few months to bring down The Collective, the men who held you hostage. He has been helping me and I could not have managed it without him. He has saved dozens, perhaps hundreds, of innocent lives. Those men will never harm another woman again because of him. He is a hero … and he loved you very much.'

I have no idea if my words will make Laura feel better. I am still adjusting to my new emotional state, but Laura smiles weakly at me through her tears.

'Even after everything I put him through … what I did to him?' she asks.

'Yes. He never gave up looking for you … until he found your note.'

Laura gulps and nods. 'I didn't want him to get involved with The Collective so I tried to push him away.'

'I attempted to do the same, but he—'

'—Is stubborn,' finishes Laura.

'Yes, unbelievably so.'

We share a small smile.

'Were you ever in India?' I ask.

She shakes her head. 'No ... I planted fake trails wherever I could, but The Collective kept tracking me down. They found me before I could kill myself and took me to that house where I've been trapped ever since. I don't know how long it's been.'

'Several years.'

'I thought as much.'

'I am sorry I could not save him,' I say solemnly.

Laura sniffs loudly and wipes her nose with her arm. 'I want to know everything. Tell me everything.'

'I will, but first let us get you clean and fed and then you can sleep. I will tell you everything soon.'

I help Laura to her feet. She clutches my arm as if her life depends on it.

'Were you and Ben ... together?' she asks timidly.

'It is a long story ...'

I help Laura remove her clothes. She is merely a skeleton covered in cuts and bruises, which only begin to reveal themselves as the warm water washes the built-up dirt away. It is a long time before the water runs clear. I wash her hair, which I think is beyond help, but I do my best. She is too weak to remain standing so we both sit under the running water while I continue to wash her; her naked and me fully clothed.

We do not speak, but it is such a tender moment and I feel an overwhelming urge to care for her as if she were my own sister.

Finally, I help her into some clean clothes and give her some water to drink and an energy bar. I need to go and get proper food for her soon. She lays down on the bed and I cover her with a blanket.

'Sleep,' I say. 'I need to sort some things out.'

Laura closes her eyes, but then swiftly opens them. 'You won't leave me, will you?'

'No, I shall be here the whole time you are asleep.'

Laura smiles as she closes her eyes and I watch her as she almost immediately drifts into unconsciousness.

I then shower myself, but my emotions overwhelm me. The warm water mixes with my tears.

I cry for Josslyn.

I cry for Benjamin.

I cry for Laura.

But I do not cry for myself.

It is not over yet …

Chapter Forty-Two

One week later ...

I have been watching the news channels religiously for days, as one by one the members of The Collective are revealed for all the world to see. It has been like watching a highly entertaining movie, but there is one man who has managed to avoid capture: Henry. I knew he would escape and I am not worried that he has. I must be patient. I have my skilled ally tracking his every movement. She will let me know when the time is right to strike. It is a media circus out there at the moment so I feel it is best that I stay quiet and let it die down before I surface.

I have not left the hotel room at all. Web Ninja has been ferrying supplies to me, which have been waiting outside the door every morning like clockwork. She even provided medication for Laura, who developed a severe cough and temperature soon after her escape, but I have been taking care of her around the clock, tending to her every need. She is now on the mend and feeling better.

I have managed to feed myself and sleep a few hours at a time, but I cannot relax yet because I know there is still work to be done. First, I must ensure Laura is strong enough to be left alone for a while.

Allow me to explain what has happened over the past week in detail.

A week ago Web Ninja downloaded the entire video from my hidden camera. She sent it anonymously to the police, along with every scrap of evidence I had gathered along the way, including all the photos and possessions Peter had collected from his victims, the folder I had found in the attic and the tape from my mother. *Everything.* It was finally time to reveal the corruption that was going on behind closed doors at Lampton Boarding School for Boys and also inside that house.

Not long after all of the evidence arrived at the police station the floodgates opened, the media were informed and over the next three days the entire school, including all the teachers, pupils and staff were questioned by the police. Stories emerged, the truth was revealed and the guilty were charged.

The Head Master had not been available for questioning (obviously), but Henry Smith was now being hunted down by the police; their number one suspect. I was not worried they would find him first.

The point is The Hooded Man finally had a name and a face and was out there for everyone to see. In total, fifteen male teachers from the school were arrested on suspicion of rape, murder, torture and kidnapping. Five students were also arrested when they admitted they were in the process of being trained to follow in their footsteps. They may or may not be let go, but that is not my problem anymore; that is for the courts to decide. I am thankful that their teaching was interrupted before it warped them into vile men.

The house was searched from top to bottom and its secrets were finally exposed. A mummified body of a woman (who was later found to be Jane Daniels) was found wrapped up in plastic and buried beneath the floorboards of the kitchen. It seemed my mother had never managed to escape her captives, even in death.

Two male bodies were also discovered in the house: Benjamin Willis and Arthur Holdings (the man I had killed in the attic). Benjamin had no family to step forward and formally identify him, but his identity was revealed eventually. However, the police had no idea what he was doing inside the house. He was labelled as a potential victim; the search for the truth is still ongoing.

A lot of female DNA was recovered from the house, including none other than Josslyn Reynolds's. Despite the previous allegations made against her the authorities and news reporters managed to put two and two together and suggested that she was possibly a victim of The Collective, and always had been. There was, unfortunately, still the small issue of her murdering her ex-boyfriend and Alicia Phillips. Of course, when the news broke that Josslyn Reynolds and Alicia Phillips shared fifty percent of the same DNA (since fraternal twins only share half and are no more genetically alike than normal siblings), it was the news story of the decade. Some stories suggest that the body under the big tree was not actually Alicia, but Josslyn and Alicia was the killer ...

It was safe to say that swarms of journalists and camera crews descended upon Cambridge, all wanting a piece of this juicy story and the truth was still being twisted and corrupted, but things were finally being set right.

The Collective was no more ...

Josslyn Reynolds was a potential victim of The Collective ...

Alicia Phillips's body was handed over to her parents and given an official burial ...

Peter Phillips is still missing, but it was confirmed that he was a part of The Collective, so he is still a target ...

Daniel Russell's body was finally buried by his parents and laid to rest ...

Benjamin Willis was given a simple funeral, but no one of importance attended because everyone who ever loved him was gone ...

And Henry Smith is on the run ...

I am now preparing to leave the hotel room and go and find Henry after receiving an email from Web Ninja earlier today. It is time ...

My Dark Self,

Henry Smith is hiding out at Peter Phillips's old house. It's empty at the moment because his parents have put it up for sale and the police have now finished their investigations. I guess they haven't bothered looking in the most obvious place yet. I tracked him through some local security footage. I suggest whatever you have planned you do it soon because the cops aren't far behind me.

Also … try not to make a mess this time. I'm having one hell of a job cleaning up after you …

Good luck.

Stay dark.

Web Ninja

P.S. Once this is all over we should totally meet up and celebrate … and maybe I'll tell you my real name. Hope Laura is okay.

P.P.S. This email will automatically be deleted in two minutes.

I finish my cup of strong coffee and place it down on the bedside table. I then pick up the hunting knife and slide it into its sheath around my waist.

Laura is still asleep; she has been sleeping a lot this week. I told her everything about me after a couple of days and she took it surprisingly well.

I am about to turn off the television when a news broadcast catches my eye. A middle-aged man talks into the camera.

'The story of Josslyn Reynolds is one that will fascinate people for decades to come. She was an ordinary woman, living an ordinary life, but she held a dark secret. She was a product of rape, of torture and neglect. As a child she was quite possibly subjected to the most horrendous form of abuse, something that is difficult to comprehend. Her mind broke, snapped … and she retreated to somewhere dark, completely blocking out her childhood before the age of six.

'Josslyn Reynolds grew up as a happy child after that with her adopted parents, but years later the cracks began to show and she quickly went down a dangerous path. She killed her ex-boyfriend, Daniel Russell, in cold blood and she tracked down her estranged twin sister, Alicia Phillips. It is possible she also killed Peter Phillips. However, it has now come to light that Peter was part of the underground rapist community known as The Collective, run by The Hooded Man, who is now known to be Henry Smith, the Head Teacher of Lampton Boarding School for Boys.

'Henry Smith is now the number one suspect for the police, but don't forget ... Josslyn Reynolds is not her real name. Her name was Alicia before the age of six and it is possible she is still out there ... So the question is ... is Josslyn/Alicia a vigilante, hell-bent on hunting down her father and murdering him for what he did to her or is she a serial killer who actually enjoys killing people? Who will get to The Hooded Man first ... the police ... or his own mentally disturbed daughter? This is Eric Bay reporting for BBC News.'

I raise my eyes slightly at the words *mentally disturbed,* but then smile ... it is the first time I have heard my name on the news before.

Now the world knows who I am ... is it time to say goodbye to Alicia as well?

Chapter Forty-Three

I stand and stare up at the building in front of me, awash with memories from the past. I see Josslyn and Oscar arriving for the first time and feel how full of nerves and excitement she was at finding out about her long-lost sister and travelling somewhere new. I see the pot plant Oscar peed on and feel a strange tug inside.

I miss Oscar ... his little wet nose against my skin, the way his whole back end of his body would shake whenever he wagged his tail, his high-pitched bark that always gave me a headache ... the way he would snuggle up against me at night like a miniature hot water bottle.

I miss Josslyn ... her constant nagging, her sarcasm, even her dependency on alcohol – speaking of which, I could really use a strong drink right about now ... which is a new sensation.

I reach the front door, remembering the moment it had opened and Peter had stood at the entrance and how Josslyn had been taken aback by how handsome he was; his perfect smile and his toned torso. He had invited her in knowing exactly who she was. All of that was so long ago now and so much has happened since then. I feel as if I have come full circle because here I am again at the same door ... back to where it had all started and now this is where it will end. It is quite poignant really when you think about it.

I knock and wait.

Henry will open the door to me; I know he will.

Several minutes pass and then I hear a faint click. I pause for several seconds before pushing the door open, gently closing it behind me. The house is dark and cold, except for the ambience of the streetlights peering through the drawn curtains. There is no furniture in any of the rooms that I can see; the police must have stripped the place bare when they conducted their search or maybe his parents had removed everything and sold it.

An ominous shadow lurks in the doorway of the kitchen. 'You found me,' it says.

'I cannot take all of the credit. I had help.'

The shadow does not move but it does speak again. 'I am disappointed in you, Alicia. You could easily have avoided all of this. Your life is over now. There is no coming back. If you had accepted my offer I could have kept you safe, the way I have kept all of my followers safe all these years, but now … now you have taken everything from me. I am exposed to the world and you … you are nothing. No one even knows you exist.'

'Is it not mandatory for a daughter to disappoint her father at some point in her life?' I reply. 'And actually, my name was mentioned on the news today.'

I square up to the shadow. Neither of us can see each other's facial expressions clearly. We are merely dark shapes, and all my other senses are heightened. I can hear him as clearly as if he were talking directly into my ear and I can smell him (a mixture of body odour and sweat, with a hint of something musty). I can even smell bleach, from when Benjamin and I had scrubbed this place clean or perhaps Peter's parents had hired a professional cleaner to spruce it up before they put it on the market.

The shadow grunts and I hear shuffling as it shifts its weight, then it disappears. I blink and wait patiently for my eyes to adjust to the darkness, but it is pointless. The dull light is doing nothing to assist me. It seems I must hunt my prey blind.

I take out the knife, enjoying the way it feels in my right hand. There is something ... intimate ... about using a knife to end someone's life. It is the weapon I have used on most of my victims. Well, apart from dear Alicia who found her sticky demise at the end of a claw hammer, but one must adapt and overcome when faced with an immediate opportunity.

I can hear my prey moving around in the darkness. I inch forwards, closer and closer ... listening, waiting ... It is what a good and patient predator does. I like to think I have evolved somewhat from the impulsive killer I once was. Gone are the days when I would kill whenever the need arose. Now I like to plan and plot and wait, biding my time, relishing the experience, soaking up the atmosphere and all the euphoria that comes with it.

My heart is pounding in my chest, but I am not afraid. I am enjoying this ... This is the moment I have been waiting for.

'I never laid a finger on you, Alicia,' I hear my father murmur loudly. It is difficult to know where his voice is coming from, but I creep forwards, peering around the corner as I do so. 'I would never hurt you,' he adds.

'You may not have ever touched me physically, but it was all your doing. There is no point in denying that obvious fact.'

I reach the bottom of the stairs and look up at the landing above, but I can barely see anything. I hear a creaking noise above … so up the stairs I go, one by one, slowly, carefully …

'You would kill your own father, your own flesh and blood?'

I smile to no one other than myself. 'You forget … I broke Alicia's jaw with a claw hammer and then snapped her neck. If I can do that to my own twin sister … just imagine what I can do to you.'

There is a long silence and then …

'You are more of a monster than I am.'

I reach the top of the stairs, my left foot stepping on a section of floor that creaks loudly—

Shit.

Something large and heavy shoves me against the nearest wall and I lose my balance, but only for a second. I duck down, the knife poised …

My prey has vanished.

He is quick, I will give him that.

I scan my surroundings, remembering the layout of the upstairs. Peter's main bedroom is just down the corridor. From what I can make out none of the doors are open. He must be somewhere on the landing with me.

I spin around at the sound of another floorboard squeaking and see the dark shadow standing at the top of the stairs, gently illuminated by the moonlight beaming in from the front door, which is located directly below.

The Hooded Man is back ...

I cannot make out anything except the large, black hood over his head.

This is my chance.

'And I owe it all to you ... Father,' I say, steeling myself for what I am about to do. This is going to fucking hurt.

I catapult myself forwards, rugby tackling him around the waist. He lets out a loud grunt as we fall backwards down the stairs, tumbling ... I keep a tight hold of him, tucking my arms and legs in as we thump all the way to the bottom, landing in a tangled heap.

I am winded and sore, but he is in a worse position than me, having taken the brunt of the impact from the wooden stairs, so I grasp the knife, raise it above my head and plunge it into his chest before he has a chance to compose himself.

The blood that erupts from his body looks like black liquid tar as it spurts over my face and chest. I do not hesitate as I bury the blade repeatedly into the large mass underneath me ... over and over and over ... destroying his body, his face, the monster that has destroyed so many lives, including my own.

There is a strangled gurgling sound, the mass beneath me twitching and jerking, but then it is still. I lay on top of him, my left ear pressed against his chest. I can hear his heart beating faintly as he creeps closer and closer to the end.

I close my eyes and listen ...

Thud ...

Thud ... thud ...

... Thud ...

... Thud ...

Silence.

The monster is dead.

Chapter Forty-Four

I slowly lift my head from the still, warm chest of my father and crawl into the closest corner, brace my back up against it, hunch my knees to my chest and stare into the darkness. The monster is still oozing dark, black blood, filling the stale air around me with its metallic smell, but it does not bother me. I like it. It smells like … victory … but why do I feel so empty? I assumed when I finally vanquished my enemy I would feel some sort of relief, or glee or something … yet all I feel is my heart thudding in my hollow chest, as if it is the only object in there.

Time slows down to a mind-numbing crawl and I know I need to leave this scene, this house, before the police show up, but my brain and body do not appear to be connected anymore, as if they have been severed by a sharp knife. Maybe I should let them take me, arrest me and lock me up. I deserve it. I have done many bad things in my life and I am tired, deeply, bone-shatteringly tired. My body is giving up; I am giving up. I want to close my eyes and sleep for a week or never wake up. I am tired of running, of hiding and of lying. I want it all to be over … Maybe it is time I stopped running and accept my fate.

But then I hear it, I feel it, I sense it … not a voice exactly, but a … *something* … and it is telling me to get up right now and leave. It is ordering me to run and hide and start over …

Josslyn … is that you?

287

The promise I made to her fills my head and now it is all I can think about. I cannot fail her ... I must keep going no matter what, no matter how hopeless the situation.

Suddenly my brain and my body reconnect and I force myself to stand. I leave the knife buried up to the hilt in the body of the monster, open the door and walk out into the cool night air, never once looking back over my shoulder.

I somehow make it back to my hotel room without being spotted. I am drenched in blood, looking a little like Carrie in the Stephen King novel, but luckily the late hour works in my favour. Laura is awake and watching the television as I stumble through the door. She gasps and leaps out of bed when she sees the state of me.

'Holy fuck! What happened to you? Are you okay?' She rushes to my side.

'I am fine. The blood is not mine.'

'Then who—' She stops and we stare at each other and then she smiles. 'He's dead, isn't he?'

'Very much so.'

Laura envelopes me in a tight hug, clearly not bothered that she is transferring blood to her clothes and skin too. I hug her back, feeling slightly awkward (I am not sure I will ever get used to hugging people).

'What happens now?' she asks me.

'Are you well enough to leave the room and travel?'

'Yes, I think so.'

Laura does look much better than when she first arrived a week ago. In the end we had to cut her hair short to get rid of the tangles and matted hair. She is still very thin, but is no longer in danger of collapsing under her own frail weight.

I nod, knowing we cannot hide here for much longer.

'Leave it to me,' I say as I begin to strip off my clothes, piling them in a heap on the bathroom floor. I step under the shower and allow the water to do its magical thing. I think I told you once before that water has always calmed me and as I watch the water turn from red, to pink, to clear, I feel the weight of the world draining away down the plughole with it.

An hour later I emerge from the bathroom, a towel around my chest. I spy my phone on the side table, which is flashing at me.

A message ... Actually, an email ...

My Dark Self,
You certainly know how to cause a scene! The police are there now. It's over. I suggest you get out of the area as soon as possible. I can help.

You and Laura need to meet me in one hour at Walker's Park by the big oak tree. I'll have everything you need.

Stay dark,
Web Ninja
P.S. We finally get to meet! Remember ... you owe me like a gazillion drinks!

I sigh as I lower the phone. Clearly I am not meant to ever sleep again. There is a small part of me that does not trust this woman, but I know I cannot live this way forever, always avoiding people who want to help me. Josslyn would not want me to live like that. It is time to put my faith in humanity and take a risk on my future happiness.

I tell Laura to get ready to leave while I reluctantly get dressed in clean clothes (wishing I could crawl into bed instead) and begin to pack all my belongings into the backpack. I pick up my new ID and stare at the name ... Lucy Adler ... I can think of worse names.

I make an attempt to clean the hotel room, especially the bathroom, to remove any trace of blood, but I am so tired I can barely focus on the job. I do not even care.

Fuck it.

Laura and I leave and head to the park, which is approximately a twenty-two-minute walk away.

The big oak tree is an ominous presence, towering over every other tree in the park. There are scattered streetlamps lighting the paths, but Laura and I stick to the shadows, not because I think we are being followed, but because I have grown accustomed to being in darkness.

Laura is shivering beside me as we approach the tree. We both spot the black shadow standing under the canopy of leaves at the same time. It is slight and slim; the shadow moves towards me.

'Web Ninja, I presume,' I say.

'My Dark Self,' is the reply. The voice is light and friendly. 'It's nice to finally meet you.'

The shadow steps into the light from the nearest streetlamp so I can finally see her face. The thirty-something-year-old woman standing in front of me is nothing like I imagined. Her hair is short, a rough grade two all over. Gold hoop earrings dangle from her ears, as well as several other dozen studs which are embedded into various body parts: nose, lip, eyebrows. She is wearing an over-sized dark jumper and a tight, black skirt along with biker-style, leather boots that reach up to just below her knees.

She looks ... fucking awesome.

'Likewise,' I say. 'I must say that without your help I could not have accomplished my mission. I owe you a great deal of thanks and gratitude ... and many drinks.'

The woman laughs. 'Yes, you fucking do, but don't mention it. You gave me back someone I thought I'd lost forever and for that ... for that I owe you my eternal gratitude.'

At this point another female-shaped shadow steps out from behind the tree. I allow my eyes to adjust, but I immediately recognise the long, dark hair hanging like curtains down the side of her face. She does not speak.

'Rebecca,' I say with a happy smile.

I can see her smiling back at me in the dim light. She stands next to Web Ninja and links her arm through hers, snuggling up to her side. She still looks very pale and nervous, but there is a glimmer of something in her eyes that was not there before: happiness.

'This is Laura Willis,' I say. Laura steps forwards and nods timidly. 'She's the sister of Benjamin who came with me to visit you,' I tell Rebecca.

I see Rebecca frown.

'Benjamin was killed by Henry,' I add.

She lowers her eyes to the ground, looking sad.

'I am sorry about your friend,' says Web Ninja, 'but now that The Collective is gone Rebecca felt safe enough to leave the hospital.'

'That is good news.'

'In fact ... all four of us have something in common now,' continues Web Ninja. 'We all wish to remain hidden and we're all hiding from the law for some reason or another.'

Laura steps forwards a pace. 'It's not that I want to hide ... I just have no one left to stick around for. My whole family is dead. My friends abandoned me years ago. I have no one.'

'You have me,' I say.

Laura smiles. 'Whatever you have in mind ... I want in.'

Web Ninja inhales deeply. 'I have a plan, but ... it will take some time to sort out, so you'll have to be patient.'

'What is the plan?' I ask.

'We disappear. All of us. Forever. I can make it happen. I can make it so that no one ever finds us, like what

I did for Rebecca, but we won't be staying in a mental hospital. We can have a life, start families ... start over. We can all go together or we can go separately, whatever you want. You're the one who's enabled us to have a second chance at life. It's all down to you ... and I don't even know your real name,' she says with a laugh.

I extend my hand for her to shake it. 'My name is Alicia.'

She shakes it. 'No last name?'

'No.'

'My name's Vicky Simmons.'

I nod. 'I like Web Ninja.'

Vicky laughs out loud. 'Yes, well ... a girl has to protect her identity somehow. How'd you come up with My Dark Self?'

'It is a long story.'

'I'd love to hear it sometime.'

'You shall.'

'So ... what do you want to do, Alicia?'

I sigh and take a moment to think. I can barely believe what I am hearing. A family ... I have the chance of having a real family, a real sister and real friends. I have the opportunity to start over and become anyone, do anything ... but am I putting these three women at risk if I choose to stay with them? Should I walk alone the way I always have or should I take the risk?

Vicky begins talking again. 'We want you to come with us, Alicia. Rebecca tells me you're her half-sister. You're family now. Laura too. Please ... come with us.'

The four of us stand quietly in the darkness.

To be honest my mind was made up ages ago.

'Yes,' I say. 'I will come with you. All of us should be together and start over.'

Everyone smiles, but then Rebecca steps forwards and hugs me. She looks at me, opens her mouth and after a few seconds manages to say, 'T-Thank ... y-you.'

It seems that all of us are finally on the road to recovery.

Vicky claps her hands together. 'Right ... let's get this show on the road. It's time to say goodbye to your old life.'

I inhale deeply. 'I am ready to say goodbye.'

Goodbye, Alicia.

Chapter Forty-Five

One year later.

Ah, there you are. I have many things to tell you ... If you passed me in the street you would not recognise me. I am no longer Alexis, or Josslyn or even Alicia. Vicky was able to formally and officially change all of our names via deed poll without anyone batting an eyelid. How, you may ask? I do not know. Do you even care? However, to keep things from becoming overly complicated I shall use the names you are used to hearing.

The others and I are now small business owners and live in Jasper, Alberta. Yes, that is in Canada. I told you I had many things to tell you. I shall try and be as succinct as possible. We own and run Snowy Lodge, a quaint hostel/Bed and Breakfast situated in the middle of the Jasper National Park, the perfect location for holiday makers who wish to escape to a quiet getaway and do a spot of skiing in the winter months. It is an ideal location, a place to hide away from the stresses of the world, which is exactly what we have been doing for the past six months.

The six months before that were spent moving around a lot, never leaving a trail behind. Vicky knew what she was doing so I trusted her and I have to hand it to her ... she came through on her word. She promised that within a year of leaving the United Kingdom we would be settled somewhere remote, living an honest, carefree life.

And here we are.

Vicky has given up her Web Ninja lifestyle (although she admits to still keeping an ear to the ground on occasion, but has never revealed exactly what this entails) and now lives her life relatively technology free. She gave Rebecca, Laura and I three rules to follow in order to keep us all safe, which we follow to the letter.

Number one - We are not allowed to use the internet to look up the news in the United Kingdom to keep an eye on the trials going on for the convicted men or the continued search for Josslyn Reynolds. I was the one most at risk of being found, so I have had to cut all ties with my old life (not that I had any in the first place).

Number two - No social media for personal use. This was not a particularly hard rule to follow because all four of us had always kept a low profile on social media anyway. Besides, I had no friends who would follow me. Yes, we have a website for the hostel and a Facebook page, but there are no pictures of any of us, anywhere.

Number three - Never mention to anyone about our previous lives, which I suppose is an obvious rule, but a very important one. We do not even discuss our old lives between ourselves. I told Vicky, Rebecca and Laura all about Josslyn and what I had been through and they told me their stories, but after that we buried the past. We now have a back story to provide to anyone who asks us why four British women have moved to Canada to set up a hostel business, which no one appears to question.

So far the rules have kept us safe and we have had no problems.

It is off season now – mid-October, which means the temperature barely raises above five degrees, often plummeting to minus ten during the night. The hostel is quiet with only five of the rooms presently occupied. It has fifteen rooms in total and during the peak season we are often fully booked. This is not a place for families to visit; it is solely catered for adults to come, unwind and enjoy themselves.

I am awake before my alarm sounds, so I turn it off, sit up and swing my legs over the side of the bed. I feel the soft, thick woven rug between my toes. I touch the floor and then bring my legs up and count to five ... before placing them back down again.

Let me explain ...

About eight months ago I began to ... *change*. Some would say I have changed a lot already from the person I once was, but this was different. Not only did I change my hair (it is now long and dyed dark red), but my mannerisms and voice began to change. It was barely noticeable to Vicky, Rebecca and Laura because they hardly knew me at the time, but it was certainly noticeable to me. Benjamin would have noticed it ...

I smile now and even tell jokes. I drink alcohol because I enjoy it (and have become drunk on a few occasions), I sometimes skip my workouts because I just cannot be bothered and yes ... I began to do the foot tapping thing Josslyn always used to do. The first morning I did it without thinking. I stopped suddenly, my heart thumping hard in my chest. Did it mean that Josslyn was coming back? No. She was gone, but what it did tell me was that she was now a part of me, even more so than before.

I am no longer Alicia, the hard-talking, no-nonsense, rude woman who speaks formally and refuses to have fun. Nor am I a complete alcoholic like Josslyn who never speaks up for herself and does not exercise. I am … a mixture of the two.

Oh … and the biggest difference … well, you shall find out soon …

I stand up and stretch my arms above my head, feeling my pyjama top riding up my bare midriff. I click my neck from side to side and pad out into the hall, following the scent of freshly brewed coffee. Rebecca is always the first one of us up. She and Vicky have their bedroom down the hall and Laura and I have a small one each on the other side of the hostel.

Vicky and Rebecca are such a cute couple. Yes, I used the word *cute*. They are married now and seeing them together makes me feel all warm and happy inside. They have changed their outward appearances too; Vicky has grown her hair to a stylish short bob and Rebecca has chopped hers off to shoulder length.

Rebecca looks up as I walk into the kitchen and prop myself up on a stool at the breakfast bar. She has four cups set out in a line. She pours coffee into one and hands it to me.

'G-Good morning,' she says. Her speech has improved dramatically over the past year. She can now hold proper conversations, despite stumbling over certain words. However, after a few minutes of talking she finds it exhausting and goes back to sign language (which we all learned during the first six months we were together in order to communicate effectively with her).

'Morning,' I say. 'Sleep well?'

'Y-Yes, thank y-you. We have two arrivals today at noon, young c-couple. Oh ... and Vicky s-says she has a surprise for us l-later.'

I take a sip, feeling the warm liquid trickling down my mouth. 'A surprise?'

'Y-Yeah ... I have no idea what it could be. Y-You?'

'No idea, but knowing Vicky it'll probably be a big one.'

We continue to chat for a few moments, mainly discussing how quiet it has been lately and then Vicky appears, looking as fresh as a daisy, dressed in her usual combat trousers and checked shirt.

'Morning!' she exclaims. She gives Rebecca a peck on the cheek, takes her coffee and perches on the stool next to me.

'What's this surprise Rebecca tells me about?' I ask. 'It's not another blind date is it?'

Yes, before you ask ... when I speak out loud I use contractions just like Josslyn used to do. I told you it was a big difference. I no longer sound like a robot.

'No, it's not a blind date, although you should really call Luke back. He really liked you.'

'I'm not ready to date yet.' And quite possibly never will be.

'But he was really cute.'

'You're married … and gay … like you really notice how cute a guy is,' I mutter sarcastically.

The girls laugh.

'Hey, just cos I'm gay it doesn't mean I don't want one of my best friends to go without dick for the rest of her life.'

I choke on my mouthful of coffee and manage to swallow most of it before it sprays across the counter. 'Gee … thanks.'

'Just call him,' pleads Vicky.

'No.'

'Please,' pipes in Rebecca.

I glare at both of them. 'I don't call guys. Never have, never will.'

'Then text him.'

'You really aren't going to let this go, are you?'

'No,' says Vicky.

'N-Nope,' says Rebecca.

I sigh in annoyance, although I am far from annoyed. In fact, I love bantering back and forth with these two. 'Fine … I'll text him.'

'Yes!' Vicky and Rebecca high-five each other.

Vicky begins wiping up the few drops of spilled coffee.

'So about this surprise,' I say finally.

'You're all going to love it,' answers Vicky.

'Gonna love what?' says a sleepy voice. Laura has just appeared, looking bleary-eyed, her hair sticking up as if she has been dragged through a hedge backwards. 'Coffee ... need coffee.'

Rebecca plants a cup in front of her nose. 'Vicky has a s-surprise for us.'

'Oh fuck ...'

'Why are you all so against my surprises?' The three of us exchange glances, wondering who is brave enough to speak first. 'Look ... just trust me, okay? It's not a blind date or anything weird or dodgy ... not like last time. Trust me!'

Chapter Forty-Six

The next few hours are spent doing the usual routine; setting up the new rooms, serving breakfast for the guests, tidying their rooms. It can get a bit monotonous, but I do find having a routine soothing and rather enjoyable. It reminds me of when Josslyn had her routine at her vet practice or when I had mine at the vineyard.

When the four of us finally stop for lunch Vicky receives a text message, which causes her to leap from her seat in excitement.

'He's here!' she shrieks.

'He?' I ask, almost slopping tea down my front at her sudden exclamation. 'I thought you said it wasn't a blind date.'

'It's not!'

I roll my eyes. 'Oh God.'

'Don't be like that. All of you ... wait here!' She runs off, leaving myself, Rebecca and Laura in silence while we continue to eat our lunch.

I look around at the two women in front of me; both of them look so happy and content. From the outside you would never know the horrors they have been through, the pain, the torture. Yes, they have physically recovered well over the past year. Laura is no longer skin and bones and has a healthy sun-kissed glow to her skin whereas Rebecca is still as pale as ever, but she asserts herself with such confidence now that it makes her whole body stand up straighter, even her voice is slowly coming back. I feel a swell of pride; I did that … I helped them … Josslyn and I helped them. We saved them, just like she saved me.

At that moment Vicky bounds into the room like a kid at Christmas, a beaming smile across her face, holding a … oh shit …

'Here he is! Everyone meet … Jasper!'

Rebecca leaps from her chair, excitedly joining Vicky in welcoming the cat into our home. Laura hurriedly slurps her tea down and begins cooing and stroking the animal. All three of them are using high-pitched voices and squealing with joy.

Why a cat? Why could it not have been a dog?

It is a black and white short-haired feline that looks to be approximately a year old; not quite an adult cat, yet not still a kitten. It squeaks and meows as Vicky, Laura and Rebecca shower it with love and affection, planting kisses upon its soft head.

I stay exactly where I am and avoid eye contact with any of them.

'Alicia! Come and meet Jasper!' says Laura, beckoning me with her hands.

'I'm allergic to cats.'

'No, you're not. Get over here,' argues Vicky. 'I rescued him. The guy in the local shop said he couldn't keep him, so I said I'd take him.'

I sigh and slowly rise to my feet. 'Didn't he have a dog you could've adopted instead?'

'You don't like cats?'

'Let's just say I have no issue with cats, but they don't like me.'

'Just give Jasper a chance to get to know you. You'll be fine … come on.'

I slowly inch my way closer to the cat, which is still nestled in Vicky's arms, but then it sees me and freezes. No one makes a move. It hisses and leaps free, scurrying under the nearest cabinet. The girls try to tempt it out with a piece of ham leftover from lunch, but it refuses to budge.

I sigh loudly. 'I told you cats don't like me. I'm more of a dog person.'

'Weird,' they all say.

That evening, after the dinner rush has ended and all the jobs have been completed for the day, Vicky and Rebecca leave for their monthly date night. They usually go to the local town to their favourite restaurant and then onto a bar that serves ridiculously strong cocktails, so I am expecting them to be quite drunk when they return later.

Laura is in her room with her new boyfriend, although I use that term loosely. She rarely keeps these men around longer than a few weeks, but they do not appear to complain. I am sure one day she will break some poor guy's heart, but in the meantime she is enjoying her freedom.

I pour myself a glass of white wine (pinot grigio, obviously) and take a seat in my favourite armchair by the roaring fire that Rebecca kindly lit for me before she left. I also retrieve the book I am currently reading (Darkly

Dreaming Dexter by Jeff Lindsay) from my bedroom and settle in for the evening. The warmth from the fire is soothing and quite pleasant after the long day of tidying up the garden area so the guests can enjoy a beverage or two in the open air, although at this time of the year it is far too cold to be sitting outside ... but each to their own.

I take a refreshing sip of wine and breathe in the fruity aromas, thinking how much Josslyn would have enjoyed this moment. I may not get drunk and watch serial killer documentaries like she used to ... but apparently now I drink and read about them instead.

This sitting area is specifically for us to use so there are no guests around, which suits me perfectly. I still do like to be by myself a lot. There is something cathartic about spending time in one's own company, but at least now I do not actively avoid the company of others.

My mind flashes to Luke and the conversation I had with the girls earlier. Maybe he did like me, but did I like him? He was pleasant enough to talk to, quite good-looking, had a killer body from what I could make out under his thick jumper and enjoys being outdoors in nature. He also has a beard that made him look like a lumberjack. I could do worse ...

I pick up my phone and send him a text before I change my mind.

Then I close my eyes for a second, but almost immediately hear a creaking sound, like a rickety floorboard. My eyes flash open ...

Jasper is crouched in the middle of the room looking slightly pathetic and lost. My phone pings almost immediately; it is from Laura (clearly walking from her room to see me is far too much effort).

Can you look after Jasper for a bit? He was getting in the way xx

I roll my eyes as I place my phone down, ignoring the incoming text from Luke for now. I sigh in annoyance at my potentially ruined evening as I place down the book and the wine. I lean forwards in my chair and slowly extend a hand as a peace offering. The cat shrinks back ever so slightly and lets out a low meow, but then … takes a tentative step forwards … then another … and another …

Now it is a mere inch from the tip of my outstretched fingers. I do not dare to flex a single muscle as it gradually touches its wet nose to my skin, sniffing, sniffing, and then … a lick. Jasper shuffles a few more steps forwards and proceeds to rub his face and neck against my hand. I smile as I tickle him behind his velvety soft ears.

'Care to join me by the fire?' I ask.

I sit back in my chair and assume the position. It takes several minutes of patience, but eventually Jasper jumps up onto my lap, sniffs my wine and then promptly curls into a ball and goes to sleep.

I suppose cats are not so bad after all.

I check my phone.

Hey, was beginning to think you'd forgotten about me. How bout dinner tomorrow at mine? I'm a decent cook x

Of course he can cook ...

At midnight I take myself off to bed. Laura still sounds as if she is occupied, so I allow Jasper to follow me. He makes himself at home on the blanket at the bottom of my bed. I smile as I begin to get undressed. Vicky has placed a pile of neatly folded clean clothes on my dresser, so I pick them up, open my wardrobe door and stretch up on my toes to reach the top shelf. While shoving the clothes wherever they will fit I accidentally dislodge some items, which tumble down to my feet. One of the items is my old black backpack. I retrieve it from where it fell and gently stroke the fabric; it is worn and faded after having seen a lot of action. I reach my hand inside to check it is empty because I shall throw it away tomorrow. I have not used it since I have been here. My hand touches something. I pull the item out from the bottom of the bag ...

It is a white envelope. Well, at least it was white a long time ago. Now it is crumpled, dirty and slightly disintegrated in places from getting damp. I search my memory ... the envelope from the attic. I never opened and read it. To be perfectly honest I had forgotten all about it until now. I must have kept it with me in my backpack while I had been travelling around.

A part of me wants to take it and throw it into the dying embers of the fire in the sitting room. My old life means nothing to me now. I am no longer that person. Vicky told us to leave everything behind and start over and that is exactly what I did ... but this envelope ... I should

307

have read it there and then. I do not know what made me ignore it, almost as if it were not the right time and place. Maybe right now is the perfect time ...

I take the envelope, sit on the bed and stare at it for several minutes, contemplating my next move. Then I open it ... and read ...

Epilogue

Dear Alicia,

I don't even know where to start with this letter. I never thought I'd have to write it, but I feel that now is the right time. You should know the truth. You deserve to know. Your mother ... I mean ... Amanda, my wife, never wanted you to know the truth. She's always been against telling you, but only because she only ever wanted to keep you safe. She knew the truth might hurt you if you found out too soon.

I know you don't really think of us as your real parents. Josslyn is the girl we raised as our own. We nurtured and protected her, taught her at home so she wouldn't have to go to school and be around other children. It was for her own protection ... and theirs.

But the truth is Alicia ... Josslyn may have been the girl we raised ... but you were the girl we adopted and rescued. I don't know how much you already know, but I'll try and explain it from my point of view. All I will say is … please forgive me.

We didn't adopt you as a newborn baby like we told you. You were nearly seven when we took you in. You were so very broken. You didn't speak when you first came to us. Amanda and I could tell how troubled and confused you were. We knew about your past, at least some of it. Your biological mother was called Jane Daniels and she was raped by an awful man. We never knew his name, but when you and your sister were born your mother immediately put her up for adoption. Her name was Josslyn, but we later found out that your birth certificates had been switched so she was called Alicia. For what reason we don't know. It could have been a complete accident. We always knew she was Alicia Phillips.

From what the adoption agency told us you were found wandering the streets by yourself and were taken to a police station. No one ever came forward to claim you as their own, so you were taken to an adoption agency. We didn't expect to adopt an older child, but when the lady told us about you we knew we wanted to rescue you and help you. You had a few possessions when you came to us, but you wouldn't let anyone touch them, so I told you that I'd hide them away in a box until you were ready.

We didn't know the full trauma of your past, only that something terrible must have happened to you. Whenever I looked at you I could see how empty you were inside. There was nothing there and we were worried, so we took you to see a specialist doctor, a doctor who specialised in helping sick children overcome their traumatic experiences. Her name was Doctor Channing. She worked with you and told you that in order to get better you needed to build a wall inside your mind and put all the bad things behind that wall. She told you to build the wall so tall and so wide that it went on for eternity, that way, the bad things could never come back.

Eventually you began to interact with her, but only her. The doctor even worked with you to come up with a ritual to do every morning to help focus your mind and keep the wall in place. It was only a simple thing, silly really. You started touching your feet to the floor as soon as you got out of bed, then bringing them back up and counting to five.

At first we didn't think it was working. You didn't speak at all and you merely stared at nothing. You just held on to your teddy bear, but you started squeezing and destroying bits of it, but you wouldn't give it back to us. One day Amanda asked you if you'd like some orange juice and I believe her exact words were 'Alicia, would you like some orange juice?' It was at that point you turned to her and spoke for the very first time. You said 'My name's Josslyn, not Alicia.'

Well, you scared Amanda half to death and when she screamed I came running. But you spoke! We were so happy, so excited. We took you back to the doctor who said that creating a new name for yourself was your way of building your wall and she believed you would recover remarkably well, which you did, but it was a long process.

There were times when you switched to a very dark personality, but usually not for long. Eventually Alicia disappeared completely and Josslyn took over. Josslyn was happy, she played, she sang, she loved animals and she loved being outside, but we knew we had to try and protect her as much as possible, so we moved to a small farm in the countryside, away from civilisation and took it upon ourselves to homeschool her. We made sure she had lots of animal friends and she seemed happy, although there were times when she became lonely. She didn't seem to remember her mother or anything about what had happened, so we never spoke about it and never told her the truth.

One day she told us that she'd made a new friend called Alicia. Amanda and I were so scared that things would start to get bad for her again, but they didn't. She was happy to talk to her invisible friend, so we didn't say anything more on the subject. She was a perfect and content child. There was that time we heard a scream in the barn and she said she'd seen a rat. However, I found a knife covered in blood a few days later and her cat, Tornado, never came home again. Cracks were beginning to form, but we ignored them. We shouldn't have. We should have taken her back to the doctor to get more help. She needed constant psychiatric attention, but we did nothing. I blame myself.

I'm going to skip forward to the day Josslyn found the ultrasound photo in the box in the attic. I wanted her to find it. I couldn't live with myself any longer. I could see the battle that was going on inside her head. Josslyn's personality was beginning to break down and she needed answers. I often found her staring at nothing or sometimes speaking to herself. I knew what was happening, but I did nothing to stop it.

I don't know the full extent of what you've done Alicia, but I know not all of it is good. I know what you are or what you claim to be. You're not a psychopath. You're a very troubled young girl trapped inside her own mind who just wants to be free. Amanda never wanted you to find out the truth so when she realised Josslyn had found the box and the photo she nearly had a breakdown. But I held it together and we told Josslyn part of the truth. I believed it would be better for her in the long run if she found out bit by bit. Your mind was very delicate and I didn't want the entire wall you'd built to come crashing down all at once. It was too dangerous. So we lied. And yes, we lied again later on after she told us she'd found Alicia Phillips (or more appropriately Josslyn).

There was one thing I didn't see coming though and that was Josslyn's story about the foetus in fetu. I must admit Amanda and I were quite shocked when she told us. I couldn't get my head around it so I listened while Amanda fed her some more lies, but also drip fed her a little more of the truth. Please believe me when I tell you that I hate myself for lying to you and Josslyn, but I honestly believed it was for your own good. I realised Josslyn had made up this entire story in her head and was using the discovery of the foetus in fetu as an answer to who Alicia really was. She was still trying to protect herself and keep the wall up, but I had to let it happen. Josslyn wanted to remove the tumour and I knew it would go one of two ways. Either she'd remove you and Alicia would truly be gone and Josslyn would be the true owner of the body, or ... you'd come back.

As soon as I set my eyes on you after the operation I knew it was you. You still had the same dark stare as you did when you first came to us. I

314

openly admit that I was afraid of you. Amanda could see you'd changed, but I believe she was living in denial that Josslyn had truly gone. We played along with your game of pretending to be Josslyn. You were good, but you weren't that good. You spoke differently, acted differently, but you were a fully functioning adult now and you needed to make your own choices. We were heartbroken when you told us you were leaving, but I finally convinced Amanda to let you go. We couldn't have stopped you even if we'd tried. I helped you sell the vet practice and then you left without telling us where you were going. I worried about you daily. Maybe I should have done more to help you, but I knew you were strong, so I trusted you to make good choices.

When Amanda died my life fell apart. I didn't expect you to ever come back so I wasn't upset when you didn't. We'd already put you as the sole benefactor in our wills years and years ago. I wanted to find you, but I didn't know where to begin. I never have been good with technology and the Internet. I thought about hiring a private investigator, but then decided against it. When you were ready I believed you would come home, so I made sure the box in the attic still held all the items I'd originally put in there for you. I must admit I never listened to what was on the tape or looked through the scrapbook. It wasn't my place to know. That was for you and only you. Maybe I should have … I don't know.

That's why I'm writing this letter now. I'm going to add it to the box. One day you'll find it. I know you will. The answers you've been looking for will all be here, waiting. I don't know how long it will take you to find it. I may not even be around by then. I've been diagnosed with cancer and I don't have much time left. The guilt I feel about keeping this from you all these years is eating me up inside. I've even become paranoid that someone is following me, but maybe that's just my old brain playing tricks on me. The point is I'll probably never see you again and it genuinely breaks my heart.

I hope this letter gives you some of the answers I know you've been looking for. I'm sorry you suffered through such a traumatic childhood, but I'm so glad we found you and gave you the chance at a normal life, even if it was only for a while. I'm not sure how you'll react to this news. I know you've probably done bad things in the past Alicia, but I want you to know that Amanda and I … your mother and I … we're so proud of you and the woman you've become. We love you. And we loved Josslyn too. She may not have been real, but she was real to us and I hope she knew that we loved her. I feel like we let her down, but this was never really about her. This was about you. It's always been about you. You'll always be our daughter, Alicia.

Never forget that you had a family who loved you.

You are Alicia Reynolds.
From your loving father,
Ronald Reynolds
xx

Leave A Review

I really hope you enjoyed reading My Real Self, the third and final novel in the "My ... Self" series.

If you liked this book please feel free to leave a review on the Amazon page or Goodreads.

Leave me a review on Amazon

Leave me a review on Goodreads

Connect With Jessica

Find and connect with Jessica online via the following platforms.

Sign up to her email list via her website to be notified of future books and receive her monthly author newsletter: www.jessicahuntleyauthor.com

Follow her page on Facebook: Jessica Huntley - Author - @jessica.reading.writing
Follow her on Instagram: @jessica_reading_writing
Follow her on Twitter: @jess_read_write
Follow her on TikTok: @jessica_reading_writing
Follow her on Goodreads: jessica_reading_writing
Follow her on her Amazon Author Page - Jessica Huntley

Printed in Great Britain
by Amazon

18438569R00190